THE HIDDEN TREASURE

THE HIDDEN TREASURE

TREASURE

Or, Found at Last

LUCY ELLEN GUERNSEY

WILDSIDE PRESS

Published by Wildside Press LLC.
wildsidepress.com

CHAPTER I.

THE GOLD MEDAL.

It was growing toward evening on a mild day of early spring in the year 1527. The sun, which had been hidden all day, peeped out of a rent in the curtain of gray cloud, and did his best to make beautiful the town of Bridgewater, by gilding the tops of the houses and the tall tower of the beautiful church of St. Mary, lighting up the boats and vessels in the river, and sending his rays on all sorts of frolicsome errands through the streets and alleys of the sober old town.

In pursuance of these errands, a set of bright beams found out and entered the shop of John Lucas, the well-known master baker in Bridge Street, and finding therein abundance of well-scoured boards, bright earthenware and burnished pewter, did so disport themselves, that at last they attracted the attention of Master Lucas himself, who was knitting his brows over certain crabbed-looking accounts, apparently trying to extract some meaning from them, by the help of a huge pair of horn spectacles. The moment Master Lucas raised his head, the aforesaid frolicsome beams at once forsook, as it seemed, all their former playthings, to dance about his portly person, light up his gray hair, and make little mimic suns in his eyes and glasses. And certainly they might have gone a long way, and have seen nothing pleasanter than the old man's face.

"Heyday!" he exclaimed. "Here is the sun at last, to be sure, and a welcome sight after all the cloudy days we have had of late. Well, well! The sun always shines at last, that is one comfort. Eh, Mary Brent?" he added, addressing himself to a pale and poorly clad woman who had just entered the shop.

The poor woman shook her head sadly. "I suppose it does, somewhere," said she, "but little of it comes my way of late years."

"And that is true," said the baker kindly. "You have had your troubles and trials these many years; but your children will soon be growing up to help you, that is one comfort; and nobody ever had an ill word for you, that's another. You will be wanting one of my new brown loaves now. Here, Simon, a brown loaf for Dame Brent."

"Not so, Master Lucas," replied Mary Brent. "You are very good, but I dare not take the loaf. I owe you more now than I shall ever be able to pay—"

"Nonsense, woman!" interrupted the baker. "The children must eat."

"And I came to ask you if you would just wait on me a little longer. I hope my son will be home and bring me some money next month; he is a dutiful lad for all they say of him; and till then we must rub on somehow."

"Look here, dame!" said the baker, in a somewhat angry tone. "Have I ever asked you for my money?"

"No, Master Lucas, you have been very forbearing, but—"

"But me no buts!" interrupted Master Lucas. "Take the loaf and go your way, woman, unless you will stop to supper with us; and as for the money, when I want it, I will ask for it."

"I thank you with all my heart," said the woman, evidently relieved from some great anxiety. "My poor children must needs have gone supperless to bed, but for your bounty."

"How then?" demanded the baker. "Did you not get your share of the dole at the convent gate this morning? I saw old Margery carrying home a fine beef-bone, and surely you have as good a right as she—the old mumping beggar that she is!"

"Nay," replied poor Mary, smiling sadly. "I get nothing now from the convent, less or more. The fathers were so angry with poor Davy for preferring rather to go to sea than to become a lay brother, that they say they will do nothing for me. And that is not the worst either. They say my husband was a believer in the new doctrines, and accuse me of the same, though there is no one in Bridgewater who keeps her church more closely than I. New doctrines or not, he was a good husband to me, and never let me want, or lost a day's work through drink or idleness."

"And that is more than many of them can say," returned the baker. "Out on them one and all for a set of lazy crows, preying on other folks' substance!"

"Well, I am surprised to hear you say as much, Master Lucas. I had thought you were ever a favorer of the religious houses. Mistress Cicely told me that your Anne was to enter the convent where she had her schooling, and that she was a wonder for her gravity, her penances, and piety; and also that your son Jacky was likely to follow the same course."

Master Lucas shook his head. "It is by no good will of mine, dame, that Anne turns her thoughts towards the cloister. The girl is well enough, if she would but laugh or speak or do anything else in a natural way, and not go round like a waxen image or an animated corpse. As for Jack, poor fellow, I much fear he will not be long for this world in any vocation. Look at him now coming along the street, so pale and spiritless, never looking above or around him. When I was of his age, I should have raced all the way, and come in as hungry as a wolf. I much fear the lad will die in a waste like his mother before him."

"Why now, Jack, what ails thee?" he continued, as a delicate, pale boy of fifteen came slowly into the shop and dropped his strap-load of books on the counter. "Art thou ill, or have the examinations gone so much against thee? Fie, never take it to heart, lad! Better luck another time. One failure is no such great matter to break one's heart about. Many a man goes well enough through the world who never learned to know great A from little B."

"But I have not failed, dear father," said John, smiling, and, leaning on his father's broad shoulder, he drew from his breast a gold medal, and held it up before him. "See, I have gained the prize!"

"Gained the prize!" exclaimed the baker, starting. "Not the gold medal, and over the heads of all thy fellows! That can never be, surely!"

"But it is even so," replied Jack. "See, here it is. Sir William says in another year I shall be able to go to college."

"Bless the boy! And have you won the prize, and come home to tell of it with such a step as that?"

"I am so tired!" said Jack wearily. "I can think of nothing but resting just now. It seemed ten miles from the schoolhouse to the head of our street."

"And you are as pale as new-bolted flour," said his father. "Sit you down in my great chair. Here, Cicely—Anne—where are you? Bring the lad a glass of ale, Cicely—or, stay, wine be better. A glass of wine, Cicely; and Cicely, bring the smallest of the pies was baked this morning. Here, Anne, my girl, do you see what has happened? Your brother has won the gold medal."

Anne came slowly forward from the back room, where she had been sitting, busily engaged in needle work. She was a tall, fair girl, with regular features, blue eyes, and a face which would have been both handsome and engaging but for its formal, repressed, and self-conscious expression. She looked like one who would never make a natural or spontaneous movement, or speak a word without thinking over all its possible consequences at least twice beforehand. She presented the greatest possible contrast to her jolly, cheerful father, as well as to her maiden cousin Cicely, who now came bustling in, carrying a goodly pasty, which, if it were the smaller of two or three, spoke well for the size of Master Lucas' oven. She was thin and wrinkled as a last year's russet apple, but her somewhat hard features were lighted up with good-humored smiles, and the roses of her youth were well dried into her cheeks.

"Lackaday!" she exclaimed, in a clear, high-pitched voice. "And so our lad has gained the prize. Lady! But who would have thought it, and he so mum and quiet about it all the time! Well, well! Would his dear mother had lived to see the day! But doubtless it is better as it is. What shall I do with the pasty, Master Lucas?"

"Pop it in Mary Brent's basket, to be sure," replied the baker. "What better place could there be? Nay, dame, you must needs take it, or you and I shall fall out. Yourself and the young ones must keep Jack's feast—eh, my lad?"

Mary Brent said no more in opposition, but withdrew with a far brighter face than she came in.

"And that's just like you, Master Lucas, and a good deed too," said Cicely. "Poor woman, I fear she often has short commons at home these days."

"Well, I must say, I wonder my father should give so largely to her—a woman whose husband died without the sacrament, and suspected strongly of heresy," said Anne.

"And suppose her husband was a heretic, is that any reason his widow should starve?" demanded her father with some heat. "Or is there any reason why I should not do what I will with mine own, or why my own daughter should take me to task in the open shop?"

Anne colored deeply. "I meant no offence, father, only—"

"Only thou art a peevish wench, and I am a fool to be ruffled by thee," said the baker, recovering his good humor. "Come, look at Jack's medal."

Anne regarded the medal with a mournful expression, not as if she were at all interested in it, but as obeying a command of her father's. "'Tis a great honor, no doubt," said she, "but the honors of this world are hardly worth striving after."

"By'r Lady! But they are," said her father. "Another such victory makes Jack an Oxford scholar, and that is worth striving after in more ways than one. But thou art ever a wet blanket," he muttered between his teeth, "taking no pleasure thyself, and doing all thou canst to damp that of other people. Come, son, drink your wine and eat this manchet therewith, to stay your appetite till supper. And do you, Cicely, provide us with right good cheer this night, and send the 'prentice boy to bid my old crony, Master Luttrell, and his wife, to sup with us. They will be glad to hear of Jack's good fortune—eh, my lad? But you look worse and worse. Cicely, bring some of the cordial I got from Captain Davis."

"I should like to go to bed, father, if you please," interrupted Jack, trying to rouse himself. "My head is so heavy and drowsy, I shall be no good company for anybody. I dare say I shall feel better after a good night's rest."

"To be sure, dear lad. Sleep is everything—worth all the doctors in the world. Anne, get your brother's room ready, and make his bed comfortably.

Yes, go to bed, my son, and sleep well, with thy father's blessing upon thee," added Master Lucas, laying his broad hand on the boy's head, while an expression of gentle benignity made his honest, open face still more attractive. "This I will say for thee, that from the day of thy birth till now thou hast never wittingly grieved thy father's heart, or given him a moment's uneasiness."

Jack took his father's hand in his own thin fingers and kissed it. "I should be a wretch indeed, to grieve you, father. You have been father and mother both to me ever since my mother died. I only wish I could do more for you in return."

"Tut, tut, lad! What could any one expect of you more than you have done? Only get well and strong, and never fear but you will do enough. Anne, why do you not see to the lad's chamber, instead of standing there like an image of stone?"

"It is nearly time for evensong, father," replied Anne. "Betty can make Jack's bed as well as I."

"Tell me not of evensong, girl! It is quite time you should learn that your father's word is not to be disputed. Go and do as I bid you, or it will be the worse for you. There, I meant not to be over-sharp, Anne, but you must learn, my maid, that so long as you are under your father's roof, his word is your law."

"Dear father, do not be sharp with poor Anne," pleaded Jack, when his sister had left the room. "She means no harm, poor girl, only they have taught her at the convent to think nothing is of any account in comparison with church observances; and they are right, for aught I know, if it is as the priests tell us."

"It was an evil day when I let her go to the convent at all," said the baker. "She has never been the same joyous girl since. And now, I warrant, you too will be thinking of the church—mayhap of the cloister—and I shall be left alone, a childless old man."

"Never, never, dear father!" exclaimed Jack, starting up and speaking with an energy which brought a flush to his pale cheeks. "Never will I leave you for the sake of becoming a lazy drone, like the monks yonder, or a proud priest like their prior, who rides abroad in such state upon his mule, and grinds the faces of poor men, and robs widows and orphans as he does. I would rather be a shepherd on the hillside all day like my old uncle Thomas, or a sailor like Davy Brent, or a miner underground, than live such a life!"

"Well, well, boy, I am glad on't with all my heart, but you need not speak so loud or put yourself in such a heat about it. The priests are not all alike neither. Never was a better man than our Sir William."

"That is so, father; and yet I would not be in his shoes. I hear the others are complaining that he preaches too much, and that he sets a bad example in not exacting all his dues. They say he would not take the last dues from Prudence Wither when her husband died, though she offered it. 'Nay, dame,' he said, 'it were more fitting I should give to you than you to me.' And he will take no christening gifts or marriage fees, because he says the sacraments should be free to all."

"'Tis a wonder if they do not accuse him of heresy before all is done!" muttered the baker.

"Well, here comes cousin Cicely to tell us that your room is ready, and I dare say she has brewed a fine posset for you—eh, old girl?"

"That have I, that have I, John Lucas!" replied the cheery old woman. "And made up his bed with clean well-lavendered sheets to boot. So come along, Jacky, if you will not sit up to supper—and truly your eyes are rarely heavy."

"You will spoil me among you," said Jack, gratefully. "I am not worth so much care. Well, good-night, dear father. I dare say I shall be well enough in the morning."

CHAPTER II.

THE SHEPHERD.

Jack's prophecy was not destined to be fulfilled. For many days, he tossed restlessly on his bed, or crept from it only to recline in the great armchair which had been placed in his room.

In vain did Cicely prepare her most tempting delicacies, and brew her choicest sleeping draughts—he could neither eat nor sleep. In vain did Anne, more awake to sublunary matters than she had been for a long time, try to divert him with legends of saints. He could not care for them any more than for the news of the school and the town which his playmates brought him.

He grew thinner and weaker day by day. The physician talked learnedly of degeneration of the animal spirits, and so on, but confessed that he could do no good. He feared there was a hereditary tendency to consumption, which nothing would counteract, and being a wise and humane man, he forbore to torment his patient with useless drugs.

One day, Sir William Leavett, the parish priest, came in to see him. Jack had been rather better for a day or two, and had managed, with his father's help, to creep down into the sunny shop, where he sat or rather reclined in his father's armchair, pleased with the change from his dull chamber and languidly amused by the bustle in the street and the people coming and going; for it was a market-day, and Bridge Street was unusually thronged.

"Why, this is well, my son," said the priest, kindly. "I am glad to see you down-stairs. Nay, sit still," he added, as Jack would have risen from his seat. "I will take the will for the deed."

So saying, he drew up a stool and sat down by the side of the sick boy. He was a kindly-looking middle-aged man, with iron-gray hair, and a face full of benevolence, but sad and somewhat puzzled in its expression. He took Jack's hand, felt its pulse, and questioned him as to his feelings.

"You have no pain, you say?"

"No father, at least very little," replied Jack. "I seem to be tired all the time. If I could only be rested, I should feel well."

"You are overwrought, my son. You worked too hard for the medal, I fear."

"I did not know how hard I was working, not till afterwards," said Jack. "No one was more surprised at my getting it than I was. I never thought it possible."

"So much the better, so much the better, my son!" said the priest. "You worked for the learning, which was its own reward, and which will last you, it may be, when this same bit of gold is rust and dust."

"Shall we then carry our learning with us into other world?" asked Jack, abruptly.

The priest smiled. "Who can tell that, my on? Yet it may be so. That which we truly earn becomes, as it were, amalgamated with our minds and a part of them, even as the food we eat becomes a part of our bodies. Have you not found it so?"

"Indeed I have, father," said Jack. "I cannot forget, if I would."

"Well, then, since our minds and souls are immortal, why should not this same learning, which has become a part of them, be immortal too? But these are deep themes, far beyond the reach of us mortals. This much I think we may rest assured of, that we shall forget nothing which it is profitable for us to remember. Master Lucas, good-day to you," as the baker entered the shop. "I am glad to see our young scholar better and able to be down-stairs."

"He is not much to boast of yet, poor child!" replied Master Lucas sadly. "I would give all his school learning to see his cheeks as round and rosy as yonder shepherd lad's. Nothing can make up for the want of health."

"Ay, ay!" said the priest musingly, looking over Jack's head into the street. "And speaking of shepherds, Master Lucas, why do you not send this lad out into the fields to try what country air and country fare can do for him? They work wonders sometimes. Has he no relations or friends to whose care you could commit him for the summer?"

"I have been thinking of that same thing, Sir William," replied the baker; "but where to send him I know not, unless it be to his mother's uncle, old Tommy Sprat at Holford. He is a good man, though plain and somewhat austere perhaps in his manners, and wonderful sparing of his words in general, as I think indeed shepherds are apt to be."

"Ay, their occupation, by its silence and solitariness, doth naturally dispose them, if they be at all men of parts or understanding, to contemplation and musing. Hence, perhaps, the favor shown them of old in making known to shepherds the first news of the Birth at Bethlehem. David, too, the great king and sweet singer of Israel, was a shepherd."

"Was he really?" asked Jack, much interested, "that King David who made the Psalms?"

The priest assented.

"And was he the same you told us of in school one day, the young lad who killed with his sling and stone the fierce giant who defied the king's armies so long?"

"Even so, my son," answered the priest, smiling at the boy's eager interest. "King David was for many years a shepherd lad, and wandered over the hills and plains with his father's flocks and herds, even that same David who wrote:"

"*'The Lord is my shepherd, I shall not want.'*"
"*Our Lord, too, is called the shepherd of His people.*"
"*'I am the good shepherd, the good shepherd giveth his life for the
   sheep.'*"
"*'My sheep hear my voice, and they follow me, and none is able to
   pluck them out of my hand.'*"
"*'He shall feed flock like a shepherd, He shall carry the lambs in
   His bosom.'*"

The priest seemed to have forgotten where he was, as he repeated these words, and then became silent, looking out of the window with a rapt and joyful expression, as if he saw more than met the eyes of others.

Jack and his father exchanged awe-struck glances, but did not venture to speak.

It was whispered among his flock, that the pure and saintly life of William Leavett had not been unrewarded even in this world, that he had more than once been favored with visions of heavenly things, and that angels had visited his dreams.

"I crave your pardon, Master Lucas. I fear I am unmannerly," said the priest, at last, coming out of his abstraction, with a sweet smile. "I am somewhat absent-minded, you know, and I think that the infirmity increases upon me with years. My advice, Master Lucas, if I may venture to give it unasked, is, that you send our scholar here, to keep sheep with this uncle of his in the country, and see if the June air which blows over the hills will not bring the color to his cheek and the light to his eyes."

"I believe your reverence is right, and I will set about the matter this very day," said Master Lucas. "I dare say Uncle Thomas will be in town, as it is a fair day, and very likely he may look in upon us. And in good time, here he comes!" he added, as a rustic-looking man presented himself at the shop door. "Come in, come in, uncle! The sight of you is good for sore eyes, as the saying goes. Craving your reverence's pardon," he added, in a lower voice, "if you would but stop and sup with us, the old man is good company, and Cicely has a fine pair of fowls."

"I would gladly do so," replied the priest, smiling and inclining his head in answer to the shepherd's greeting; "but I have promised to go and see Mary Brent, and only looked in on my way thither. The poor woman has had a bad fall, and I fear it may be a long time before she walks again."

"Poor soul! Poor dear soul! And she with all those children. Cicely must go see her, and I will send the lad down with bread and meat for their suppers. I trust your reverence to let me know if aught else is wanted. You know I esteem it a favor when you call on me."

"Ay, truly, 'tis a favor I do not spare you, Master Lucas," and bestowing his blessing upon the company, he left the shop.

"There is a priest now, worth bowing to!" said the baker. "A true shepherd, and no hireling fleecing the poor sheep to the very bones, ay, eating their flesh and drinking their blood to supply his own greed and luxury. If there were more like him, we should not hear such complaints of the decay of religion, and the spread of heresy. No man was ever the worse for him, nor woman either, and he hath ever a kind word and a blessing for the poorest and youngest, as well as for the rich and great."

"Yet I hear he is no favorite with his brethren," said Jack.

"Ay, that is because they are rebuked by his poverty and his industry. But come in, come in, Uncle Thomas; I have matters of importance about which to consult you, after supper, that is. We will not talk of business, fasting. Sit you down and talk with Jack, while I draw the ale and see to the mulling of the wine."

The shepherd was an old man, somewhat bent with years and rheumatism, but still tall and stately, with white hair and beard, clear, somewhat dreamy blue eyes, and a firm and kindly mouth.

Jack felt attracted toward him directly, and was delighted to hear him consent at once to the proposed arrangement.

"My house is but a plain place, and my fare coarse and homely compared to yours, Master Lucas; but I can give the lad good beef, bread and milk, and mayhap the change itself will be well for him. My housekeeper, Margery, though somewhat of the deafest, is yet clean and a good cook, and I will care for Jack as if he were my own. More I cannot say."

"And more need not be said," answered the baker heartily. "I know you well, Thomas Sprat, for an honest, godly, and kind-hearted man, and I shall feel as easy about my lad as if he were in his own chamber. So then we will consider the matter settled, eh, Jack? And thou shalt learn to keep sheep, like the king the good priest was telling us of, he that wrote the Psalms—what a head I have, to be sure!"

"King David," said Jack. "But there will be no giants to fight at Holford, I am afraid."

"There are giants to fight everywhere, dear lad," said the shepherd, "yes, and dwarfs, too, worse than the giants."

"Dwarfs and giants in Holford! What does the man mean?" said the baker. "Oh, I see—this will be some of your parables!" he added, with a jolly laugh. "I am but a plain man, and don't understand such matters. You and Jack will suit exactly, I dare say. Well, then, it is settled, and as soon as the lad is able to ride so far I will bring him out to you."

"There is one thing for which I should like to be a priest," said Jack the next day.

He was lying at length on the settle in the sitting-room, and Anne sat sewing at the window.

"Only one?" said Anne.

"Only one that I know of now. I should like to be a priest, that I might read the Bible. Did you ever see a Bible in the convent, Anne?"

"No, never," replied his sister. "I dare say there might be one in the library, for they had great store of books both written and printed; but no one ever meddled with them, except that the librarian used to take them out and dust and air them once or twice a year."

"But what did you do?" asked Jack. "You must have had a great plenty of time."

"Not so much as you think. There were the daily services, and the hours of silence, and the embroidery, and the making of sweetmeats and comfits for sale and for feast-days, and other things besides. There was very little time for reading."

"But you had reading at meals," persisted Jack. "What did they read to you?"

"Homilies, and lives of the saints, and such like," replied Anne.

"And were not some of those taken from the Bible?"

"How should I know, when, as I told you, I never saw a Bible?" asked Anne, in a tone of some little irritation. "The Bible is not for common folks and laymen like you and me. Father Barnabas said it was by reading the Bible in the vulgar tongue that the rebellion was got up long ago in the days of Lord Cobham and the Lollards."

"That is curious, though," said Jack, meditatively.

"What is curious?"

"That reading the Bible should make men rebels and traitors. The priests say—at least Father William says—that the Bible is the Word of God to men, given them for their salvation; and I cannot see how reading and knowing the word of God should make men wicked."

"I'll tell you what, Jack, you are getting into a bad way, and meddling with things which don't concern you," said Anne, laying down her work. "Sister Alice asked some such questions of one of the elder nuns, and a fine penance she got for it. She had to kneel on the stone floor of the church all one winter's night."

"That must have done a great deal toward convincing her of her errors," said Jack, dryly; "though I should say it was more likely to give her the rheumatism."

"She had no business to need convincing," replied Anne; "that was what Father Barnabas said. Her duty was to submit to her spiritual superiors. I suppose the Bible is like medicine. Medicine is good to take when the doctor gives it to us, but if we should go to taking drugs at our own fancy, without knowing their qualities and uses, we should soon poison ourselves."

Anne delivered this illustration, which, indeed, was part of one of Father Barnabas' sermons, with a tone of authority which silenced Jack for a time. But he was not one quickly to let drop an idea which had taken firm hold of his mind, and later in the day he began again, upon another branch of the same great subject, which was indeed occupying many more minds than that of the baker's lad.

"Anne, did not somebody say that Mary Brent's husband was infected with the new doctrines?"

"Yes," said Anne. "So much the worse for him!"

"Why?" asked Jack.

"Because he died a wretched heretic without the sacraments, and was buried like a dog—as he deserved," replied Anne, bitterly. "Well for him that he fared no worse, as he would have done had Father Barnabas been the parish priest instead of Sir William Leavett."

"But Mary says her husband was a kind husband and a good man, and never let her want for anything," persisted Jack. "I wonder where he learned these new doctrines?"

"Among the sailors and merchants in Germany and the Low Countries, as I have heard," said Anne. "From the monster Luther himself, for ought I know."

"Did Luther believe in allowing people to read the Bible?" asked Jack.

Anne put down her work, and coming to the side of Jack's bed, she kneeled down and put her arm round him.

"Dear Jack, what has got into you?" she asked. "Who has been putting these notions into your head?"

"What notions?" asked Jack.

"These notions about reading the Bible, and this curiosity about heretics and about the new doctrines. Oh, brother dear, don't meddle with poison! Don't touch pitch lest you be defiled! Think of your immortal soul—of your friends and your father. Be warned in time—" Anne laid down her head on the bed, and her whole frame shook with convulsive sobs.

"Dear Anne, don't cry so!" said Jack, wondering at his sister's emotion. "What have I done to make you so unhappy? I have no notion of running after the new doctrines, and even if I did wish to read the Scriptures, why should that trouble you?"

"Because—because I know what comes of it!" said Anne, lifting her colorless face, and speaking in a low tone. "Jack, I had a friend in the convent—the dearest friend I ever had. She was one of the young sisters, and taught me to embroider and to write, and though she was of good family, and I but a baker's daughter, she took a liking for me, and I loved her with my whole heart."

"Well!" said Jack, breathlessly, as Anne paused, for there was something in his sister's tone which awed him.

"She went home for a few weeks," continued Anne. "When she came back she brought with her a certain book. It professed to be part of the Holy Scripture—Heaven knows what it was—but Agnes read in it every spare moment. She would have had me study the book with her, and I did read a few chapters. Then I grew frightened and would read no more, and I begged Agnes to burn the book, but she would not—ah, woe is me! She would not."

"Well!" said Jack again, as Anne made another pause.

"The poison entered into her soul," continued Anne, speaking in a still lower tone, and shivering as with horror. "She became infected, and she spoke profane and slighting words of the saints, and of our Lady herself, even declaring that there was no warrant in Scripture for asking her intercession. More she spoke that I cannot repeat—that I dare not think of. Oh, would that she had never spoken to me of the matter! Would it had not been my lot—"

"Anne, you did not betray her!" cried Jack indignantly. "You did not betray your friend?"

"What could I do?" murmured Anne, her face once more hidden. "I must needs go to confession, and answer the questions which were asked of me. I was her confidant, and the priest knew that, and questioned me shrewdly. I was obliged to tell, and—oh, woe is me! Woe is me! Why was I ever born? She was called before the prioress and the priest, all the sisters standing by, and there she avowed her heresy, and spoke out boldly. She was a modest, shamefaced girl in general, but she was fearless enough then. Never, never shall I forget her face and her voice. They dragged her away at last, and as she was going, I fell at her feet—I could not help it—and implored her forgiveness."

"She looked down upon me with her sweet eyes full of tears. 'I forgive you, Anne, if there is aught to forgive,' said she. 'You could not help yourself, I suppose. These are the days spoken of by our Lord, when the brother shall betray the brother to death; but whosoever shall endure to the end shall be saved. Pray for me, dear Anne, as I shall for thee.'"

"Then they drew me away with bitter words of reproach, and I knew no more till I found myself in my cell, with kind old Mother Paula watching over me."

"And what became of Agnes?" asked Jack.

Anne shivered again. "That I never knew. I did venture to ask once of Mother Paula, but she only crossed herself and shook her head. She may yet be alive in some lonely cell, or her bones may be mouldering in the vault below the convent. I dare not ask or think."

"What did they say to you?" asked Jack.

"Father Barnabas was very hard upon me, and gave me many severe penances. I know not what might have been done, had the prioress not stood my friend. But she was a tender-hearted lady; more than that, she was a daughter of my lord, and a person of weight and authority, so she had her own way. She sent me home at last for a change, as she said, that I might recover my health and see somewhat of the world before taking the veil."

"Now, Jack, you know what nobody else knows outside the convent wall. You know why my life is one long prayer and penance. I would I could make it more so than it is. I would have gone a pilgrimage on foot—ay, on my knees to the Holy City, had not my father forbidden, if so might win forgiveness for myself and my friend. I would sleep in my grave every night—I do lie on ashes upon hard boards—I would perform the vilest offices for the poor or the sick; but when think of what Father Barnabas said—that he feared lest the lowest depths of purgatory should be too good for such as she—" Again Anne bowed her head and wept bitterly.

Jack would have given the world to comfort his sister, but he knew not what to say. He saw no comfort himself. He had been brought up to think heresy the worst of sins, beyond even the purifying fires of purgatory. Yet as he heard Anne's tale, and thought of the fair Agnes Harland betrayed by her friend, however innocently, perhaps to a horrible death, perhaps to a living grave worse than any death. As he saw, and understood at a glance, the whole explanation of Anne's conduct—her prayers and tears, and the penances which were wearing out her young life—his whole heart and mind rose in furious rebellion against the faith in which he had grown up. His soul demanded freedom from this intolerable yoke, while at the same time he saw no way of escape.

He turned, and groaned in anguish.

"I have done wrong to tell you this story," said Anne, recalled to some degree of calmness by her brother's agitation. "I have worried and excited you; but oh, dear Jack, if you will only take warning!"

"I am not likely to need the warning," said Jack, with a faint smile, "since I know not how or where I am like to get a sight of the Bible; unless, indeed, I become a priest, and that," said Jack, with sudden vehemence, "I will never do. I will rather keep sheep all my days, or go for a ship's boy, like Davy Brent."

"Hush!" said Anne, imperatively but yet kindly. "You must be quiet, dear Jack, or you will be worse, and my father will blame me. I am glad, in one way, to have told you this tale. I seem to have relieved my mind of a little of its intolerable load. But, dear brother, you must never breathe a word of what I have said, or you will bring me into terrible trouble."

"I never will—never," replied Jack, throwing his arms round his sister's neck and kissing her. "I am glad you have told me this tale, sad and horrible as it is, because it makes me understand many things which have troubled me and puzzled me. But oh! Anne, it does seem to me as if there must be some other way—some way of escape."

Anne held up her hand to check him. "Not a word of that. Let us say no more."

And, Dame Cicely coming in at the moment, Anne made her escape to her own room.

When Jack saw her again she was pale and calm, and seemed to have once more put on the icy mask of reserve which she had worn so long. But Jack had seen behind that mask, and had found out what it covered. Henceforth he was always ready to take Anne's part, to shield her from remark and blame, and to divert his father's attention when the old man, jovial spirit was vexed with his daughter's asceticism, and he was ready to break out into one those windy gusts of reproof which only made matters worse between the father and child. He would gladly have questioned Anne as to what she had read in Agnes Harland's book, but the only time he ventured to approach the subject with her, she showed so much distress and horror that he determined never to allude to it again.

CHAPTER III.

THE SHEPHERD'S TALE.

"Uncle Thomas," said Jack, "did you ever see a Bible?"

Jack Lucas was lying on the short, elastic grass on the side of Holford Hill, helping his great-uncle, Thomas Sprat, to watch the large flocks of Sir John Brydges, the greatest man in these parts. Four or five weeks of country air and country faire had done much to restore the roses to his cheeks and the strength to his muscles. He began once more to feel that life was worth having for the mere sake of living; to feel a keen enjoyment in climbing the steep hills, in following the sheep in their devious wanderings over the unenclosed pastures, and recalling to a sense of its duty any one of them which showed a disposition to stray too far.

The brown bread and milk, the boiled beef and greens, and ale, which deaf Margery set before him, had a flavor which he had not found for many months in the dainty cookery of his cousin Cicely. In those days the English peasants knew little, in ordinarily good seasons, of scarcity of food. Foreign travellers record their wonder and admiration at the "great shins of beef," the quantities of bread and animal food, consumed by the English yeomen and cottagers, and much of their superiority in battle was supposed to be owing to this circumstance.

Jack and his uncle suited each other very well. The old man was rather sparing of his words, but he was a pleased and indulgent listener to the boy's prattle, and when he did speak, it was always to the purpose. Sometimes in the evening, or when they were alone on the hillside, Jack would catechise the shepherd, and draw from him accounts of what he had seen in his younger days.

For the old man had not always been a shepherd on the hillside. He had followed his master to foreign wars, and helped to uphold the honor of England on more than one stricken field. He might have ended his days in peace and idleness in the knight's hall corner, for Sir John was a liberal and worthy man, and honored the old retainer of his father; but Thomas had no fancy for an idle life. He was hale and strong, and quite able to perform the duties of a shepherd, and he preferred living in the old cottage where his father and grandfather had lived before him.

Sir John was not one of those who insist on doing people good against their will or exactly in his own way and no other. He was content to let the old man please himself. Thus it came to pass that Thomas Sprat, had a home of his own to share with his great-nephew; and, as I have said, he made it very pleasant for the lad.

Anne's tale had produced a very different effect upon her brother's mind from what she had intended. Instead of putting an end to his curiosity and his mental questionings, she had given them a new impulse. Again and again, he went over in his mind the story of Agnes Harland. He recalled the words she had spoken, the account which Anne had given of the girl's constancy and bravery under trial, and wondered if it was anything in the words of the mysterious book which had given her so much courage, and whether that book was really a copy of the Holy Scripture.

And why should her superiors have been so angry with Agnes for reading the book, supposing it to be the Bible? Was it true that the word of God was so dangerous? Was it indeed like a poisonous drug, only to be touched by a skilful physician, and even then with caution? Or—Jack put away the thought with horror, but it returned again and again—was it true that the monks knew themselves condemned by its pages; that their pretensions to absolute authority over the mind and conscience of men had no ground or support in Holy Writ, and, therefore, they were afraid to put the book into the hands of the people? And, if this were true, how much more was true? What if Luther and the German heretics were right after all?

Jack's mind was like a seething caldron with these and similar thoughts and conjectures, and had been so, ever since he had heard the tale of Agnes Harland. He had never dared heretofore to mention the subject, and he hardly knew how he had ventured to begin upon it now. But there had already sprung up a very warm and intimate friendship between the old man of fourscore, grave, silent, and somewhat severe in his manners, and the fresh-hearted impulsive schoolboy, with his head full of the classical learning he had acquired at school, and the tales he had heard from his father and Cousin Cicely.

Deaf Margery remarked with some little jealousy, that Master Thomas said more words to Jacky in one day than he had done to her in a month; forgetting, poor woman, that Master Thomas might as well have tried to keep up a conversation with one of his own sheep.

Thomas himself was conscious of a new flavor, as it were, given to his quiet life by the advent of his young kinsman, which repaid him tenfold for any trouble he had taken in the matter.

On this particular day, Jack and his uncle were alone on the breezy side of Holford Hill, looking over a beautiful prospect of meadow, waste and woodland. The old man sat on a flat stone, leaning back against a great stunted oak tree which grew very conveniently just behind this his favorite seat, and, with his hands folded before him, seemed lost in meditation. Jack lay at full length on the thymy and springing turf, gazing up into the blue sky, and watching now the rooks, now the great sailing white clouds which passed over it. Suddenly he spoke out:

"Uncle Thomas, did you ever see a Bible?"

The old man started and turned round with a look of surprise, somewhat as if his own thoughts had found an echo in the boy's words.

"A Bible, lad! And what set thee to thinking of a Bible?"

"Oh, I don't know exactly. I should so like to see one. There must be such fine tales in the Bible," replied Jack, feeling his way, as it were. "Tales of St. George and St. Patrick and such like."

The old man smiled and shook his head shrewdly. "I am not so sure of that, my son. I never saw or heard any such. I doubt whether St. George and St. Patrick are in the Bible at all, though they may be there for all that."

It was now Jack's turn to start. "Then you have seen a Bible!" he said, raising himself on his elbow and looking earnestly at the shepherd. And as Thomas did not answer, he repeated again, "Then you have really seen a Bible?"

"Ay, lad," replied the shepherd. "I have both seen a Bible, and held it in my hands, and read it too."

"But where? But how?" asked Jack.

"Raise yourself up and look about you," said the old man. "Do you see any one near?"

Jack started to his feet and gazed around him in every direction. "I see nobody," he said at last, "nobody but the falconer from the Hall, exercising his hawks in the waste half a mile away, and old Margery bringing water from the Lady-well. Nobody can come upon us here without being seen."

"Sit down here by me, then, and I will tell you the tale. I cannot think it will harm you. I had thought to carry the secret to my grave, since I have no son to whom I may leave it. But I have learned to love you as my own son, and all I have will be yours when I am gone. It will not be much; only the old cottage, and what little gold I have saved; but, if you have the cottage, you must have the secret of the cottage as well. So sit you down, and you will, and hear the old man's tale."

Jack obeyed, and prepared to listen with breathless attention. The old man once more glanced warily round him, and then began his narration.

"You asked me, dear boy, if I had ever seen a Bible. Yes, I have both seen and handled the Word of God in the vulgar tongue. It was not a printed book such as we have now; it was written by hand on parchment, and bound in leather with heavy iron clasps, like the enchanter's book in your legend of Merlin. But it was no enchanter's book. It was the real, true, living Word of God, done into English by good Master Wickliffe of Lutterworth."

"It happened first in this wise. I was a young boy of nine or ten years old, and sharp for my age as any lad in these parts. I had learned to read from my father, who was a substantial yeoman, and could both read and write. But there was little to read in those days, only a ballad now and then or some such folly, which my father did not greatly favor."

"About this time, I began to notice that though I was always sent to bed with the chickens, yet my father and mother and my elder brother, a boy of sixteen or thereabouts, sat up much later. I used to lie awake and listen after a while, and I could hear a low murmur of voices, as though some one were reading aloud. I dared not ask any questions, for I stood much in awe of my father and mother, more than is the fashion in these days," added the old man with a sigh.

"Well!" said Jack, fearful lest the shepherd should fall to moralizing on the degeneracy of the times, an exercise of mind as common then as now and quite as reasonable.

"Well," said the shepherd, "as I told you, I listened thus for several nights, now and then catching a word which roused my curiosity still more, till at last I could bear it no longer. One night (it was Easter-even of all the nights in the year), I rose softly from my bed, and putting on my clothes, I slipped carefully down the stairs, till I could peep through the door at the bottom. There sat my father and mother, surrounded by three or four neighbors. You have seen the little footstool which always stands by my great chair in the chimney corner?"

"Yes," replied Jack, wondering what the stool could have to do with the matter.

"My father had this stool turned upside down on his lap, and upon it lay a great book from which he was reading in low, reverent tones, the story of the raising of Lazarus from the dead. I noticed in one glance, as children do notice everything, that the door was barred and the window carefully darkened so that no gleam of light should appear without, and also that my brother seemed to be on the watch. I stood still in my hiding-place and listened to that wonderful tale, not losing one word, till my father came to that place where he that was dead came forth bound hand and foot with grave-clothes. Then I could no longer bear the excitement, and I cried out aloud. In another moment, my mother had drawn me out of my hiding-place, and I stood in the midst of the company."

"I was terribly frightened. I thought when I saw my father's grave face that I had done something dreadful; and I fell down on my knees at his feet and prayed him to pardon me. I shall never forget his look and tone as he raised me and placed me between his knees. It was seventy years ago and more, yet I seem to see and hear him now as he kissed me—a rare thing for him to do—and said to me—"

"'My dear son, I am not angry with you. You have unwittingly intruded into a great and dangerous secret, a secret which concerns men's lives, and you must now show that you are able to keep it.'"

"I was none the less frightened for this address. My head was as full of tales of enchantment as ever yours was, and I could think of nothing but that my father and his friends were engaged in some unlawful art, and I glanced fearfully around me, expecting to see I knew not what frightful appearance. My father seemed to perceive that I was frightened, for he passed his arm round me and bade me not be afraid."

"'This book,' said he, laying his hand on the volume, 'this book, my son, is no other than the Word of God, done into English by that good priest, Master Wickliffe of Lutterworth, in the days of my father, thy grandfather, for whom thou art named. My father held this book as his most precious treasure, albeit he suffered both persecution and loss of goods for its sake; and when he died, he bequeathed it to me. If I were known to possess it, the book would be taken and destroyed, and not only thy father and mother, but these neighbors, might be burned at the stake. So you see, my child, into what a perilous secret you have intruded yourself.'"

"'But, father,' I ventured to ask timidly, 'are you sure that this is really and truly the Word of God?'"

"'Yes, my son,' he replied, 'I am well assured of it.'"

"'How then?' I asked. 'I thought that only heretics were burned, and how should a man be accounted a heretic for reading the Word, of God?'"

"My father and his friends smiled, and one of them said, 'Truly, my dear lad, that is a question which has been asked by older heads than yours.'"

"''Tis indeed a grave question, and I will strive to explain the matter to you another day. Meantime, my son, attend to me. As I tell you, the lives of your father and mother depend upon your discretion. If you speak of what you have found out to any one, you may expect to see us burned alive at the stake. Do you know what that means?'"

"I did know, only too well. Only a year before, I had played the truant to see some great sight, I knew not what, which had drawn together a crowd of people over there on the border of the waste. I had slipped between them till I reached the front rank, and I had never forgotten the sight which met my eyes—the body of an aged woman consuming in the flames. The sight and the smell had haunted my dreams at times ever since."

"'I never will betray you, dear father; never,' I cried passionately. 'I will never breathe one word, if only you will let me hear God's Word.'"

"From that time, I was a regular attendant at the evening readings, nor would I have missed them for any reward which could have been promised me. My mother could repeat whole chapters of the Scripture, especially of the New Testament, and she caused me to learn them also; for she said—"

"'You may not always have the book. It may be destroyed, or you may have to leave home, but what is stored in your memory no man can take from you.'"

"Accordingly, she caused me to learn by heart large part of the sayings of our Lord, with the account of his miracles."

"Did our Lord work miracles like the holy image at Glastonbury, or like those we read of in the lives of the saints?" asked Jack. "Was he seen gliding along over the treetops, or kneeling a little way up in the air at his devotions, like St. Catherine; or did he live a whole week on five orange seeds, like St. Rose; or—"

"Nay, our Lord's miracles were very different from most of those related in the lives of the saints," replied the shepherd. "They were mostly performed to heal the sick, or to help those who were in some strait for want of food, or the like. But at last, the time came when I must go forth to seek my own living. My father was not rich, and had suffered, like almost every one else, by the long civil wars. So I was sent to keep sheep on the Stonehill farm, across the waste yonder, and quite on the other side of the parish. I did not come home for a year, and then it was upon a mournful occasion. My father had been arrested and thrown into jail for a heretic, and though my good master, Sir John Brydges, interceded for him, he could not save him. My brother was obliged to flee for his life, and what became of him I cannot say. I never saw or heard of him again."

"I was permitted to see my father and receive his blessing, but only in presence of witnesses. His enemies would gladly have pushed matters to extremity, and have turned my mother and me out into the world to wander as beggars, if indeed they had left us that resource, but again Sir John stood our friend. May God bless him for it, and give him his portion among the saints! He was a man of weight and power, and he used his power well. The cottage where my father and grandfather lived was assured to my mother for her life, and I was taken into the good knight's service, he thinking, I suppose, that I should be safer attending upon him."

"I followed his fortunes faithfully for more than forty years, and I supported his head when he died. His son, the present knight, has ever been kind to me. He would have given me a home in his own hall had I desired it, but I was ever a lover of solitude, and found more pleasure in following the sheep on the hillside than in sitting among the servants in the great hall. Besides, I have always cherished a secret hope that I might find my father's great book hidden somewhere about the old cottage."

"Then it was not destroyed?" said Jack.

"Not that I know of. It was never found. My father, fearing for its safety, had bestowed it in some new hiding-place the day that he was arrested, and he had no time to tell my mother where he had placed it."

"Then it may be in being now," said Jack. "Oh, uncle, if we could but find it!"

"Would to God I might!" replied the old man, looking upward and clasping his hands. "I would depart in peace, could I but once more hold the Word of God in my hands. And, son Jack—for dear you are to me as my own son—I know not if it may not be a fond fancy, but by times something tells me that I shall see it again before I die."

CHAPTER IV.

SEED BY THE WAYSIDE.

From this day forward Jack had a new interest and a new object in life—to find the old Bible. Day by day, he explored every possible hiding-place, turning things upside down in all directions, and rummaging, old Margery declared, worse than a rat or than the goblin which haunted her father's barn. Over and over again, did he take the false bottom out of the little footstool, where the book had once been concealed, and gaze into the empty space, as if he thought he might somehow have overlooked the cumbrous volume, and might perhaps find it by more careful search.

The book haunted his very slumbers. Often did he dream of finding it, and once the dream was so vivid, that he went before sunrise to the little dell where he had seemed to discover it under a flat stone. But, alas! There was no such stone to be seen, and he came sadly back a little ashamed of his own credulity, and having gained nothing but a prodigious appetite for his breakfast.

Jack had but one consolation, and that indeed was a great one. He made the shepherd repeat to him all that he could remember of Holy Scripture. The old man's memory, though somewhat impaired as to late occurrences, was as vivid as ever for all those things which had happened in his youth, and he was able to repeat whole chapters of Wickliffe's version of the Bible, which, rude and imperfect as it was, had been as a savor of life unto life to many hungry souls.

Jack was astonished at the things he heard, and still more at those he did not hear; and not a little grieved to find that some of his favorite legends of saints had no place in the Scripture at all.

"Tell me of St. Anne, our Lady's mother," he said one day.

"There is only one place about St. Anne," replied the shepherd, and he repeated the story of our Lord's presentation in the temple.

"Is that all?" asked Jack in a disappointed one. "I do not see that it says a word about her being our Lady's mother."

"Nothing at all," answered the shepherd.

"Perhaps the story is in some other place," Jack suggested.

But the old man shook his head.

"I have read the New Testament all through," he said. "There is not a word said about our Lady's mother, and very little about our Lady herself."

Jack looked startled. "But do you think it could have been the true and right Gospel, Uncle Thomas?" he said. "The priests tell us more about our Lady than about our Lord himself; and I am sure that Anne says ten prayers to her for one that she says to our Lord."

The old man did not answer immediately, and Jack repeated his question, "Do you think it could have been the true Gospel after all?"

"I have been thinking, Jack—" said the shepherd, after a little silence, and without answering or seeming to hear the question, "I have been thinking that I have perhaps done wrong in this matter."

"How?" asked Jack.

"Because the knowledge I have given you, may bring you into danger. Because the questions I have raised in your young mind will not be lightly laid again. And how shall I answer it to your father, if anything happen to you?"

"But, Uncle Thomas," said Jack, after a little silence, "your father did not fear to expose you to the danger."

"No, because my father was fully persuaded in his own mind. He esteemed the true knowledge of God and his truth worth every danger which could befall. I well remember his words to me, whispered in my ear as he gave me his last embrace, 'My son, remember the words of our Lord: Fear not them that kill the body, and after that have no more that they can do; but fear him who is able to cast body and soul into hell!'"

"I cannot but think he was right," said Jack, with decision, after a little pause. "I cannot but think the truth must be worth any danger that can come upon us for its sake. Nor can I yet understand why reading God's Word should make men heretics. The priest at the convent says it is because ignorant men know not how to use it, and that it is like a poisonous drug which can be safely touched only by a physician."

"Ay, I have heard that story often enough," said the old man; "and how that the giving the Scripture to the common folk is a casting of holy things to the dogs and pearls before swine. A pretty saying indeed, to call those for whom Christ died, dogs and swine!"

"Do they then christen little whelps and pigs?" asked Jack, shrewdly. "Methinks that were as great an abuse of holy things as reading the Bible to the vulgar people."

The shepherd smiled. "Thou art a shrewd lad. Take care that thou make thy wit keep thy head instead of losing it."

"I will take care," replied Jack, with all the confidence of fifteen. "But, uncle, according to all that you tell me, the holy apostles were but common men like ourselves. St. Peter and St. John were fishermen and worked for their bread; and yet our Lord's sayings were spoken to them."

"Yes, I have often thought of that," replied Thomas Sprat. "Those they called the Pharisees were learned men, it would seem, and yet our Lord did not call His apostles from among them. He even told them that the publicans and the harlots should go into the kingdom before them. Strange how the words come back to me more and more!" continued the old man, in a musing tone. "I would not have thought I could repeat so many: 'But the Holy Ghost shall teach you, and shall bring all things to your remembrance, whatsoever I have told you.' I well remember how my mother repeated to me those words when I first went from home to the Stonehill farm. I was deploring my fate in being obliged to go away where I could no longer hear and read the Word of God, and saying that I feared that I should forget all that I had learned."

"'My son,' said she, 'remember that you carry with you a teacher who is able to make you wise, even without the words of this book, and without whom even the book itself can teach you nothing. I mean the Holy Spirit of God. Our Lord promised this Spirit of truth to His disciples, and said:'"

"'"He shall teach you all things, and bring all things to your remembrance, whatsoever I have told you."'"

"'Ask constantly for this Spirit, my son, and it shall be given you.'"

"And so verily have I found it. I have been exposed to many dangers and temptations in my long and wandering life, and, woe is me! I have sinned often and grievously; but in times of the greatest trial, there have been brought to my remembrance words of my father's book which have kept me back from sinning, or encouraged me to return when I had wandered away."

"And do you think," asked Jack, in a tone of awe, "that it was the Holy Ghost which brought these words to your mind?"

"I cannot but think so, my son."

"But, Uncle Thomas," said Jack, "is it not—"

"I believe I know what you would say, my son," said the old man, as Jack paused. "You would ask if it is not presumption to suppose that God Himself teaches and governs us. I cannot think so. It would be so, doubtless, if He had not given us warrant for it in His Word; but so long as He says, He is more ready to give the Holy Spirit to them that ask Him than earthly parents are to give good gifts to their children, I think we are bound to believe Him."

"'If ye then, being evil, know how to give good gifts to your children, how much more shall your Heavenly Father give the Holy Spirit to them that ask Him?'"

"Jack," added the old man with energy, "I thank God that I have been led to open my heart to you, for the repeating of the Scriptures to you has so refreshed my memory of them, as I could not have believed possible."

"And I am thankful too," said Jack. He sat musing for some minutes, and then added, "Yes, I am thankful, and shall always be thankful, even though the words of Scripture should bring me to such a fate as they did poor Agnes Harland."

"Who is Agnes Harland?" asked the shepherd.

Jack started.

"I am wrong," said he. "I promised Anne I would never tell the tale again. It was something which happened in the convent."

The shepherd nodded sagaciously. "Ay, ay. I can guess," said he, "but say no more, dear boy. Remember that a promise broken without great necessity is a lie told, and beware, of all things, of lying. But this is the conclusion of the matter: God is always ready to hear the prayers of His children, and to help them at their need."

"But, Uncle Thomas, suppose one should wish to pray for something, and should not know any prayer which said what he wanted."

"Then I suppose he must make a prayer for himself, as David did, and as other saints have done. I know no other way."

That night when Jack went to bed, he prayed that God would show him where the old Bible was hidden, or send him another.

A few days after this conversation, Master Lucas made his appearance at the shepherd's cottage, mounted on his easy ambling mule, and followed by his man Simon.

"Well, well," he exclaimed, with his usual jolly laugh, as Jack ran to help his father dismount. "Why, this is fine, to be sure! This is a sight for sore eyes. Uncle Thomas, you are worth all the doctors and wise women in Bridgewater. Bless thee, boy, thy father's heart is glad to see thee again."

"It is but little that I have done," said Thomas Sprat. "The credit of Jack's cure belongs to the fresh air of the hill far more than to me. But come in, come in, cousin Lucas. You must be in need of refreshment. You do not often ride so far from home."

"Why, no, not of late years," replied the baker, bowing his head to enter the low door of the cottage. "I do grow too stout for journeying. Ho! Dame Margery, how goes all with you? Why, you look so young and well-favored, we shall have you fitted with a gay bridegroom next."

"Fie, fie! Master Lucas!" replied the old woman, chuckling nevertheless at the compliment. "Well-favored is far past my time of life. But you yourself are looking purely, Master Lucas, and your voice is like the knight's hunting horn. 'Tis not often I hear any one so plainly."

"Come now, I cannot have you young folks bandying fine speeches," said the shepherd. "Bestir yourself, Margery, and provide refreshment for Master Lucas and his man and for the beasts."

"Don't trouble yourself about the beasts," said Master Lucas. "The fine fresh grass will be a treat to the poor things. I have brought thee some linen and such like, my lad, and Cicely has packed a whole pannier of good things. Bid Simon bring them into the house."

"And Anne, dear father?" asked Jack. "How is Anne?"

Master Lucas's face clouded at mention of his daughter. "Why, well in health—that is, think she would be well if she would let herself alone and live like the rest of us; but she is wearing herself into her grave with her penances. 'Twas but the other day, I found out that she slept on the hard boards every night, and, not content with that, she must needs strew ashes on them. I know not what to do with her, and that is the truth. But there is great news about the gray nuns' convent where she learned all these ways. It is to be put down by order of my lord cardinal, along with many others—some forty, they say—all small ones like this."

"For what reason?" asked Jack.

"I do not understand, exactly. For the founding of some college or other. Anyhow he has the order from his Holiness the Pope, and so the nuns must budge, will they nill they. Poor old girls! I wonder much what will become of them all. I don't love them too well, but it pities me to think of them turned out all among strangers, and I have told Anne if she has any special friend among them she may ask her to stay with us till she can have time to turn herself."

"You are the very best man in the world, father!" said Jack. "I do believe there never was such another."

"Tut, tut, lad! I trust there are many better in our good town. I will say for Anne, she was very grateful, and thanked me prettily enough, poor child. But you and I have lived to see many changes, Uncle Thomas. 'Tis but a little while since folks were wondering over hearing the Creed, the Lord's Prayer, and the Commandments said in English in the churches. Who knows what may come next? We may live to hear the whole Bible read, as they say the Lutherans do."

"Not in my time, I fear," replied the shepherd. "But is not this a strange move of my lord cardinal's? There is much discontent already with the religious houses, and the monks complain everywhere of the disrespect with which they are treated. To my mind, this measure is a little like showing the cat the way to the cream."

"Maybe so! Maybe so! I fear me the cat will find her way to that cream-pot without showing, some of these days," said the baker. "But anyhow, the gray nuns must troop, bag and baggage, and there is talk of my Lord Harland buying the house and lands. They say he brought home much treasure from the Low Countries, and some pretend to affirm that he is a favorer of the new doctrine. Anne, poor maid, went off into a fit of weeping when she heard the story. I suppose it is but natural she should be grieved at seeing the place go into secular hands."

Jack thought he understood better the cause of his sister's grief. He remembered the sad tale of Agnes Harland, and could not help wondering whether she were still alive and whether the suppression of the convent might prove her release.

"But even if she be living, they will doubtless make sure work with her before that day comes," he thought. "She will have secured her martyr's crown before this time."

Meantime Dame Margery's exertions had spread the board with a hearty and substantial meal, to which the travellers did full justice. Master Lucas praised everything, declared that such milk and butter were well worth the ride, and shouted compliments to Margery till the old woman fairly blushed. He was one of those happy people who are always disposed to see the bright side of everything, and who come like a broad beam of sunshine into every house they enter.

"Well, we must even be jogging homewards," he said, at last. "My mule is not swift at best, as how could she be, poor creature, with such a load on her back? We must not be late, or the women will imagine all sorts of dangers and horrors."

"And indeed, I would not have you out after dark," said Thomas Sprat. "The waste here harbors many vagrants—gypsies and the like, who bear none too good characters."

"I will go with you a part of the way, father," said Jack. "I suppose Simon can foot it a mile or so, and I will ride his beast and walk back."

"That can I, indeed, and will do so with a right good will," said Simon the journeyman, who, truth to say, was something the worse for his unusual equestrian exercise, if so it could be called, and who looked forward with no great pleasure to mounting his mule again. "I would gladly walk half the way back to Bridgewater."

In a short time the mules were saddled, the last good-bys said, and Jack and his father were riding soberly side by side on the road to Bridgewater, while Simon trudged after them on foot, keeping at such a distance as not to overhear their conversation, yet as near as was consistent with "manners." Their talk was of home matters and of the news of the town.

Jack begged his father to send him some of his books. This the old man at first flatly refused to do, saying that if Jack had his books he would spend his time poring over them and would soon be as bad as ever again; but upon farther entreaty, and on Jack's representation that he should have to be out of doors with the sheep all day, at any rate, and that he should forget all he had learned, his father so far gave way as to say he would consult Sir William about the matter, and if he thought best, the books should be sent; and with this promise Jack was fain to be content.

Presently they met and passed a man mounted on a serviceable riding hack, and followed by a mule loaded, as it seemed, with merchandise. The traveller was dressed like a merchant, and Jack did not fail to notice that he held a small book in his hand, which at their approach, he put into his pocket.

"There's a man after your own heart, son Jack," said the baker. "He reads as he travels along the highway. Good-day to you, sir!" he added, addressing the traveller as they came within speaking distance. "Methinks your horse must be a steady one, since he allows you to study upon his back."

The stranger smiled and bowed courteously. "My horse and I are old companions and well acquainted," he replied. "Nevertheless, I do not often make a reading chair of my saddle. I did but refresh my memory as to a passage on which my mind was running. May I crave to know if this is the road to Holford and the house of Sir John Brydges?"

"You are just in the road," said Jack, "but the knight is not at home. He went up to London the day before yesterday."

A shade of disappointment passed over the stranger's grave face. "Then we have passed each other on the road. I am very sorry, for my business is somewhat pressing. Do you know, my young sir, how long he will be gone?"

"About a month, I heard them say at the Hall."

"Well, I must needs go on my way, nevertheless," said the stranger. "Doubtless there is some house of entertainment in the village where I can abide for the night."

"There is indeed, sir, and a very decent place, too, the Appletree Inn kept by Widow Higgins. But if you go up to the Hall they will care for you hospitably," said Jack. "They turn no one away, gentle or simple, who comes before eight of the clock. Men say the knight's house is as open as his heart and hand."

"Jack, Jack, how your tongue runs!" said his father. "I pray you pardon the lad's forwardness," he added, addressing the stranger. "The knight hath been kind enough to notice him, and he is one who thinks much of a small favor."

"'Tis a small defect if it be one at all," replied the stranger kindly. "And I am not disposed to find fault with the tongue which runs only with good words. Good-day to you, sir, and the peace of God go with you!"

"A grave and godly man, no doubt," said the baker, as they parted company. "I wonder if he is really a merchant after all. He rode a fine horse, and I noticed his gown was of superfine cloth, and trimmed with costly fur; but these London merchants, many of them, are as rich as the great lords, and live in far greater comfort and luxury than our country knights and squires."

"I wonder what book he was reading," said Jack. "He must be a learned man to carry a book in his pocket."

"I am not so sure of that," said his father laughing. "A man may not certainly be a good baker because his coat is covered with flour."

"But he spoke like a scholar, father," said Jack. "Did you not think so?"

"There was something uncommon about him, for certain," replied Master Lucas. "He had the look of a man who is always thinking of great and grave subjects. To my mind, his face had something the look of our Sir William."

"Sir William had a cousin in London, I know," said Jack, struck by a sudden thought. "Perhaps this might be the same."

"Like enough! Like enough! But, my son, you have gone far enough seeing that you are to walk back. My blessing on thee, dearest lad. Take care of thy health, be dutiful and obedient to Uncle Thomas, and learn all that thou canst from him. Learning is light to carry about, and no kind ever comes amiss. Remember thy duty to God and thy father; say thy prayers every day, and thou wilt never go far astray."

Jack loaded his father with love and messages to all at home, from the good priest and his sister down to the old cat, whose infirmities of now and then helping himself out of the pantry and shop, he besought his father to pardon.

"Never fear; never fear!" said his father, laughing. "The poor beast shall live out his days in peace, I promise thee, for all me. He does but act after his cattish nature, and we must keep temptation out of his way. Once more, my blessing be upon thee."

Jack had begun to feel very manly of late, but all his manliness did not prevent his shedding a few tears at parting with his father, nor was Master Lucas free from a similar weakness, which, however, disguised itself under a sharp criticism of the style of riding of poor Simon, who, he averred, sat his mule like one of his own meal-sacks.

Jack had wiped the drops from his eyes, and was walking briskly on when his foot stumbled on something at the edge of the footpath. He looked down, and quickly picked up the object which had arrested him. It was a small but thick book, bound in parchment and with brazen clasps, and he had no difficulty in recognizing the book he had seen the stranger reading.

He debated for a moment as to whether he ought to open it, but a new book was a rare sight in those parts, and curiosity got the better of his scruples, and he unclasped the volume. The first words he saw arrested his attention, and he walked on reading till he was aroused by some one speaking to him.

"So you have found my book, my fair son. I was coming back to look for it, and am right glad to see it safe. But you seem greatly interested."

Jack looked up with wide-open eyes full of eager interest and a kind of reverential awe.

"Oh, sir, please tell me—forgive me if I am forward—but do please tell me, is not this book a Bible?"

CHAPTER V.

THE CHRISTIAN BROTHER.

The stranger paused a moment before answering Jack's question, and scrutinized his face.

"Why do you think it a Bible?" he asked.

"Because, sir, I find words here like those I have heard before, and which I was told were in the Bible. Here is the very tale of that son who left his father and his home, and went away to waste his goods in a far country, which Uncle Thomas told me. And here are those other words, 'Fear ye not them which kill the body and be not able to kill the soul.' Oh, sir, is it not really a Bible?"

The stranger dismounted from his horse and walked slowly along by Jack's side.

"My dear boy," said he gravely but kindly, "will you tell me from whom you have learned so much of Holy Scripture? Nay, I will not ask, if it is a secret," he added, seeing Jack hesitate. "I am a stranger, and cannot reasonably ask you to trust me at sight. Nevertheless, I will trust you, and answer your questions. This book is a part of Holy Scripture, that part which contains the life and sayings of our Lord, and the letters of His Apostles, lately translated, and done into English, that plain men may read that which it concerneth their salvation to know. It is to be hoped, in time, that we shall have the whole Bible in English, but the New Testament is put forth first as being the most important to Christian men."

Jack walked on in silence, still looking at the precious volume. "I would give all I have," said he at last, "for such a book as this."

"Would you, indeed?" asked the stranger. "That is verily in accordance with Holy Writ, which saith, 'The kingdom of heaven is like treasure hid in the field, the which a man found and hid it; and for joy thereof goeth and selleth all that he hath, and buyeth that field.'"

"But, dear lad, you are but young and tender, and the possession of this book hath its dangers. There be many who look upon it as the work of the devil and his servants. Sir Thomas More, himself—albeit in many respects a good and wise man—would gladly burn both the books and their authors and readers. Such risks are not for children like you."

"But, sir, does not this very book say we are not to fear them which kill the body?" asked Jack. "Did not the man in the parable you have just spoken sell all he had to buy the treasure hid in a field?"

"Even so, my son."

"My uncle's father was burned for having in his house and reading an English Bible," pursued Jack, "and he went to his death with joy. Oh, sir, I have so longed and prayed to see an English or Latin Bible!"

"Ay, so! You can read your Latin Bible," said the stranger, "You are, then, a scholar?"

"No great scholar as yet, though I can read Latin well enough," said Jack, with not unjustifiable pride. "I took the gold medal at Bridgewater grammar school, and Sir William Leavett says I can go to Oxford in another year, if my health fail not. I came to keep sheep with my uncle in Holford because I was sickly with too much study, but I am quite well now."

"And was it your uncle or your father from whom you parted but now?"

"My father, sir, and, I do think, the best man in all the world. My uncle lives in a cottage just under the hill yonder."

"And you are of Bridgewater, and know my cousin, Sir William Leavett?" continued the stranger. "I purpose to visit him before my return. Is the good man well?"

"Quite well, sir, my father says. He is indeed a good man, and beloved by gentle and simple among his own flock. He has promised to come and see me one day, but his hands are always full of business, what with the school, and the poor and sick, and the Greek studies which he greatly affects."

"Ay, does he so? And you, do you know any Greek?"

"But very little, sir: only the letters and a few rules. My father is somewhat afraid of it, because one of the monks—Father Francis, the sacristan, who sometimes comes to see us—told him that Greek was a heathen language, not fit for Christians to learn. He said he was cast into a deep sleep only by trying to make out the forms of the letters, and so forgot to ring the bell for evensong," added Jack gravely, but with a certain spark of fun in his eyes. "But Father Francis is fat, and likes a humming cup of ale, and mayhap it was something else which put him to sleep."

"Very like, very like," said the stranger smiling. "My counsel to you is to learn all the Greek you can, and then you may read the New Testament in the original tongue. But that is a knowledge to which common men cannot well attain, and for that reason certain well-learned persons are advised to put forth this translation which you are now reading." (For Jack still held the book in his hand). "But if you will raise your eyes to the clouds, you will see that we are threatened with a storm of some violence, and that before many minutes are past. Can I reach the village or Hall, think you, before it breaks?"

"I fear not," replied Jack. "Your best way will be to come at once to my uncle's cottage, which is close at hand, and where, I am sure, you will be heartily welcome, if you can put up with so plain a place."

"I thank you, and will accept your offer," said the stranger, "if I shall not put your uncle's household to inconvenience."

"I am sure he will be glad to see you," said Jack. "But make haste, for the storm will quickly be upon us."

In effect, the traveller had hardly entered the door of Thomas Sprat's cottage, before the rain fell in torrents. Old Thomas was in the house, and made his guest courteously welcome.

"You were best bring your merchandise into the house, sir," said he. "We have no locks upon our stable door."

"Have you, then, dishonest neighbors?" asked the merchant.

"As to that, the place is much like other places," replied Thomas Sprat. "We have both good and bad neighbors, but the waste yonder harbors a sort of vagrants and masterless men, of whom our good knight has not been able altogether to rid us. I would ill like to have my guest robbed under my roof."

"And I would ill like to be robbed," said the merchant; "therefore, though the contents of my packs are not such as to tempt common thieves, I will, with the help of my young friend here, bestow them in the house. It will not be the first service he has rendered me, short as our acquaintance has been. He has restored to me a precious treasure, which my carelessness suffered to fall by the wayside; and not only so, but he has shown an acquaintance with its value which has much surprised me."

The shepherd looked surprised in his turn, but he said nothing till the packages of the traveller were safely placed in a corner, and the table spread with such food as could be provided from the resources of the cottage, aided by the stores of Cicely's hamper. The stranger said grace, and sat down to his meal, which he discussed with a good appetite.

"I find your grandson—or nephew I think he called himself—a good scholar," said the stranger, addressing the old shepherd. "He tells me that he can read Latin and has begun to learn Greek."

"Yes, the lad has profited at his book," replied the shepherd. "I am no scholar myself, beyond reading and writing, but they tell me Jack is a good one for his years and has won high honors at the school in Bridgewater. But I fear, Jack, the stranger will think you over-forward, if you are so ready to boast your own learning."

"It was through no boasting of his, but through my own questioning, that I learned as much," said the stranger. "He picked up a book which I let fall, and coming back to seek it, and finding him engaged in reading it, we naturally fell into conversation. I was much surprised and pleased to find him already acquainted with its contents."

"Indeed! It will be some of his school Latin books, doubtless."

Jack looked at the stranger with a gesture and glance of entreaty.

"Oh, sir, may I not show my uncle the book?" he asked. "Old Margery is deaf. She will not hear a word or notice anything. May I not show him the book?"

"You may do so, if you will," replied the stranger, with a benevolent smile. "I see no harm it can do, since it is to your uncle you tell me you owe all your knowledge of its contents."

The shepherd looked wonderingly from one to the other. Jack opened the volume haphazard, and put it into his uncle's hand. As the old man examined the page his expression changed from one of surprise and uneasiness, to a look of joyful awe and thankfulness. Clasping his hands and raising them to heaven, while his eyes filled with tears, he exclaimed, "I thank thee, O Lord! Now lettest thou thy servant depart in peace, for mine eyes have seen thy salvation. May the blessing of God rest upon you, sir, whoever you are, since you have brought to my eyes what they hardly expected to see again—the Word of God in the vulgar tongue. Sir, I know not who you are, you are a rich man belike, and I am but a poor shepherd; but if any treasure I possess can purchase this book—"

"Say no more, my good brother," replied the stranger. "With this book I cannot part, seeing it was the gift of a dear friend; but another copy of the Scriptures, in better print and more easy to your eyes, you shall have and welcome, and right glad am I to put it in such hands. I am, as you have said, a rich man, and I know not how I can spend my wealth better than by helping to spread the Gospel in this land which longs for it as a thirsty land for the rain of heaven."

So saying, the merchant undid one of his mails, and from under the rich silks and stuffs with which it was apparently filled, he drew forth a large copy of the New Testament and put it into his host's hands.

"To this book, as I said, you are freely welcome," said he. "It is the New Testament newly done into English by that learned clerk and godly man, Sir William Tyndale. I need not tell you that it is a treasure to be kept and used with caution, since many of the bishops and priests, not less than the King himself, are bitterly opposed to the reading of this translation."

"It is then a service of some danger you undertake in carrying these books about with you, Master—"

"My name is Richard Fleming, at your service, a merchant of London," said the stranger, as Thomas Sprat paused. "It is indeed a service of danger as you say. Yet it is not my own danger which at times appalls me and makes me almost ready to give up that which I have undertaken. It is the thought that these books, precious as they are, bring danger of persecution and even death to those who receive and read them. Even now, for aught I know, I may have thrust a firebrand into the thatch of your peaceful dwelling, or have, as it were, lighted a death-pile for this fair boy. When I think of these things I am ready to say: 'It is enough, Lord! Take away my life!' And yet the burden is laid upon me, yea, woe is me if I help not to spread the Gospel."

"I understand your feeling," said Thomas Sprat, as the stranger paused. "I have myself felt the same toward my young kinsman here, whom yet I have instructed so far as I was able in the words and meaning of Holy Scripture. Our blessed Lord knew it also doubtless when He said to His followers: 'they shall lay their hands on you, and persecute you, delivering you up to the synagogues and into prison, and bring you before kings and rulers, for my name's sake.' Yet I cannot but think that the boon is worth all it costs twice told. Shall we refuse to suffer for Him who died for us? Methinks you are a man to be envied, since you are permitted to spend your time and substance in thus spreading abroad the Word of God. I had thought the merchants of London too busy with their goods and merchandise, with the care of their gold, and the enjoyment of luxury in their fine houses, to care for aught else."

"It is alas! the case with too many of them," replied the stranger. "Yet are there many among them who are of my mind, and esteem the riches of God more than all the treasures of Egypt, who spend their time and their substance freely for the spread of His Word. An association has been formed among them called the Christian Brothers, of which I am a member; and we are pledged to devote ourselves and our goods to spreading a knowledge of pure Gospel truth in this land. I trust we have already sowed seed which shall spring up and bear fruit unto everlasting life, though we may not be spared to see its full fruition."

"It was a blessed hap which brought you here this day," said the old shepherd fervently. "Oh, how earnestly I have longed and prayed to see and read once more the Word of God which I knew and read in my youth. Son Jack, our prayers have been answered sooner than we hoped, though in a different way."

The Association of Christian Brothers, formed about the time of our story among the merchants of London, makes of itself a sufficient answer, if indeed an answer were needed, to those who sneer at trade and the pursuits of commerce as ignoble and unfitting the mind for great deeds. The object of these men was to disperse abroad among the people copies of the New Testament, and portions of the writings of the Reformers, as fast as they could be received from the printing-presses Antwerp and other Flemish and German cities.

For this end, the Christian Brothers and the agents travelled through the length and breadth the land, bearing their perilous yet precious commodities concealed among their goods, and disposing of them as they had opportunity. Of course the service was one of great danger. If any man were found circulating the Lutheran books, as they were called, public penance and disgrace and ruinous fines were the least he had to expect; and the flames and smoke of the stake were always in the background of the picture.

Nevertheless, those devoted men, the Christian Brothers, abated not a whit of their diligence; but availing themselves of their opportunities as merchants trading to Germany and the Low Countries, they brought over not only the New Testament in English, but other books and tracts in great numbers, which were carried throughout the whole of England, and eagerly caught up and read both by gentle and simple. Tyndale's prophecy, made years before in a dispute with a Romish priest, seemed in a fair way of being fulfilled: "Ere many years are past, the very plough-boys of this land shall know more of Holy Scripture than thou dost."

In our days, when the Bible lies on almost every shelf and may be had by every man, woman, and child in the land, when we can hardly remember our first acquaintance with the sacred text, it is difficult for us to enter into the feelings of those who read the Bible for the first time. To us, it has become as familiar, and it is to be feared often as tedious, as a twice told tale; and it requires all our reverence for the book as the written and authentic Word of God, to fix our attention upon our daily lesson.

To those who received the English New Testament from the hands of Tyndale and his followers, it possessed all the charm of novelty. They had heard at the best only short and garbled extracts from the Holy Book, and what little they knew was so overlaid and mixed up with legend and fable, that the whole gracious story was to them a new revelation, startling and arousing them alike from what it said and from what it did not say. The doctrine of purgatory, with all its tremendous consequences, fell at once to the ground. So did that of the invocation of saints; and especially the almost divine honors paid to the Blessed Virgin were seen to be wholly without foundation.

To many an overburdened soul painfully striving by prayers and penances to escape from the wrath to come, the knowledge of justification by means of faith in the Son of God, of free forgiveness through His own oblation of Himself once offered, came with an overwhelming sense of relief from an intolerable burden; while to another it brought a feeling of deep humiliation and mortification that all the self-made sanctity for which he had perhaps been celebrated and held up as an example to his fellows was of no avail or value in the eyes of God, not worth so much as a cup of cold water given in the name of Christ to one of His little ones.

Welcome or unwelcome, loved or hated, the Word of God went on its way. It was like the leaven which a woman took and hid in three measures of meal. No man who received it could hide it wholly within his heart. Consciously or unconsciously, it affected his conduct and appeared in his conversation; and thus the new ideas spread from one to another, even among those who were the most bitterly opposed to them.

CHAPTER VI.

A FALL AND A NEW FRIEND.

Long after old Margery had retired to her chamber wondering at her master's unusual waste of candle-light, did the other two inmates of the cottage sit listening with rapt attention while Master Fleming read and expounded the Holy Book, or told them tales of the deeds and sufferings of the friends of the Gospel at home and abroad.

At last, in a pause of the conversation, Jack exclaimed—

"Oh, if I could but go with you and help you in this great work, how gladly would I give all my time and strength to the spread of God's Word among the people! I used to wish I had lived in the days of chivalry when the valiant knights went forth in search of adventure, and to succor the helpless and oppressed wherever they were to be found; but this is a greater work still, and better worth one's life and substance."

"You say well," replied Master Fleming. "It is indeed better worth the spending of life and substance than any of the often fantastic enterprises of your favorite knights; and neither is it without sufficient danger to life and goods, though there are no more dragons and enchanters to overcome. But the work of the Lord has this advantage, that it may be done by simple folk as well as gentle folk, and as worthily in the humblest vocation as in the highest. The lowliest life, the commonest task, if sanctified by an earnest and honest intention of doing God service, is as much accepted and blessed by Him as that which is highest in the sight of men. Our Lord Himself has said that a cup of cold water, given in His name and for his sake, is given to Him."

"But I would so like to devote myself to this work," said Jack. "It seems such a noble way of serving Him."

"I fear your motives are not altogether clear, son Jack," said the shepherd. "I fear a part of your zeal arises from love of adventure and novelty."

Jack blushed, and the merchant smiled.

"And if it were so, you have no cause to blush, my son," said he kindly. "The love of novelty and adventure is natural to youth, and is doubtless given by Heaven for some good purpose. But you must remember that, as the soldier does not choose his work or his place, but goes whither he is sent, and upon whatever service his commander orders, having no will of his own, so must it be with the soldier of Christ. He must be as ready to abide by the stuff as to go forward upon the stricken field; to keep the few sheep in the wilderness, as to fight the giant of the Philistines before the armies of Israel."

"Sir William told us that tale," said Jack, "and how King David overcame the giant with his sling and stone. But there are no giants in these days."

"No, but there are dangers as terrible, ay, more terrible than any man meets in the stricken field. If it be true in all ages, as doubtless it is in some sense, that they who would live godly in Christ must suffer persecution, it is doubly so at this time when he that departeth from evil maketh himself a prey, and men are condemned to the dungeon and the stake but for desiring to acquaint themselves with the Word of God. You say, my dear son, and doubtless with truth, that you would gladly help forward this work; but think of yourself as torn from all that you love and cast into a loathsome foul dungeon, without light or fire or fresh air, subject to the scourge and the rack at the will of your oppressors, daily tempted with all the rewards of this world, if you would abjure your faith, and threatened with the pangs of a horrible and shameful death, if you did not. Do you think you could hold fast the profession of your faith without wavering?"

Jack sat looking at the fire for a few moments without reply. Then he lifted his head, and a new light seemed to exalt and illuminate his somewhat plain features as he spoke.

"I would be far from boasting of my manhood, sir. I know well that it has never been tried, and that I am but a young and simple boy. Nevertheless, I have read in this book already, that our Lord said to one of His apostles who was in some strait: 'My grace is sufficient for thee, for my strength is made perfect through weakness,' and again 'God is faithful who will not suffer you to be tempted above your strength, but shall in the midst of temptation make a way to escape out.' I would be far from boasting of mine own strength or manhood, since I know how oft I have failed under very easy trials of temper and patience; neither would I run heedlessly into danger. But if God should call me to such works as those of which you speak, might I not think that He would be faithful in giving me strength to do them?"

"Verily, thou hast given me a good answer, and, as it were, out of mine own mouth," replied Master Fleming, with his grave smile. "You are, no doubt, in the right. I trust your faith will never be tried in such ways; and yet it is well to be prepared for whatever may come. I would advise you to read and ponder the tenth chapter of St. Matthew's Gospel, and to pray constantly and earnestly for grace to stand when the day of trial arrives."

"It may not come," said Jack.

The stranger shook his head. "The trial is sure to come in one way or other," said he. "It may not be in the way of persecution, perhaps it may come in the opposite direction from the temptation of this world. In these days the seed is perhaps as likely to be choked with care and riches and voluptuous living as in any other way. But in whatever way the temptation comes, we shall need all the strength which our Lord hath to give, to fight the battle of life withal. But the hour waxes late, and I must needs rise early and go on my way."

Jack gave up his own bed to the visitor, and slept on the great wooden settle by the fireside. His sleep was not sound, and toward morning awaking suddenly he heard, as he thought, some one speaking earnestly as though pleading for, some great boon, and willing to take no denial. He stole softly to the foot of the stairs and listened. The voice was that of the stranger guest, and Jack presently perceived that he was engaged in fervent prayer. A feeling of delicacy prevented him from listening; but, as he lingered for a moment, he caught the words:

"Not this one, Lord, not this one! If there must needs be a sacrifice take the old tree, broken and withered in thy service, but spare the young and tender plant."

Jack's reverence deepened into awe as he perceived that Master Fleming was praying for himself, pleading with God as a child with a tender parent, that he might be spared the horror and pain in which the "gospellers" too often ended their lives.

Jack stole back to his bed and sat thinking for a long time. He remembered how he had ventured to pray in somewhat the same way for sight of the Scriptures, and how his prayer had been answered in the sense and realization of God's presence at the time he was praying, as well as in the apparent chance which had brought the stranger to his uncle's house. Would Master Fleming's prayer be granted in the same way?

Or would he be called to witness for God at the stake and on the rack, like some of those confessors of whom he had lately heard? And if so, would strength be given him according to his needs?

And what would become of him afterward? Should he be taken to paradise or to purgatory? Was there any such place as purgatory? Was he fit for heaven? How could he make himself so?

Master Fleming had seemed to speak but slightingly of penances and pilgrimages and such like exercises, and had intimated that there was another way, sure and easy. What then was that way?

These were but a few of the questions which rose in the boy's mind as he sat in the chimney corner under the slowly dawning light. He was a grave and thoughtful lad at all times, sober beyond his years to a degree which had often troubled his father, and made old Cicely declare that her nursling was not long for this world. The religious teaching he had received had been mostly given him by Sir William Leavett and had been of a character unusually spiritual and pure for that time.

Then his uncle had taught him a great deal concerning the Bible during his residence at Holford; and altogether his soul was like a watered garden, ready to receive the seeds of eternal truth and to bring forth fruit to everlasting life.

Now, as he sat and thought, seeking in vain for satisfactory answer to the many questions which arose in his mind, he remembered what the shepherd had told him concerning the teachings of the Holy Spirit, that this Spirit could guide his mind into truth even without the written Word, and that unless he had such teaching from on high, all other instruction, yea, the Holy Book itself, would be of no avail. He took the volume from the safe place where it had been deposited, and opening it at haphazard, he read in the now quaint English of Tyndale's translation—

> "Axe and it shalbe geven you. Seke and ye shall fynd. Knocke and it shalbe opened vnto you. For whosoever axeth receaveth; and he that seketh findeth; and to him that knocketh it shalbe opened."

Jack read on to the end of the paragraph. Then it would seem that all he had to do in order to receive this wonderful teacher, was to ask for it. His heavenly Father was as ready to give it him as his own father would be to give him food when he desired it. Jack was happy in that he was able to reason from the goodness of an earthly to that of a heavenly Parent. He could not remember that his father had ever denied him any reasonable request, and the argument was thus a strong one.

> "'If ye then being evil know how to give good gifts to your children—'"

Why then should he not ask at once for what he felt he so much needed?

Jack restored the book to its place; and then, seeking the retirement of the little shed where Master Fleming's beasts were accommodated, he knelt in one corner and prayed long and earnestly and in simple faith that God would teach him all that it was needful to know. He was so absorbed as not to mark the passage of time, and he started to his feet and blushed deeply when the stranger gently opened the door and entered the hovel.

"Nay, never blush, my son," said Master Fleming kindly. "No man has cause to blush for being found on his knees. Rather let them be ashamed, who, pretending to be reasonable and immortal beings, live like the poor brutes that perish. But you have risen early."

"I have been up a long time," said Jack. "I could not sleep, and I have been reading in the book you gave us. Oh, sir, I would I might go with you, or that you would remain with us. I need so much instruction."

And thereupon, he poured out to his new-found friend some of the questions and thoughts which were seething in his brain.

Master Fleming listened patiently and with grave interest to Jack's confession and inquiries.

"Dear son, it would require more hours than I have minutes to spare, to answer all your questions. Nay, of many things you must be content to remain in ignorance, since they are beyond man's feeble understanding. I will leave with you certain treatises of Master Tyndale and, other good men from which you may gain much instruction, and you do right to ask for the illumination of the Spirit of God, which you will doubtless receive. But, my son, you must be prepared to learn from that teaching, many things which will be displeasing to you, ay, things against which your pride will rise up in rebellion. No man ever sees the wickedness and weakness of his own heart till the Spirit reveals it to him, and the sight is not a pleasant one. Yet it is necessary that we behold it, or we shall not feel our need of the remedy without which we must be lost indeed."

"And that remedy—" asked Jack.

"Is found alone in Christ Jesus, the way set forth by our Father for the forgiveness of sins. His blood, when we believe in Him and receive Him for our Saviour, cleanseth us from all sin which we have committed, so that for His sake we are freely pardoned and justified before God. Not as there were any merit in faith itself, but because it is only by faith that we accept Christ and receive Him into our hearts."

"See here, I must needs go on my way at present. I would gladly take you with me, and, as you say, let you help in this great work. But that would not be right. You are the only son of your father, and yet in your nonage, and your duty lies in obedience to him. Go on then doing your work in that place where God has put you, and remember that He will accept your service and make you His helper in building up His kingdom, whether he call you like the Jews of old to build on the walls of the spiritual Jerusalem with a sword in one hand and a trowel in the other, or in the quiet dells of the mountain to quarry out the stone for the temple, or even to carry food for them who are more actively engaged."

"It is the great blessing of work in our Divine Master's service, that nothing done for Him is ever thrown away, no, not even when the workman would appear in the eyes of men to have failed utterly. He will account nothing a failure which is done with a hearty and humble desire to serve him. Do you, therefore, watch and pray, read and meditate, strive for holiness of heart and purity of intention, and let your light so shine before men that they may see your good works and glorify your Father in heaven."

"I will give you for your own, a copy of the New Testament containing Master Tyndale's glosses and notes, which will be a great help to you in understanding the Word. It may be that we shall meet again, for I purpose to remain some time in this country; but if not, I charge you, my son in the faith, if I may call you so, that you keep your loins girded about, and your light trimmed and burning, and you yourself as one who waiteth for the Bridegroom, that, when the day of account shall come, I may meet you at the right hand of the Throne."

For the whole of that and many succeeding days, Jack was like one in a dream. He seemed to have lost all taste for his usual pleasures, bird's-nesting and fishing, while he strove with punctilious accuracy to fulfil all his daily duties and to take every possible care from his uncle. In fact, a new world seemed to be opened to him.

His imagination, always a strong part of his mental constitution, revelled in the scenes to which he was introduced and made them real to him. He walked the streets of Jericho and Jerusalem, and sat with the apostles at the board with their Lord; he was among the crowd which stood around the sepulchre when Lazarus came forth, and entered with the chosen disciples into the inner chamber where the ruler's young daughter was raised from the dead.

Nor was it the narrative alone which interested him. As Richard Fleming had told him, he began to have some sense of his own real nature, to realize his own sinfulness, and to wonder whether it were possible he could ever attain to the inheritance of the saints in light. At times he felt a profound discouragement, and was ready to despair of himself; then he found help in such passages as these contained in Tyndale's notes:

"Ye shall not thynke that our dedes deserve ani thynge of God as a laborer deserueth his hyre. For all gode thynges come of the bounteousness, liberalitie, mercy, promyses and truth of God in the deseruing of Christes blood only."

"The eye is single when a man in all hys dedes loketh not but on the will of God, and loketh not for laude, honor, or ein other rewardes in this worlde. Nother ascrybeth Heven or a hyer roume in Heaven unto hys dedes; but accepteth Heven as a thing purchased bi the blode of Christe, and worketh freely for loves' sake onlie."

"As a natural sonne that is his father's heyre, doth his father's will not because he wolde be heyre, that he is already by birth— but of pure love doeth he that which he doth. And axe him why he doeth any thing that he doth, he answereth, my father bade, it is my father's will, it pleases my father.' Bonde servantes work for hire, children for love; for there father, with all he has, is there's already. So doth a Christen man freely all that he doeth, considering nothing but the will of God and his neighbour's wealth only. If I live chaste, I do hit not to obteyne heaven therby, for thus should y do wronge to the blode of Christe. Christes blood has obtayned me that." [1]

By such like instruction, by comparing one passage with another, and by help of the teaching of his uncle, Jack began at last to arrive at some clear notion of salvation by Jesus Christ, to cease to place any confidence in his own works or deservings, and to understand and feel somewhat of the blessedness of an accepted child of God.

"Oh, how I wish Anne could come to see this," he said one day, after a long conversation he had been holding with his uncle on the hillside. "She is killing herself, as my father says, with prayers and penances, that she may win forgiveness and heaven for herself and her friend. If she could only be brought to see this plain and easy way!"

"What was the story of her friend?" asked the shepherd. "Ay, I remember, there was some secret in the matter. I would, indeed, the poor child could be led to see that her Lord hath done all for her. Perhaps you may find some way of enlightening her when you return home."

"I should hardly know how to begin," said Jack, thoughtfully. "Anne has such a horror of heresy. She was distressed because I only said I should like to be a priest in order to read the Scripture; and she tried to make me promise that I would never look at any heretical books if they came in my way."

"I think Anne was convent bred, was she not?" asked the shepherd.

"Yes, at the gray nuns' convent, that my father spoke of, the one my Lord Harland is to buy. It was by no good will of my father, who never loved the religious houses; but my mother wished it, and he would not cross her. Anne would have taken the veil ere this, I doubt, but for the prioress herself. Anne's health failed, and the lady sent her home, saying she should have time to see more of the world before leaving it. But it is little she has seen of the world, poor child. She lives as closely as any cloistered nun and fares as hardly. It is a great trouble to my father, who would have none but cheerful faces about him. Anne thinks it is her duty to deny herself all pleasures, and so she will not taste any of the good things Cousin Cicely is so fond of making, nor sing to the lute as my mother used to do, though it is my father's greatest delight to hear her."

---

1   This passage occurs in Tyndale's defence and not in his notes.

"I doubt there is some self-will at the bottom of her heart," said the shepherd, "else she would perceive that there is a truer and purer self-denial in giving up her own tastes and inclinations in indifferent things, and conforming herself to the will and wishes of those about her."

"I see," said Jack, thoughtfully. "Then it might be that eating a piece of Cousin Cicely's gingerbread when she did not really care for it, rather than mortify the poor woman by refusing her dainties, would be a more useful penance than going without anything."

"For Anne perhaps," replied old Thomas, smiling.

Jack laughed. "Truly I never found any mortification in Cicely's gingerbread myself, save when I had eaten too much of it. But, indeed, Uncle Thomas, Anne does mean to do her duty faithfully. She would not do anything wrong for the world, and if she happens to make any little slip she grieves over it for days, and redoubles her penances. But, oh! She is so unhappy. If it had not been for Sir William Leavett, I almost think that living with Anne would have made me hate all religion, because it seems to make her so miserable. I do wish she could be brought to read this book."

"Well, dear son, we can but pray for her, and perhaps a way may be opened. Jack," said the shepherd, lowering his voice to a whisper, "don't turn your head now, but in a minute look yonder. Is not someone in hiding behind you thornbush? I have seen it move two or three times, and I am sure I caught sight of a gown."

Jack waited a moment, plucking up a pretty good sized clod of earth and grass as he did so. Then, suddenly turning, he hurled the clod with a good aim at the bush, saying, "There is an owl abroad in the daylight."

A hasty exclamation, but not in the owl's language, was heard from the bush, which stood on the edge of a steep grassy declivity, and was followed by various gurgling sounds of distress.

Jack rushed to the spot, followed more slowly by the old shepherd; and as he reached the bush, he burst into uncontrollable laughter. There was the fat priest of the little church at Holford rolling over and over down the slippery grass slope, clutching vainly at the short herbage, and uttering at intervals cries and interjections, some of them not exactly of a clerical character.

"He will tumble into the brook," said the shepherd hastily. "Run down by the path, Jack, and be ready to help him out."

Down by the path Jack ran like a deer, but another was beforehand with him. Bevis, the big sheep-dog, was first at the spot, and as the poor priest plunged into the somewhat deep pool at the foot of the slope, Bevis jumped after him and dragged him out with as little ceremony as if he had been one of his own wethers. Jack came to the help of the dog, and between them they got the unlucky father on dry land, and seated him on a sunny bank.

"How do you find yourself, father?" said Jack, speaking gravely, though he was choking with laughter.

"Oh—ah—ugh!" spluttered the priest. "Alack! I have broken my bones, I sink in deep waters! And that accursed brute hath torn my new gown."

"He meant no harm," said Jack. "He only wished to pull you out of the water and mud, which is deep enough to smother you."

"Eh—oh—the tender mercies of the wicked! I am wet through—I shall catch my death."

"You had best go home to my cottage and send for dry clothes, or go to bed while these are dried, good father," said the shepherd, who had just arrived at the scene of action.

"Jack, run and tell Margery to have the bed ready and warmed, and then come back, and bring with you the bottle of strong waters your father brought me. It will revive his spirit, and keep him from taking cold. How is it with you now, Sir John? I trust you have no bones broken by your fall."

With many a sigh and many a dolorous groan, the unlucky father raised himself on his feet and ascertained, by stretching himself, that he had sustained no serious injury.

"How did you fall?" asked the shepherd.

"Ah—eh! It was the clod of earth that unlucky lad threw at me."

"Were you behind the bush, then, father?" asked Jack, who had returned with the bottle and a cup, into which he was pouring a goodly portion of strong waters, alias brandy. "I humbly crave your pardon, but I took you for an owl."

"An owl, indeed! An owl in the desert, a sparrow on the housetop," said the priest, quoting at random. "Do I look like an owl?"

"Verily, I think you do, and a drowned owl at that," said Jack to himself. "I crave your pardon once more, father," said he aloud. "Pray you, drink this. It is good of its kind, for my father gets it of one of his cousins who trades with the Low Countries."

The priest drank off the contents of the cup with a readiness and gusto which seemed to show that he was not altogether unaccustomed to such medicines.

"Verily, thy father knows what is good," said he in a mollified tone, returning the cup and smacking his lips. "I would I could have to do with that same merchant, for the trader in Bridgewater sells villainous stuff, and wofully dear. Ah, alt that warms one's heart, certainly."

"Take another portion, an't please you," said Jack, replenishing the cup once more. "When I return home, or have a chance of sending, I will ask my father to send your reverence a bottle, and I am sure he will do so with pleasure."

"Thou art a good lad after all," said the priest, whom the second cup of spirits put into high good humor. "Only beware thou meddle not with things too high for thee, lest thou fall into the snare of the wicked; and the next time you throw a stone, see where it is going to light. Oh, I am marvellously restored. I think with the help of your arm, I could walk to the tree yonder where I left my mule."

"Shall I not go home with you to your own house?" asked Jack, who saw that the priest's head was beginning to be affected by the liquor he had drank. "You may be attacked with giddiness by the way, and perhaps have another fall."

"Do so, do so, my dear son," replied Sir John. "Why, you are a good lad after all, as I said but now, and surely no heretic as that pestilent conceited clerk of mine pretends. 'Twas he got me into this scrape, a plague upon him! I should have never thought of listening but for him."

"Oh ho! Then you were listening," thought Jack, "and I dare say Master Sacristan has been listening too. I will cut down that thorn tomorrow, and set old Bevis to watch."

"If folk would only mind their own business, there would be none of this trouble," continued Sir John, whose tongue was thoroughly loosed. "Here is Father Barnaby now has been lecturing me about seeking out heretics in my parish and watching who comes to mass. I am sure, if the heretics will let me alone, I am willing to let them alone; and as to the people coming to mass, let them come or go as it pleases them, so long as they pay their dues and live in peace. Say you not so, my son?"

"Indeed I do, father," replied Jack; "and besides, it stands to reason, that if people pay their dues they can be no heretics; does it not?"

"Right, right!" exclaimed Father John. "You reason as well as an Oxford scholar. If they pay, they are no heretics, because if they were heretics, they would not pay; 'tis clear as Aristotle. All my parishioners pay their dues, therefore there are no heretics in the parish, and Father Barnaby may go hang! Say you not so?"

"That I do with all my heart," replied Jack, gravely. "But here we are at your door. If I might venture to advise, your reverence will go at once to bed, and take a hot posset to keep off any farther effects of cold. I will bring the strong waters the first time I go to Bridgewater."

All the way back to the hill Jack laughed over the adventure, but the shepherd looked very grave on hearing the poor priest's words.

"I do not like the look of it," said he. "There may be no harm in poor Father John, who is, with all reverence, fonder of his table and his comfortable cup of spiced ale, than of anything else in life; but I know something of Father Barnaby. He has a keen scent for heresy, and he will be none the sweeter in temper for this suppression of the convent. We must be very careful."

The next day, Jack cut down the thornbushes and levelled the ground.

"I hope I am not shutting the door when the steed is stolen," he thought. "How could I be so careless as not to think of the thornbushes?"

CHAPTER VII.

FATHER JOHN AT HOME.

TWO or three days after the descent of Father John into the brook, Jack had an opportunity of sending home, by one of the knight's servants who was going to Bridgewater market. He wrote a note to his father stating that he had had the ill-luck to offend the parish priest, and begging for a bottle of strong waters as a peace-offering. He received more than he asked, for Master Lucas not only sent the bottle, but also a mighty and well-seasoned pasty on which he had expended all his skill, and a basket of sweet cakes and confections such as were in fashion, with a small parcel of sugar candy, then a great luxury, and some rare spices.

Armed with these provisions, Jack presented himself at the parsonage. He was received by the priest at first with a certain conscious stiffness and formality, which, however, gave way at once as Jack spread the contents of the basket before him and gave his father's message.

"Truly, truly, I said thou wert a good lad, though thou dost throw stones inconsiderately. But boys will be boys, and we were all young once; all, at least, but Brother Barnaby, who I do verily believe was born with a shaven head and fifty years old at the least. Truly your father is a man of taste and good sense, and no doubt has brought you up well. You can say your cat-echism now, I dare say?" asked Sir John, as though suddenly remembering his priestly character.

"Oh yes, your reverence," replied Jack promptly, determined to concil-iate the old man if possible. "I know my catechism well, and the Penitential Psalms both in Latin and English. Shall I say them, your reverence?"

"Another time, another time," said the old man hastily. "But now tell me, of what were you and your uncle talking that unlucky day, eh?"

"Of my sister, sir, who is out of health, and the causes of her illness."

"And of what else do you talk?"

"Nothing wrong, I trust, sir," replied Jack. "My uncle often tells me of his travels and adventures in foreign parts when he was abroad with his master; and sometimes we talk of things I have read in my books."

"Well, well, I dare say there is no harm. I trust not, for look you, my boy, you are a scholar and quick for your years, and like to be taken with novelties; and I would ill like to have any harm come to you, though you did take me for an owl," said the father chuckling. "I have no notion myself of peeping and spying into other men's matters. If they be heretics, why so much the worse for them; but there is no need to blaze abroad the matter, and so make two where was one before. You don't know any heretics in this parish, I dare say?" said the old man, looking wistfully at Jack.

"No, your reverence, that I do not," replied Jack, glad that the question was put in such an answerable shape. "You know I have been here but a little time, and seen very few, scarce any one but my uncle and the knight's household."

"True, true, your uncle is no ale-bench haunter, and you are more likely to be taken with some tale of chivalry than with the talk of country clowns, or with volumes of divinity either, I should say. Tell me now, can you construe Latin?"

"Oh, yes, your reverence," replied Jack. "I have read Caesar his Commentaries, and Virgil, and a little of Horace, and I am to read more so soon as I can find a book."

The old man rose and went to his cupboard, from whence, after some shuffling of papers, he brought forth a letter sealed with a gorgeous coat-of-arms.

"See here," said he. "The Abbot of Glastonbury has sent me this epistle all in Latin. As far as I can make out, it is about certain lands which the abbey possesses in this parish. But, our Lady help me, I never was the brightest scholar in the world at my Latin, and I have forgotten all I ever knew, save so much as may serve me for mass. Do you think now you could construe this letter for me, and say nothing about it?"

Greatly delighted with the turn things had taken, Jack promised secrecy, and proceeded to translate and expound the letter, not without sharply criticising in his own mind the Latinity of the reverend writer.

"He writes like a booby of the fourth form," said he to himself. "Wouldn't Master Crabtree give it him for his concords?"

"And you are sure now that you have the right sense?" asked Father John.

"Oh, yes, sir. That is the whole of it."

"And now he will be expecting an answer in Latin," groaned the poor father. "And how I am to compass that, I cannot guess. I might ask Brother Barnaby, but then—he is a good man, and learned, but he hath short patience with the mortal infirmities of other folks, seeing that he hath none of his own. He would be sure to deliver me a lecture and—"

"So please your reverence, if you will give me in English the substance of your answer, I will put it into Latin for you," said Jack, who began to feel a great kindness for the poor, good-natured old man.

"Oh, my dear son, but are you sure you can do it to the Abbot's satisfaction? He is a great man, you know, is the Abbot of Glastonbury."

"I think I can, your reverence; I was accounted a good scholar in Bridgewater grammar school, where I took the gold medal last term," said Jack, adding to himself, "I am sure I never should have got it if I had not written better Latin than the abbot's secretary."

"Well, well, I will think of it, and inquire about the land, and tell you what to say. And now see here."

Father John opened once more the cupboard where he kept his papers, and brought forth a book beautifully bound and clasped.

"You say you want a Horace. Well, here is one which was left me by an old college friend. I cannot use it, and you can, and it were better in your hands than mouldering away in this old nook. Take it then, my son, and the saints bless you. Surely I never thought to like you so well when you tumbled me into the brook the other day."

Jack could hardly believe in his good luck. Such a beautiful Horace, with illuminated letters and title. Sir William himself had nothing like it among his treasures.

"There, there," said the priest, interrupting his thanks. "Say no more, say no more. Who is this stopping at the door?"

"It is Father Barnaby as I think," said Jack, looking from the window. "I have seen him in Bridgewater. Yes, it is he."

"Alack! What has brought him here just now?" groaned Father John. "He will see the pasty and spices, and there will come a lecture on fleshly appetites. Do you take the pasty into the next room; or stay! Let it remain, but hide the abbot's letter there in the cupboard. And oh, dear son, mind what you say to him. He is a hard man."

Jack hastily arranged the table in order, put away the letter, picked up the priest's breviary which had fallen on the ground, and laid it open before him, and then assumed a respectful position behind Father John's chair, keeping his beloved Horace in his hand. Presently Father Barnaby entered. He was a tall, dark, thin man, who looked indeed as though good eating had little charms for him. He returned Father John's meek, flustered greeting with a certain air of condescension and authority, and Jack's scarcely at all.

"Will you not take some refreshment, brother, after your ride?" asked the elder priest. "I am better provided than usual, thanks to the liberality of this good lad's father, Master Lucas of Bridgewater."

"Nothing for me, thank you, brother," replied Father Barnaby. "I eat nothing between meals. To you, who lead a life so much more laborious than mine, the case is different."

Jack saw the old man wince at the sarcasm, and resented it for him.

"Whatever you know," thought he, "you have not learned one thing, and that is to respect your elders."

"So you are Master Lucas's son of Bridgewater," said Father Barnaby, turning his dark eyes on Jack with no very friendly expression. "I have heard of you, young sir, and am glad to meet you. I must have some conversation with you before we part. But I must send my attendant brother with a message to the Hall."

"Hark ye, dear son, don't anger him," whispered Father John, as Father Barnaby left the room. "Don't contradict him or give him a handle against you. He is a devil when his temper is up, the saints forgive me for saying so! And he is as keen after heresy as a terrier after a fox. Be on your guard, there's a good lad."

"I will, your reverence," said Jack, and, wondering whether the trial Richard Fleming spoke of had arrived already, he lifted up his heart in prayer for strength and wisdom. But the trial was not to come just yet.

Father Barnaby came back in a moment, and seating himself in the hardest chair in the room, he called Jack to stand before him, and bent his eyes upon him as though he would look him through.

Jack sustained the glance with modest confidence, and waited to be spoken to.

"They tell me you are a scholar," said Father Barnaby, "and I hear of you that you have an appetite for novelties and would fair pry into high and sacred matters."

"Who told you as much as that, I wonder?" thought Jack, but he held his peace.

"I do assure you, brother, the boy is a good boy," said Father John, timidly and anxiously. "He can say his creed and questions, and is regular in his duties."

"Say you so? Then you have examined him?"

"Oh, yes," replied Father John hastily, "and he can say the seven Penitential Psalms."

"That was a bit of a fib," thought Jack, "but after all, I dare say he thought he had."

"I am glad to hear as much," said Father Barnaby, though he did not look so. "But I propose to examine him myself, always with your leave, good brother. I would not for the world trespass upon your rights and duties, especially the latter which you are so careful to fulfil."

Jack was trying hard to keep his mind in a calm and proper frame for the trial which he supposed was coming; but he could not help thinking that he should like to break the monk's head for his insolence to his old friend. He felt that Father Barnaby meant to intimidate and confuse him; and he was determined to be neither confused nor scared. After another interval of silence, the younger priest began again—

"I have heard something of an ill report of you, young man; and I desire to discover whether there is any foundation therefor. So answer my questions plainly and directly, and let me have no evasions."

"So please your reverence, I will do my best to satisfy you," replied Jack, modestly. "I trust I have been well taught both at home and at school, as well as by our parish priest."

"Umph!" returned the priest. "It takes more than good teaching to make a sound Christian. Now tell me—but what book is that you are hugging so closely under your arm?"

"My Horace, an't please you," replied Jack, producing the volume.

Father John had declared that Father Barnaby had no infirmities, but in this he was mistaken. Father Barnaby did possess one unregulated affection, and that was love for the Latin poets, above all, for Horace. If anything could draw his attention from a controversy or make him forget his canonical hours, it was a new edition or a disputed passage of his favorite author. He had read all that had ever been written on the subject, and had himself written a treatise on the question as to whether Leucothoe in the eleventh ode was a real person or a figment of the poet's imagination, and also upon the Babylonian numbers in the same ode.

"So you read Horace, do you?" he asked, in quite another tone of voice.

"But a little, your reverence," returned Jack. "I had but just begun it when I left school; and I fear I shall find it too hard without some help."

"How far had you gone?" was the next question.

"I am just at the eleventh ode, but I do not understand it very well," said Jack, not less pleased than surprised at his catechiser's change of tone and manner.

"Find your place, and I will explain it to you," said Father Barnaby. "I have bestowed much study upon it—too much, some might say, for a churchman; and I can, no doubt, help you."

For more than two hours, till the lay brother he had sent to the Hall returned with his message, did Father Barnaby expound to his willing and attentive pupil, divers different and disputed passages in his favorite author, delighted to find that Jack understood and appreciated him. Then bestowing his blessing, and promising to send Jack a copy of his own treatise, he rode away in high good humor, and was half way back to the convent where he lived before he remembered that he had forgotten after all to question Jack as to his theology.

"But I can do it another time," he said to himself. "I dare say the lad is sound enough. How cleverly he understood the points in dispute between myself and Brother Thomas of Glastonbury, and how clearly he perceived that I was right. I will certainly send him the treatise."

"Well, the saints be praised!" said Father John, when his visitor was out of hearing. "He has for once gone away in a good humor. How glad I am that I thought of the book! I am sure I never cared so much for a book before. He was a heathen, I doubt, this Horace," he added, looking dubiously at Jack.

"Yes, your reverence," replied Jack, suppressing a smile. "He lived before our Lord was born into the world."

"Ah, well, then he could not be blamed, poor man. He has done us a good turn this day, at any rate."

"Will you give me the notes for the answer to the bishop's letter?" asked Jack.

"Not to-day, not to-day, my son. My poor old pate buzzes like a bee-hive with all this learning. Go, lad, and come again; let me see, ah, come on Saturday. Be a good lad, and above all meddle not with heresy. My blessing be upon this Horace whoever he was," he murmured, when Jack had taken his departure. "I will certainly say some masses for him when I have time. And it does no good, it can do no harm."

CHAPTER VIII.

JACK GOES HOME FOR A VISIT.

Jack described his visit to his uncle with considerable glee, but the old man shook his head and looked grave.

"I am glad Father Barnaby was diverted for once," said he; "but I fear he will not be so easily turned aside. From whence could he have gotten the notion that you were curious about heretical books?"

"I cannot guess," replied Jack. "I have never spoken a word to any one but you and Master Fleming. Surely he could not have played us false!"

"I think not. Did you not tell me once that you had talked with Anne, and said to her that you would like to read the Scriptures? And is not Father Barnaby her confessor?"

Jack started and turned pale. "Surely, surely, Anne would never betray me!" he said. "And yet—"

"If she were questioned, she might not be able to help answering," replied the shepherd. "Such minds and consciences as hers are as wax in the hands of a confessor like Father Barnaby. Many a time hath the brother betrayed the brother to death, and the father the son, without thinking they were doing any harm, or that their confession would be used against them. However, all may yet be well, and we will not borrow trouble. 'Each day's trouble is sufficient for the same selfe day,' our Gospel tells us. You have gotten the right side of Sir John, and that is something."

"I cannot help liking the poor man, in spite of his laziness and love of eating," said Jack. "He seems so good-natured, and he was so anxious that I should get on well with Father Barnaby, who by the way treated him with scant civility. I thought he might reverence the old man's age at any rate, for Sir John is old enough to be Father Barnaby's father. I wonder what in the world brought him up there behind the thornbush the other day."

"Not his own good will, I dare say," replied the shepherd. "I should not care if he had been the only listener, but I shrewdly suspect that sacristan of his has been before him. He is a sharp fellow, that same sacristan, and I have heard he was placed here by Father Barnaby to keep a lookout upon matters in the parish. It has been whispered—take good heed you whisper it not again—that our good knight is a favorer of the Gospel, like his father and grandfather before him; and I suspect Father Barnaby may have put this Brother Jacob about Sir John as a spy not only on him, but upon the family at the Hall. He had better not let our knight catch him at any spy work!" added the old man, smiling somewhat grimly, "Or he will get a worse fall than poor Father John's."

For two or three weeks all went on quietly with our friends at Holford. Mindful of another probable encounter with Father Barnaby, Jack studied his Horace with diligence, and stored his mind with hosts of queries to be answered and difficulties to be solved, should he meet the father again. He was a good deal startled and shocked by some things he encountered in his studies, and could not but wonder how two churchmen like Father Barnaby and Father Thomas of Glastonbury could bestow so much time and thought upon ladies of such at the least dubious character as some of those celebrated by their favorite author.

"Yes, I have often thought of that same thing," said Father John, when Jack remarked as much to him one day. "Here is Brother Barnaby ready to condemn one to I know not what, if one so much as looks at a pretty girl in the parish or gives her in all innocence a red apple or a flower, and yet he can pore for hours over all sorts of love stories, and those none of the nicest, as far as I can understand, and it is all right because they are in Latin. For my part I could wish there had never been any such language as Latin, unless just enough for the mass perhaps. I don't know what it is good for, except to puzzle men's brains and procure whippings for little boys, who when they grow up remember the whippings and mostly forget the Latin."

"And now about the abbot's letter, your reverence," said Jack. "If you had the notes ready, I would write it for you."

"Oh, dear, my son! You are as bad as Father Barnaby himself—no, not as bad, because you are good-natured and don't lecture me."

"I should hope I knew my duty far better than to lecture my elders and betters," said Jack. "I would not hurry you for the world, only you know great men like the abbot are sometimes offended at delay in their business, and he might speak about it to Father Barnaby—"

"Yes, that is true indeed," said the priest with alacrity. "That would be worse than setting the dogs on me. Well, I will make the necessary inquiries this very day, and you shall begin the letter tomorrow. It is a fine thing to be a scholar, though it sometimes brings people into trouble, as you see. If you did not know Latin, you would not be burdened with writing letters for me."

"I am sure I am very glad to do as much and more for you," said Jack, honestly. "You have been very kind to me, besides giving me that beautiful book, and I owe you amends for that unlucky mistake of mine on the hillside the other day."

"As to that, the mistake was mine, for I had no business there," replied Father John frankly. "I never should have thought of such a thing if I had not been worried into it by that pestilent sacristan of mine, who I wish was in Rome or farther away. He hath somehow—Just open that door, will you?"

Rather startled by the priest's tone, Jack threw open the door so quickly that the sacristan, who was close behind it, had no time to get out of the way. The heavy door opening outward and coming upon him unexpectedly gave him a smart blow on the head, and caused him, after staggering a few paces backward, to assume a sitting posture with more haste than was either dignified or convenient. As the poor clerk sat rubbing his forehead with a dazed expression, Father John burst out laughing.

"Truly, eavesdropping is a business which does not flourish in these parts," said he, as soon as he could recover breath. "Tut, never mind it, good brother. I dare say you meant no harm, but you should be careful not to stand so near the door."

"I was but coming with a message to your reverence," said Brother Jacob, recovering his feet, and repulsing Jack who ran to his help. "Old Dame Higgins is near her end, and desires the sacraments of the Church. I did not know you had company with you," he added, casting a venomous glance at Jack.

"Your excuse is received, Brother Jacob," said the old priest, with more dignity than Jack had thought he could assume. "I shall thank you to give orders concerning my mule, and have all things in readiness. I will visit the good woman at once, and would have you lose no time in making preparations."

Brother Jacob left the room without more words, and Father John watched him till he was out of hearing. Then, closing the door, he turned to Jack once more. "Now, dearest son, listen to me," said he, laying his hand on Jack's arm, and speaking with great earnestness. "This same sacristan of mine has whispered to me, that your uncle is, and hath long been, suspected of heresy, and that he has been teaching you the same. I trust it is not so, for your own sake and his. I ask no questions. I would willingly live in peace with all men, as you know. But, since they have put Father Barnaby over my head, I am but a cipher in mine own parish; and if you or your uncle were to be attainted of heresy, I could do nothing to save you. I pray you, therefore, be careful to whom and of what you speak. Make friends with Brother Jacob if you can, though I doubt he will be harder to conciliate than I was, although he did not fall so far. And oh, dear son, for your soul's sake, as well as your body's, beware of new-fangled doctrines. Surely, what was good enough for our fathers, may well do for us. I have learned already to love you; you are like a young brother I had once, and I do not have many to love nowadays," said the old man, with a break in his voice and tears in his eyes. "It would wring my heart, if evil should befall you."

Much affected, Jack kissed his old friend's hand, and assured him that he would be careful. On his way out he met the sacristan, and stopped to apologize for his share in the accident. Brother Jacob received his apology meekly, and said it was his duty to forgive injuries.

"But I meant no injury to you," said Jack, a little vexed. "The good father bade me open the door, and I could not see through the oak plank to know who was behind it, you know."

"True, and yet—however, we will say no more about it," returned the sacristan. "I trust I am too good a Christian to bear malice or to revenge any injury done to myself, above all when it is, as you say, unintentional."

"You may be as good a Christian as you like, but I would not trust you farther than I could see you, for all that," muttered Jack to himself. "I might have guessed, when Father John bade me open the door, that some one was behind it. I think it is my luck to make enemies. I wonder whether I had better tell my uncle what the good father told me."

Jack thought on this point all the way home, and at last concluded it best to tell the story.

Thomas Sprat heard it without surprise.

"I have been expecting as much," said he "A bird of the air is always ready to carry such matters. For myself, I care little. I am an old man, far past the age of ordinary men, and my summons will soon come. It matters little to me whether I go to my Father's house from a dungeon, or a stake, or my own bed. But I am troubled for you, my son, lest I have put your young life in jeopardy."

"As to that," said Jack thoughtfully, "I do not see that it matters so much whether one's life be long or short, so it be used in the best way and spent in God's service. I wish you would not be troubled about me, dear Uncle Thomas. I tell you truly that if I should be thrown into jail tomorrow, with no chance of escaping fagot and stake, I do believe I should still thank you for all you have done for me, and should think what I have learned here worth the price ay, a thousand times over. Besides, we may after all be in no danger; I have a dozen hard places in Horace, ready for Father Barnaby, if I encounter him again," he added, smiling.

The old man smiled also, but somewhat sadly, and shook his head.

"I doubt that bait will hardly take a second time," said he. "He is an hard man—so every one says—and I heard it whispered also among the servants at the Hall, that he was set over Father John's head expressly that he might keep a lookout for heresy."

"There is no love lost between him and Father John, I know that," re-marked Jack. "I can clearly see that Father Barnaby tyrannizes over the old man, and that Father John is afraid of him. I do not believe that Father John himself would hurt a fly."

"Not unless the fly were very troublesome indeed," said the shepherd. "I would not be the fly that should keep him from his nap after dinner. These very easy-going people are sometimes hard enough on them that interfere with their beloved laziness. Well, my son, after all that has happened, I see not that we can do better than to put our trust in God and be doing good. We may be sure that what He sends or permits will be for the best in the end, since we have His word that all things work together for good to them that love Him. I wish our good knight would come home."

"I heard he was expected before many days," said Jack. "I made bold to ask my lady, the day I carried her the snails and birds' eggs for the making of her medicine, and she told me Sir John would not be away much longer. She seems a kind lady, though she is so proud and stately in her manners."

"She is a good lady, though as you say she is proud and stately, far more so than the knight himself," said Thomas. "She is more so than she used to be before the death of her son, about whom I told you the other day. I have often wished she had a daughter to comfort her. But poor Master Arthur was the only one of all her children who lived to man's estate. She did not seem to be as much bound up in the young gentleman as his father, while he lived; but she has mourned sorely for him since his death, and expended great sums for masses for him."

CHAPTER IX.

A JOURNEY.

"THERE is somebody coming up the hillside from the cottage," said Jack to his uncle, as they were sitting on the hillside a week or so after Jack's affair with the sacristan. "It is Master Fleming, I do believe."

"You are welcome, dear sir," said the shepherd, rising to greet the merchant. "Why did you not send for us to come to you, and spare yourself the trouble of climbing the hill?"

"The trouble is a pleasure, my old friend," said Master Fleming, shaking the old man's hand cordially. "I have lived in London many years, but I was bred in the north country where the hills are higher than here, and I have followed my father's flock on the mountain side many a day when I was a lad."

"I almost wonder you could endure life in London streets," said Jack. "I am beginning to marvel how I shall ever live in Bridge Street again after breathing the free country air all summer."

"I had little voice in the matter," said Richard Fleming. "My good father was killed, and our little property wholly destroyed by the marauding Scots (for we lived near the border), and my mother was left destitute with three young children. So when my mother's cousin in London offered to adopt me and bring me up as his own, she had little choice but to accept his offer. I well remember the exultation I felt, and the wonder and envy of my playfellows when it was announced that I was to go away to London and become a merchant; and my pining homesickness for the first few months of my sojourn in my cousin's house. But I grew used to the confinement and interested in my work after a time, and my cousin's family were very kind to me."

"Then I made acquaintance with a young kinsman of my own age, William Leavett, whom you, my son, know right well. We soon became sworn friends, and have always continued so, though we took different paths in life, and of late meet but seldom. I am now on my way to Bridgewater to see him, and one part of my errand here is to ask for the favor of your company on the road. I think you told me when I left you last that you were thinking of going home for a visit before long."

Jack looked somewhat doubtfully at his uncle. The prospect of riding all the way to Bridgewater in company with Master Fleming was a delightful one; but he thought of the old priest's warning, and of the sacristan, and he did not like the idea of abandoning his uncle when he might be in danger.

"I think, son Jack, you will do well to ride with Master Fleming, since you must go soon at any rate," said Thomas Sprat. "It will be both pleasanter and safer for you to travel with him than to travel alone. Nay, look not so grave upon it, dear lad. If your father think it best, you can return again by and by, and I shall come and see you in Bridgewater before long."

"But there is the Latin I was writing for Father John," said Jack, hesitating. "The poor old man will be sadly disappointed if I do not finish it, for I am sure he cannot do it himself. Good man, he did not know whether Horace were a Christian or a heathen."

"Ah, well," said the stranger, "many a man lives out his days in great comfort and usefulness who never heard of Horace. But as to that matter, it is my purpose to tarry a day or two at the Hall with Sir John Brydges, who, as I hear in the hamlet yonder, is last night returned from London."

"Is he returned? I am glad to hear it," said Thomas Sprat.

"He is then a good man," remarked Master Fleming.

"He is indeed, sir. I would all our country knights were like him; and his lady is worthy of her husband. Their household is a school of good manners and godly living to both men and maids."

"I have heard as much before, and am glad to hear it confirmed," said Master Fleming. "I have never met Sir John, but I have letters to him from mutual friends in London. I shall sojourn with him for two or three days, so you, Master Secretary, will have time to finish Father John's letter."

"I shall feel easier at leaving you, now that the knight is at home," said Jack to his uncle, after Master Fleming had taken his departure.

"Have no fears for me," replied the shepherd. "I have none for myself. My dependence for aid must be upon no arm of flesh, dear son, but on One who can as easily save by one as by many, and who will let no harm happen to me."

The next day Jack finished writing his Latin letter and copied it out fairly in his best hand, wishing in his soul that Master Crabtree could only see it. Then he carried it down to the little hamlet of Holford and called at the priest's house.

Father John welcomed him warmly, as usual, and admired the appearance of the letter, which, though he could not understand a word in ten, he insisted on Jack's reading aloud to him.

"It sounds all right, I am sure," said he. "And it is much better written than that of the abbot's secretary. It has come just in time too, for I shall have a chance to send it this afternoon by one of the brethren from the Abbey who has come to see the knight on some business. And now, son, what shall I pay you for your labor?"

"Nothing at all, dear father," replied Jack. "I should be ashamed to take a penny from you after all your kindness to me. I only wish I could do more for you before I go home. Shall I not set your reverence's books in order?"

"Nay, they are hardly worth the trouble, my son," replied Father John. "And so you are going home. Well, I shall be sorry to miss you, that is the truth. Your fresh young face comes upon me like sunshine. I fear I shall never see you again, for I am an old man, an old man, my dear, and between ourselves," he added, carefully looking round him, "this talk about heresy and the new doctrines, and all, is wearing me into my grave. Here has been Father Barnaby talking to me again about my duty—my duty, forsooth, who was in orders before he had left off his long coats, if indeed he ever wore them, which is doubtful—and the suspected spread of heresy in this part of the world; it was a good world before he came in to spoil it. I would he had been born in Germany or some of those outlandish parts where the Lutherans began, he would have enough to do there. And talking of the spread of heretical books, as if there was any danger from books where not one person in ten knows great A from little b. And to say I want discretion; I that might be his grandfather almost—what think you of that, my son?"

In his own mind, Jack was by no means sure that Father Barnaby was mistaken in this last named article; he did not say so, however, but applied himself to comforting the poor old man.

"I am sure, father, all the people of the parish love you. I know my uncle does, and so do all the knight's household. I heard them talking of it only a little time ago. I suppose Father Barnaby means to do his duty—"

"Oh, duty!" exclaimed Father John, interrupting him. "Whenever I hear folk talking about their duty, I always know they are going to say or do something disagreeable. But what have you there?" as Jack brought forward a basket.

"Fresh eggs, sir, ducks' and hens' eggs, and a pair of young fowls which my uncle sends you with his duty to your reverence. You will find them well fatted."

"Many thanks, many thanks, my son. And there now, that is the third pair of fowls I have had given me in a week. Does that look as if the parish were given to heresy? Do heretics send chickens and fresh eggs to their priest? Answer me that, now."

"I should say not, decidedly," answered Jack, suppressing a smile.

"The parish is a good parish if it were let alone," continued Father John, "but there, I must not keep you. I would you were not going, and yet mayhap it is best. Here, take this medal and hang it round your neck. It hath an image of your patron saint, and is of sovereign virtue to keep off the ague, so mayhap it may keep off heresies as well. Go, go, my son, and all the saints bless you!"

Jack kissed the old man's hand, promised to wear the medal faithfully, and went away rather wondering that he should feel sad at parting from one with whom his acquaintance had commenced so inauspiciously.

After leaving Father John, Jack took his way to the Hall to learn the hour at which Master Fleming intended to set out in the morning. He found the merchant and the knight walking together upon the terrace; and, standing quietly at one side, waited to be spoken to. Sir John was the first to notice him, and bade him good-day with his usual kindness.

"Can I do anything for you?" he asked. "Is my old friend, your uncle, in want of anything?"

"No, Sir John," replied Jack. "I came but to speak with Master Fleming, and they told me he was walking upon the terrace. I thought he was alone, or I should not have intruded."

"Nay, there is no intrusion in the case, my lad. I am glad to see you. Master Fleming tells me you are to be his travelling companion as far as Bridgewater. I am sorry you are going away. Your uncle will be lonely without you."

"I may perhaps come back and stay till school begins again," replied Jack, feeling much honored. "I have been very happy here, but my father misses me and wants me at home for a visit."

"I could find it in my heart to envy him the possession of such a son," replied Sir John, sighing as he spoke. "Dutiful and good children are a great blessing. See, my lad, that you never give your father cause to rue the day that God gave him a son."

"Remember the place of Scripture we read together this morning, brother," said the merchant in a low tone. "The prodigal son may yet come to himself and return to his father's house."

"I fear not, I fear not," replied the knight, shaking his head. "I fear he hath gone whence there is no returning. But should he come back, oh how gladly would I meet him—even a great way off!"

Jack stood by in reverent silence. He well knew to what the good knight alluded. Sir John Brydges had had but one son, and he had proved anything but a comfort to his parents. He had brought well-merited expulsion and disgrace upon himself at college, had gone first to London, and then abroad, and had been last heard of as fighting under the banner of one of the German princes. His mother believed him dead, and had caused many masses to be said for him; but his father could not wholly give him up for lost.

"You have come, I suppose, to see about our arrangements for tomorrow," said Master Fleming to Jack, after a little silence.

"Yes, an't please you," replied Jack. "I would now at what time we set out, so as to be ready."

"I propose to leave the Hall at an early hour, that we may avoid the heat of the day," said Master Fleming. "Can you be here by six?"

"By five, sir, if you desire it."

"Six will be early enough," said Master Fleming, smiling. "I suppose your luggage will not be large?"

"Oh, no, sir," returned Jack, blushing. "Only a change or two of clothes and two or three books—if you do not think that too much."

The knight smiled kindly. "They tell me you are fond of books," said he, "and that you are thinking of going to college. Do you then mean to be a priest or monk?"

"No, sir!" said Jack, with so much emphasis and decision that both gentlemen smiled. "I do not think I have any vocation for such a life. I had thought I should like to be a physician."

"'Tis a noble calling, and you do well to choose it, though it is not by any means so easy a life as the other; or so I should guess," said the knight. "Well, my lad, I doubt not you will do well. I have some interest at Oxford, and shall be glad to give you any help in my power. Now go, and be here betimes in the morning."

The next morning Jack was at the Hall even before the hour specified. He found his friend waiting for him, and a well-appointed pony prepared for his riding, while a man-servant attended to lead the sumpter mule, whose burden was considerably diminished. The knight gave Jack a fair rose-noble as a parting gift, and the lady bestowed upon him a plum bun and a handful of sweetmeats; and, fortified by a good breakfast of ale and cold beef, he set out on his journey in high spirits.

"Well, good luck go with 'em wherever they go, and the blessing of our Lady and all the saints attend them," said old Margery, sighing.

Their road passing by the cottage door, the travellers had stopped for a parting word, and Margery had done her best to insure their good fortune by throwing an old shoe after them.

"A better boy than Master Jack never breathed the breath of life; and as for Master Fleming, he is a godly, quiet gentleman as ever I saw, none of your swearing, ruffling gallants, and knows what belongs to good manners," added Margery, contemplating with much satisfaction the kerchiefs and hood the merchant had bestowed upon her. "Do you not think, Thomas Sprat, that we shall be lonesome without Jack?"

Thomas Sprat nodded a reply; and, having looked after the travellers as long as he could see them, he put his Testament into his pouch, and hastened away to the thicket in the little valley which was wont to serve him as a place of retirement.

CHAPTER X.

HOME GOSSIP.

TO our young friend, the journey to Bridgewater in company with Master Fleming was one long pleasure. It was a great comfort to pour out his heart to one who understood him fully, to bring forward all the questions which the reading of Scripture had raised in his mind, and to listen to Master Fleming's explanations and remarks.

To his extreme delight, he found that Master Fleming had been in Rome and even in Jerusalem, as well as in Germany, and the Low Countries, as Holland was usually called. Jack could have wished the road to Bridgewater a hundred miles long, he had so much to say and so much to hear.

"Oh, how I wish I could travel abroad and see foreign lands!" he exclaimed. "It seems to me as if I were just beginning to find out how large the world is."

"It is a large place, no doubt, and we have as yet seen but a small portion thereof," replied the merchant. "There are the far-off parts of India and China, and those lands over the sea which have been discovered of late by the Spaniards, and which are described as a kind of earthly paradise by those who have seen them. But here we are, as I think, at our destination. Are not those the roofs of Bridgewater?"

"They are so, and that tall steeple is that of the Church of St. Mary. I will guide you to the house of Sir William Leavett, which is by the waterside. I could wish our journey were to be longer."

"I shall remain with my cousin for a month or more, and hope to see you many times," said the merchant, "as well as to make the acquaintance of your good father. And is this my cousin's house? Truly it is a modest one."

"That large house farther up the street should be by right," said Jack, "but the old priest of St. Mary's lives in it, and hath done for forty years. He is very old and infirm, and our Father William will not let the old man be disturbed. He never thinks of himself or his own comfort."

"He was always self-sacrificing, sometimes almost recklessly so," replied the merchant. "Well, my young friend, I must bid you farewell for a time, but I will see you again. Remember what I have said to you, and be careful, for your own sake and that of others; yet let not your care lead you to the baseness of denying your Lord, be the risk what it may. Better a hundred deaths in one than that. May the Lord have you in His keeping."

Arrived in Bridgewater, Jack could almost have thought his absence a dream, everything looked so entirely unchanged. On entering the shop, however, he noticed two or three alterations. A great bowpot of sweet flowers and herbs stood on one end of the counter. The cakes and other matters in which Master Lucas dealt were arranged with more than usual neatness and taste, and an elderly kind-faced woman, dressed in black, whom Jack had never seen before, was arranging on a tray in the window some confections of a more delicious and choice description than Jack had ever seen there before. She started as he entered, and nearly let fall her tray.

"Lady! How you startled me, lad!" she exclaimed in a brisk, cheery voice. "You will be wanting Master Lucas now?"

"Is my father well, madam?" asked Jack, using unconsciously the title he would have employed in addressing a lady of rank, for there was something superior in the stranger's whole appearance.

"Good lack! You are then young Master Jack come home again. Your father will be right glad to see you. Here, Anne! Dame Cicely! Here is Master Jack come home."

Jack's wonder as to who the stranger could be was cut short by the entrance of Cicely and Anne from the dwelling-house and of his father from the bakery; and now he really felt himself at home again. Cicely kissed and hugged him, held him off at arm's length to see how well he looked, and then kissed him again. His father was not one whit behind, and even Anne warmed up for once and was almost genial. Jack thought her looking much worse than when he left home. She was paler and thinner than ever, and her eyes had a frightened, almost a guilty, expression. As soon as he was alone with Cicely, he began to question her about his sister.

"Well, she is much as usual, poor thing," said Cicely. "No great comfort to any one, nor yet to herself, poor dear. I doubt Sister Barbara was a great disappointment to her as it turned out, though she built much on her coming."

"Who is Sister Barbara?" asked Jack.

"Why, the lady that came to us when the gray nuns' house was broken up," replied Cicely. "She is going to some convent in the north, when she can do so safely; but meantime your father gave Anne leave to ask her to stay with us. You saw her in the shop when you came."

"Was that Sister Barbara?" asked Jack, surprised. "I never thought of that. I am sure she looks like a nice lady."

"And so she is indeed, and yet she was in a way a great disappointment to your sister. You see, Anne thought that when Sister Barbara came she would have someone to help her in her penances and prayers. So she fitted up the room next her own with a rood, and an image of our Lady, and I don't know what all, and there Sister Barbara was to live secluded, and Anne was to fetch her meals, and they were to have another little convent all to themselves. Your father never interfered with her, but let her arrange matters in her own fashion; only he smiled when Anne talked about Sister Barbara's living secluded, and about her having lived in the convent ever since she was three years old, and knowing nothing of earthly vanities; and he said the gentlewoman should have her way, whatever it was."

"He is certainly the best-natured man that ever lived," said Jack. "But please go on, Cousin Cicely, I want to know how it turned out."

"Well, it turned out differently and much more pleasantly than anybody expected," continued Cicely. "Sister Barbara came at the time appointed, and Anne took her up to her room where she was to be secluded. But, bless you, she did not stay there, not she. The second day, she came down into the kitchen where I was busy cooking, and overseeing the maids. She was as much interested as could be in everything, and it being a fast-day, she proposed to me that she should make some almond pottage, such as they used to have in the convent at such times, for your father's dinner. Well, my dear, I thought I was a pretty good cook—"

"And so you are," said Jack.

"But, bless you, I cannot hold a candle to her! I never saw anywhere such nice things as she makes. Well, she was a bit shy of your father at first, but pretty soon she got to dining with the family, and bringing her work down in the sitting-room, and there was an end of all the seclusion. By and by she came to me, and says she:

"'Dame Cicely, I am tired of idleness, and I want to do something to pay for my keeping.'"

"'Laws me, madam!' says I, 'Don't you think of such a thing. You are a born lady,' says I, 'and I am sure Master Lucas thinks it a pleasure and an honor to have you for a guest.'"

"'You are all very good people,' says Sister Barbara. 'I never guessed before how lovely a thing family life could be. For you see, dame, my mother died when I was but a babe in arms,' says she, 'and I was put into the convent, and have never known anything else. But now I am here with you,' says she, 'life seems so much brighter and worth so much more than it has ever done before.'"

"'Laws, madam,' says I, 'I am glad you like our homely ways, I am sure.'"

"Well, the long and the short of it was, that she said she knew how to make many kinds of sweetmeats and cakes, and she did not see why she should not make them for your father to sell in the shop; and she prayed me to mention the matter to him. Well, I did so, and says he:"

"'Let the gentlewoman have her way and please herself. Mayhap she will feel more at home and contented, if she thinks she is doing something for her own support.'"

"And so she fell to work in good earnest, and filled the shop window with her pretty dainties; and your father says she makes him a great deal of profit. And she has left off wearing her nun's robe and veil, for she says she does not want to be stared at."

"But what does Anne say to all this?" asked Jack.

"Why, she was terribly shocked at first, especially at Sister Barbara's leaving off her nun's dress; but then Father William upholds her in it, and even Father Barnaby says it may be just as well so long as she is out of her convent, and so long as she is such an old woman. Sister Barbara laughed well at that, and so did your father, for you see she is a fine lady even now and as graceful and comely as a willow tree. Many an older and plainer woman has been married. But I must say she is far pleasanter in the house than poor, dear Anne."

"You must not find fault with Anne, dear Cicely," said Jack. "She hath a great deal to trouble her, and I dare say it vexes her to see her friend so different from what she expected. But does not Sister Barbara go to church with Anne?"

"Ay, that she does, and says her beads at home as well, and works for the poor folk. And do you know, I heard her talking with Anne one day about that very matter. Says Anne:"

"'I don't see how you can find any relish in prayer and meditation, and yet be so much occupied with worldly matters.'"

"'My dear child,' answers Sister Barbara, 'I never enjoyed prayer and meditation so much in all my life as I do now, when I come to them from helping Dame Cicely in the kitchen, or making tarts and sweetmeats for the shop, or doing some little good turn for neighbor Benton.'"

"For I forgot to tell you, Dame Benton is brought to bed of twins, after so long a time, and you never did see anything so delighted as Sister Barbara was with the babies. I don't suppose she ever saw one before in all her life."

"Well," said Jack, very much interested and desirous to bring Cicely back to the point.

"Oh! 'Well,' says Sister Barbara, 'I never took so much comfort in prayer and meditation in all my life before, not when I had hardly anything else to do.'"

"Anne didn't seem very much pleased at this, and says she, 'I always thought a religious life was one thing and a secular life another.'"

"'Ah, my dear daughter,' replies Sister Barbara, 'I have been thinking that perhaps we have been mistaken in that very thing, and that all lives may be religious lives—that of the family as well as that of the cloister.'"

"I believe she is right," said Jack with decision. "Certainly God set people in families long before there were any such things as convents, as far as I can find out, and I suppose He knew what was good for them."

"Well, well, my dear lad, these are matters too high for us," replied Cousin Cicely. "Anyhow I am glad Sister Barbara is so content, and I wish she might abide with us, for she is like sunshine in the house, so she is; and as kind and pleasant with me as an own sister, for all she is a born lady and we only simple folk. I only wish Anne would take pattern by her, for she is a kind of thorn in your father's side—that is the truth."

"I think Anne looks worse than ever," remarked Jack. "She has such a scared look. Does she continue her penances?"

"Oh, yes, and increases them every day. I never saw her so strict; and now she has taken to visiting the poor folk, she just wears herself to a shadow."

"Does she visit the poor folk?" asked Jack. "I should think that might cheer her up a little."

"So it would, I think, if she went about it in a different way," replied Cicely, "but you see she makes a penance of that as she does of everything else, and somehow the poor folk seem to feel that she does, and that spoils it all. Now when I run about among them, I just do it in a neighborly way; and I gossip a bit with this one about her baby, and with that one about the new gown and kirtle she is making for her little maid, or her old mother maybe; and I hear the old folk tell their old tales about the times that were so much better than these, you know; and really I think I enjoy it as much as they do, and I come home feeling better, and disposed to be thankful for all the good things about me. But Anne, she takes no interest in all their little plans, and unless she can do something directly for them, she will not stay. She sometimes talks to them about their religious duties, and blames them for not going oftener to church, but she never sits down for a bit of neighborly talk. So they don't like her and don't feel at ease with her, and she feels that, and it makes her colder than ever."

"I understand," said Jack. "She does it like task work, and not because she loves God and her neighbor. She seems to think God is a hard master and a harsh judge, and not a kind loving Father. I wish she could see things differently."

CHAPTER XI.

NEW PROJECTS.

Jack and Sister Barbara were soon on the best of terms, and he learned to love the kind genial lady as well as if he had known her all his life. He was both amused and touched to see how she enjoyed the ease and freedom of her present life, and with what a zest she entered into all the family plans. She was very particular in observing all the canonical hours, and she fasted on Fridays, as indeed they all did, but her fasts were very different matters from poor Anne's, who ate hardly enough at any time to keep soul and body together. Sister Barbara seemed to think it quite enough to abstain from flesh, like the rest of the family, and she cooked many nice little messes for fast-days, telling Anne when she objected that they were just such as they always had in the convent. She took a deep interest in all the children in the neighborhood, especially in the babies, and showed a remarkable skill in tending the latter, which certainly must have come by nature.

"For, do you know," she said one day, "I never saw a little babe near at hand till I saw Dame Burton's?"

"Sure you never were meant for a nun, madam," said Master Lucas somewhat bluntly. "You should have married some gallant gentleman, and had a household of your own. You would have ruled it well, I warrant you."

Anne looked shocked, as she was apt to do at her father's blunt speeches and sallies; but Sister Barbara sighed and smiled as she answered—

"Maybe so, maybe so, Master Lucas. I had little voice in the matter, anyhow. I grew up in the convent, and never knew any other life, so I took the veil naturally when I came of age."

"I wish I had grown up in that way," said Anne. "I should then have known nothing else, and should have had no natural ties to keep me down and bind me to earth."

"Anne, who do you suppose did so arrange matters that you should be born in a family, and have these natural ties to bind you down to earth?" asked Jack abruptly. "Who is it that has made all these relations of parent and child, brother and sister, husband and wife?"

"God, I suppose," said Anne, after a little hesitation.

"I suppose He did without doubt, since the Psalm says that children are an heritage from the Lord, and the man is blest who hath his quiver full of them; and again, 'He maketh the barren woman to keep house and to be a joyful mother of children.' Do you not think He knew what He was about when He made all these family ties? Did He not know what was the life best fitted to promote holiness?"

"I suppose then you would have every one go on in earthly carnal courses," said Anne, somewhat tartly, and coloring deeply. "You would have nobody lead a religious consecrated life save those who have no friends or relations?"

"I would have all men and women lead religious lives, ay, and lives consecrated to God's service," replied Jack with emphasis. "I would have all they do consecrated to God, yea, even eating and drinking; but I would have them religious in the state where He hath placed them, and in the duties He hath marked out for them, instead of making fantastic duties of their own. I would have them serve Him in their own families and among their neighbors, and not selfishly shut themselves up in a cloister or hermitage. I do not believe God's Word ever gave warrant for any such conduct as that. Almost all the Bible saints that I can learn anything about were married, and had servants and horses and cattle, and overlooked them as gentlemen and farmers do nowadays."

"But it is so much easier to serve God in the cloister," said Anne, in a more subdued voice.

"I am not so sure of that, dear sister," remarked Sister Barbara, who had been listening attentively. "The temptations were of a different kind perhaps, but I am not sure but they were as trying. Think of all the little bickerings and heart-burnings we used to have among us; think how much jealousy there was of the favor of the prioress, and how many tales were told from one to another. And I am sure you can see that there were a good many hindrances even in the convent. Besides, to say truth," continued Sister Barbara, blushing a little, "I don't know how it is, but I seem to enjoy my prayers now a great deal more than I did when I had little or nothing else to do than to pray. I do believe one reason is that my health is so much better now that I run about so much in the open air, and have so many things to think about."

"I am sure you are looking better, madam," said Cicely. "You have such a fine color. I wish I could see our Anne's cheeks so red."

"I have been very happy in this house," said Sister Barbara, with tears in her bright gray eyes. "I am so thankful to Master Lucas for bringing me here, if only that I might see what a home is like. I never knew before. When I go back to the cloister, I shall take pleasure in thinking how many homes there are in the land, and how good and happy the people are in them; and I shall feel a great deal more hopeful about the world than ever I did before."

"Why should you ever go back to the cloister, madam?" asked Master Lucas. "Why should you not stay and make your home with us so long as you need one? One house is large enough and to spare, and one more makes no difference, even if you did not pay for your keeping, which you do and more too. We are but simple folk, 'tis true, and you a born lady, but yet—"

"Speak not of that, I pray you, Master Lucas, my good friend," interrupted the sister. "I will abide with you for the present, since you are so kind, and we will let the coming time take care for itself. Doubtless it will be ordered for the best. I would I could find more to make myself useful."

"Dear lady, don't fret about that," said Cicely. "I am sure you are a comfort to all of us. Why, the very little ones who come to the shop are ready to worship you, if you do but speak to them."

"Why should you not set up a school for little girls, madam, since you are so fond of children?" asked Jack.

"Hush, my son!" said his father.

"Pray let him speak," said Sister Barbara, eagerly. "What were you thinking of?"

"There are so many little maids about here," said Jack, "who are too young to be of much use at home, who yet are old enough to learn to read and work, ay, and to learn all kinds of mischief. Why should you not gather them into a school and teach them all the good you know?"

"That seems to me a good motion," said Sister Barbara. "I used to be thought good at teaching, you know, Anne."

"Yes, you were far better and more skilful than any one else in the convent, except—" Anne checked herself and turned pale.

And Sister Barbara sighed and was silent for a moment.

Jack guessed that they were speaking of Agnes Harland, and he sighed in his turn.

"I love children and young folks so well, I believe that is the secret of the matter," said Sister Barbara, recovering her cheerful tone. "I should love dearly to have a dozen or so of the little things together every day and teach them to knit and spin, and perhaps to do white seam and cut-work. It would be helping them to earn a living as well as to be useful at home, would it not?"

"It would indeed, madam; and you might teach them their religious duties at the same time."

"I will talk to the priest about it," said Sister Barbara.

"I am sure our Sir William will be pleased," remarked Cicely. "He has always wished for a girls' school. But it seems like a come down in life for you to be teaching a dame-school for children such as these, not young ladies, but daughters of tradesfolk and the like."

"I suppose our Lord died for tradesfolk and laborers as well as for gentlefolks," said Jack smiling.

"That is very true," said Sister Barbara; "and a religious person ought not to think any office too lowly which is done for the good of others. I have heard that our holy father the Pope washes the feet of twelve old men every Holy Thursday."

"Yes, with a gold basin and a damask cloth," said Jack dryly. "Master Fleming told me about that. He has seen the ceremony."

"I should like to meet this same Master Fleming," said the baker.

"He bade me say to you, father, that he desired to make your acquaintance," said Jack eagerly. "I had so much to think about, I had well-nigh forgotten the message. He is Sir William's cousin as I told you, and is to stay here a month or more. I am sure you will like him, for he has travelled a great deal, and you know you love travellers' tales."

"Ay, that I do. Well, we will go to see him, and have him and Sir William home to supper. He has been kind to you, and that is enough to make me love him."

"Then must you love all the world, and yourself most of all, for all the world is kind to me," said Jack; "but when will you go?"

"Directly, and you will go with me. I am right curious to see this friend of yours."

"Jack is graver than ever," said Cicely, when Jack had left the room.

"He seems a wondrous good lad," observed Sister Barbara. "I had thought all boys rough and cruel."

"They are so, too many of them," answered Cicely; "but our Jack was never like other boys, even before he took this last turn. And yet, though Jack is so grave and thoughtful ever since he came home, he seems happy too. I see him sometimes sit thinking by himself, and his face shines as if there were a light within."

"He is much changed," said Anne. "I cannot make him out. He is not like the same boy he was last winter."

Anne was right. In such circumstances and times as I have been describing, character develops fast, and Jack had grown from a schoolboy into a man.

CHAPTER XII.

AN EXPLANATION.

Sir William Leavett caught with avidity at the proposition of Madam Barbara, as she came presently to be called, to teach a girls' school in Bridge Street. A room was found in a house belonging to Master Lucas and suitably arranged; and here did Madam Barbara set up her sceptre over her kingdom of about twenty little maids of all ages from three to twelve, to whom she taught the arts of sewing, knitting, spinning, and reading, promising to advance the best scholars as far as white seam, cut-work, and carpet-work, and possibly even to writing.

Her school soon became very popular, as well with pupils as with parents. The mothers rejoiced in the manifest improvement in the manners and appearance of their little girls and their advancement in all useful arts, and were flattered that their children should be taught by a "born lady." The children themselves learned to love their teacher and to feel themselves exceedingly comfortable under her gentle but decided sway. It was certainly true, as Master Lucas had said, that Madam Barbara had a natural talent for managing children. She knew how to combine the most absolute authority with great indulgence and kindness. She knew that the youthful human heart has many avenues of approach, and that as much might be done by praises and rewards as by reproof and punishment. She possessed the inestimable art of prevention—she knew that it was a great deal better if possible to keep children from being naughty, than to punish them afterwards. Her sway was so gentle, as compared with that of Master Crabtree over the boys, as to arouse some murmurings among the latter, that the girls should be so much better off than they were.

"Yes, Peggy may well like to go to school," said Mary Brent's boy Peter, in reply to his mother, who had been holding up his sister to him as an example. "It is a very different thing. Madam Barbara is always kind and gentle. She hardly ever punishes the girls, and when they do well she gives them cakes and comfits; and praises them beside. Master Crabtree hardly ever says a good word to a boy, no matter how much pains he may take; and if he does the least thing out of the way, whack comes the strap across his back or hand. If Peggy went to Master Crabtree, she wouldn't be in such a hurry to get to school, I can tell you."

"No, that I shouldn't," agreed little Peggy, heartily sympathizing with her brother. "I wish Peter could go to Madam Barbara, only she doesn't take boys."

"As though I would go to school with a parcel of little maids," growled Peter; but in his heart he wished so too.

Jack meantime fell very much into his old ways, helping his father with his accounts, playing with his old schoolmates, and going to Sir William Leavett for a Greek lesson twice a week; for, to his own disappointment as well as to that of Master Crabtree, his father firmly refused to let him go into school at present.

"He will lose all he has gained if he once gets back into that close room, and with Master Crabtree to drive him with whip and spur," said Master Lucas. "I am willing to have him learn what he can at home, since Sir William is so kind as to help him; but to school he shall not go for a year."'

And as Master Lucas, with all his kindness and gentleness, was an absolute monarch in his family, Jack was fain to submit, especially as he found upon making the trial that he could not bear the confinement for any length of time. So he gave up the thought of going to school this year and to Oxford the next, and contented himself with what he could do at home. He was especially anxious to get on with Greek, as Master Fleming promised him a copy of Erasmus' Greek Testament as soon as he was able to read it intelligently; and with the help of Sir William Leavett, he made great progress.

Master Fleming still remained in Bridgewater at the house of his cousin, now and then making an excursion into the country, especially to the houses of Lord Harland and the knight of Holford, with whom he seemed to be on terms of great intimacy. He had been invited to the tables of most of the substantial citizens of Bridgewater; but while he was always ready for a friendly chat upon London matters, trade in general, or any other topic, he was anything but a boon companion and frowned most decidedly upon any light or loose conversation. He visited much among the poor of Father William's congregation, especially among the sailors' families down by the waterside, and gave a large present in money to the fund of the almshouses for the widows of mariners, which had been endowed by the will of a wealthy ship-owner some years before.

He was often to be found in Master Lucas' shop, sometimes under the pretext of storing his pockets with cakes and sweets for the school-children, sometimes merely to have an hour's talk with the kind genial old man; and he and Jack took long walks into the country on pleasant evenings, talking of everything in heaven and earth; Jack asking endless questions, and Master Fleming listening and answering with that patient kindness and sympathy which often produces in an intelligent young person of either sex, a sort of adoring reverence for an older companion. In short, Master Fleming won golden opinions from all sorts of people, from the prior of the convent, whom he informed as to the best way of supplying his house with almonds and figs, wax candles and fine cloth, to Mary Brent and her little children, to whom he gave cakes and toys and more substantial comforts.

Mary Brent's condition had considerably improved since we first met her in Master Lucas's shop at the beginning of this tale. She had recovered from her injury, and thanks to the long rest enforced by her sprained ankle, and to the generous diet provided by Dame Cicely, she found herself in better health than she had been since the death of her husband. She was thus enabled to take in the fine washing and ironing in which she excelled, and which was then a profitable business, owing to the great quantity of laces worn by both sexes.

Mary Brent was judged to be the neatest hand at a lace or cut-work falling band, or a lady's stiffened coif and pinners, of any one in Bridgewater; and thanks partly to Cicely's active patronage and recommendation, she found plenty to do. She was able to put in order her house, which had once been a good one, and to help pay her way by letting lodgings now and then to the better sort of sea-faring men. Peter and Peggy both went to school, and Master Lucas promised to take Peter for an apprentice so soon as he should be a little older, while Peggy was learning under Madam Barbara to do the fine sorts of needlework which would insure her a superior place whenever she should wish to go to service.

Moreover Mary had received letters and money from her son in foreign parts more than once—not a great deal, to be sure, but enough to be a help to her and (what she valued still more) to show that her Davy was not the scapegrace that his former masters would have made him out. In short, as Master Lucas had once prophesied, the sun was beginning to shine on her side of the hedge, and she could well afford to dispense with the charity which had been so grudgingly dealt out to her at the convent gate.

There was one person with whom Jack did not "get on" at all, and that was his sister Anne. Jack had always loved his sister dearly, it must be confessed on slight encouragement, for Anne's system of religious belief led her to look on all natural family affection with suspicion, as a thing savoring of "the world," and a hindrance to that ascetic sanctity to which she aspired. For a time during Jack's long and severe illness she had seemed to thaw toward him, and to be disposed to give him her confidence, especially after the conversation relating to Agnes Harland; and Jack had looked forward with affectionate impatience to seeing her again. But he found her, to his great disappointment, frozen up ten times stiffer and colder than ever.

At first he was unwilling to accept this state of things, and accused himself of jealousy and unkindness, but he soon came to see that it was no fancy of his own. Anne avoided him as much as possible: she would not sit down in the room alone with him, and seemed actually afraid of him.

Jack felt very much distressed, for aside from his strong natural affection toward his sister, his heart was full of the first love and joy of a genuine religious experience; and he would fain have been on good terms with all the world. He made many attempts to put matters on a better footing; but without success. Anne seemed to shrink into her shell more and more as Jack tried to draw her out of it.

At last, one day finding her alone in her room, he entered it and closed the door behind him.

"Now, Anne dear, let us have it out," said he. "Do not let us go on in this uncomfortable way any longer. Tell me at once and plainly, what have I done to offend you and make you so cold to me?"

Anne, looked round like a frightened hare for a chance to escape, but seeing none, she seemed to control herself and resume her usual icy composure with a great effort. "You have done nothing to offend me," replied she coldly. "What makes you think so?"

"Your whole air and manner," replied Jack frankly. "You avoid me at all times as though my presence carried the plague with it. You never speak to me if you can help it, and I tell you freely, sister Anne, I cannot think it right. Even if I have displeased you, it is not the part of a Christian to bear malice. The Scripture rule is, 'If thy brother trespass against thee, tell him his fault between him and thee alone.'"

"The Scripture!" said Anne, starting. "What do you know of Scripture?"

"I know that much at all events, and so do you, because Father William preached from it only last Sunday."

"I did not hear the sermon," replied Anne. "I was praying in our Lady's Chapel. It would be well, brother, if you prayed more and minded sermons less."

"And I cannot but think, sister, that it would be well for you, not perhaps to pray less, but to seek instruction more."

"I seek instruction where sound teaching is to be found," said Anne, coloring. "I do not run after novelties and novelty-mongers like Father William."

"You have no right to speak in that way of Father William," said Jack, coloring in his turn. "But we will let that pass. One of two things I am sure of," he added, fixing his eyes upon Anne; "either you think I have wronged you or that you have wronged me. Which is it?"

Anne's color grew yet deeper and then faded to paleness. She dropped her eyes, but did not speak.

"Anne, did you tell Father Barnaby that I was curious about heretical books?" asked Jack.

"That is no affair of yours," replied Anne, trying to speak in her usual tone, though she trembled visibly. "My confessions are between my confessor and myself."

"In faith, it is my affair, and is like to be an affair of moment, if your confessions are such as may bring me to the stake," returned Jack. "Father Barnaby may be your confessor, but he is not mine; and you have no right to talk of my affairs to him."

Anne grew paler and paler. She sat silent for a moment, and then whispered, "I could not help it."

"Could not help it," repeated Jack. "Could you not tell him the truth, at least? When did I ever say to you that I would like to read heretical books?"

"You said you would like to read the Bible," said Anne.

"And is the Bible an heretical book? Is not the Bible the Word of God? And how then can it be heretical?"

"There is no use in going over all that again," returned Anne. "You know as well as I that it is wrong and presumptuous for lay and common people to desire to read the Scripture. You know what comes of it."

"I know what will come of it one day, and that will be the downfall and ruin of those who so presumptuously keep it from them to whom it rightfully belongs," said Jack, forgetting his prudence. He might have said more had not Anne herself checked him.

"Jack, if you have any mercy on me or yourself, hush, and say no more such things. You will not only destroy your own soul, but mine, if you go on. If you knew all that I have borne and am bearing for your sake, you would be more pitiful to me."

"But why should you bear anything on my account, dear Anne?" asked Jack, softened at once by his sister's look and tone of distress.

"Because I would save you if it were possible," returned Anne, weeping; "because I would—but oh, it is of no use!" she sobbed, bursting into a flood of bitter tears. "I would have saved the other. I would have saved Agnes, if a whole life spent in prayer and penance would have done it—if it would have availed for her even after ages spent in purgatory; but all is of no use. Father Barnaby says she was an incurable heretic, and as such doomed to hell without remedy; and he says my love for one like her is a sin for which all my penances will hardly atone. Oh, what shall I do? What shall I do? Oh, if I could see any way of escape, any ray of hope; but no, there is, there can be none!"

Jack hesitated a moment, and then came to his sister's side. He felt that he must speak, that to keep silence would be that denial of which Master Fleming had warned him to beware at all hazards.

"Anne, believe me, there is another way, an easy and safe way to mind and spirit, whatever it may be to the body in these evil times," said he. "God is far, far more merciful than you think. All these labors which are wearing out your life are none of His appointing. They are but the cunning devices of men. He hath provided a way by which we may be saved, even by simple faith in His mercy through the blood of His Son."

"Dear Anne, our Lord hath done all for us already. He hath borne our sins in His own body on the tree; it is by His stripes we are healed, and not by those we lay on ourselves; the Scripture says so. They are the words of St. Peter himself. He came into the world not to condemn, but to save it, and whosoever believeth in Him hath everlasting life and shall never come into condemnation. He is ready to save, His ear is always open. Oh, dear Anne, come to Him—see and know Him. Leave all these devices of men which are separating you from your family, and driving you into your grave, and be at peace."

Anne looked at her brother for a moment with wide-open eyes as if she had seen a ghost. Then she said in a husky whisper—

"What do you mean? Who has been saying these things to you?"

"It is the Lord Himself who says them, Anne," replied Jack. "He tells us so in His Word, that very word which supported Agnes Harland when she was despitefully used for reading and believing it. Anne, I am putting my life in your hands by telling you these things; but I cannot see you suffering as you are without trying to help you. Oh, sister, only read for yourself—only hear—"

In his eagerness, he had thrown himself on his knees at his sister's side and seized her hand.

Anne pushed him away.

"How dare you speak so to me?" she said angrily. "Is it not enough then that you should destroy yourself without trying to destroy me?"

"It is because I would save you that I speak. Only look for yourself. Anne, I tell you, as sure as you are alive, there is no other way of salvation but through faith in Christ. If your merits were as great as those of St. Peter himself, they could avail nothing so far as that is concerned. Our Lord has Himself paid all the price of our redemption, and we have but to accept it as a free gift at His hands. Oh, sister, the way is so easy!"

"Easy! Yes, the way to hell is always easy," said Anne, with bitterness. "It is the other way that is hard. How dare you come bringing your heresies into this room where our mother died? How dare you speak them to me who am the promised bride of Christ? How dare you tell me that all my prayers and penances are worth nothing in God's sight, after all these years that I have striven to earn His favor and love?"

Jack was silent for a moment, startled by Anne's burst of passion so unlike her usual self-restraint.

Then he said gently, "His favor and love are yours already, Anne, if you will but take them. They are a free gift. The gift of God is eternal life through His dear Son."

"Oh, it is too hard—too hard," cried Anne, bursting into a fresh passion of tears. "I have heard all these things before. They rang in my ears for weeks and months after Agnes was taken from me; and now, just as they had ceased to haunt me day and night, you awaken the memory of them again. I will go far away. I will to the nunnery again—to the strictest order that I can find, and there in the darkest cell I will—" Anne's words were choked by her sobs.

Jack, much distressed, would have taken her hand to soothe her, but she repulsed him violently, and then as if her strength were exhausted by the effort, she fell back fainting in her chair.

At that moment, Sister Barbara opened the inner door which communicated with her room.

"Hush, dear lad," said she, gently and quietly. "Help me to lay your sister on the bed, and then leave her to me. She will be better presently, poor thing."

"I fear I have been to blame," said Jack, as he lifted Anne in his arms and felt shocked to discover how emaciated she was. "I have distressed when I meant to help her."

"I know, I know," whispered the good nun. "Say no more, but go and pray for her and all of us. I will bring her to herself, and she will be better."

CHAPTER XIII.

"THEY THAT SOW IN TEARS."

Jack left the house and went out to walk, feeling the need of solitude to compose his thoughts. He was distressed at his sister's condition, and a little frightened when he thought of the way in which he had put himself in her power; and yet, in considering the matter, he did not see how he could have done otherwise. He was so deep in thought that he started on being spoken to, as if a bolt had fallen from the sky.

"A fair evening, my young brother," said Master Fleming. "Yet you do not seem to be enjoying it greatly. Your eyes are on the ground as if your thoughts were heavy."

"They are so in truth," said Jack. "I am right glad to meet you, Master Fleming, and would willingly have your advice and opinion on a grave matter."

"Both are at your service," said Master Fleming. "I trust nothing unpleasant has chanced."

In reply Jack told him the whole story, to which Master Fleming listened with grave attention.

"I cannot see that you have done wrong," said he at last. "You might perhaps have used more caution, and yet caution is not always best. You say no one heard you but your sister?"

"Nobody unless Madam Barbara might have caught a few words," replied Jack. "Her room is next my sister's. I hardly think she could have done so, or she would not have spoken so kindly and gently to me."

"What did she say?" asked Master Fleming.

"She bade me go pray for Anne and myself—pray for us all, were her words, I think. She is always a kind lady; but, methinks, as I remember it, there was an unusual tenderness in her voice and glance."

"That is strange, if she did really overhear you," said the merchant. "You do not think your sister would betray you?"

"Never, if she were left to herself," said Jack, warmly; "but you see, there is just the rub. She will not be left to herself. I have good reason to think that she has told tales of me already, from what Father Barnaby said to me at Father John's house in Holford."

"How was that?" asked Master Fleming.

Jack repeated the story, to which the merchant listened with attention, laughing heartily as Jack recounted with considerable humor his encounter with Father Barnaby, and the way in which he had been thrown off the scent by means of Horace and the Babylonian numbers.

"Well, my brother, you certainly owe Horace a debt of gratitude," said he, when Jack had finished the story. "You say you have not seen the priest since that time?"

Jack replied in the negative.

"I see nothing that you can do but to wait in hope and trust for the result," said Master Fleming. "It may be that your words will be blessed to your sister after all, and that she may have grace to turn to the only source of comfort and light. Poor young maid, my heart is sad for her. Meantime I need not tell you to treat her with all kindness and forbearance, and to pray earnestly for her."

"I never mean to be out of patience with her," said Jack, "and yet she does anger me sometimes so that I can hardly forbear speaking sharply to her—not for my own sake, but for that of my father and my Cousin Cicely. She is such a continual grief to them."

"There is nothing gained, but a good deal lost by that, my young brother," said the merchant kindly. "I dare say your good father does not lose patience with his unhappy daughter."

"Not often," replied Jack. "He treats her always with the greatest forbearance and kindness, puts up with all her ways, and indulges her in everything; and yet she does not seem to have the least notion of it."

"I dare say not; few people have," said the merchant dryly. "But do you take pattern by your father, and remember that you have a double call to exercise kindness and love. Let me tell you what to do. When your patience seems like to fail, do not dwell upon and aggravate in your own heart the offence of your sister (as I know by my own experience one is apt to do), but lift up your heart in prayer for her, and then recall to mind your own offences against God, and His gracious and free forgiveness, and remember our Lord's saying, 'not till seven times, but till seventy times seven.' Above all pray that your heart may be filled with love to God and man, for therein lies the great remedy for sin in every form."

"I will," said Jack, brushing the tears from his eyes. "Oh, what shall I do for a counsellor when you are gone? I wish you could abide with us always."

"That can hardly be," replied Master Fleming. "I must go back to London before long. But I trust some friend will be raised up to you."

"I wish I could go with you," said Jack. "It would be so much easier to be good with you."

"It is not the part of a good soldier to choose the easiest way," replied Master Fleming, smiling. "Besides, Jack, it is usually a mistake to think that you could serve God and do better in some other place than the one where He has put you. It is this very error which has driven so many into the cloister. Others it has led out into the dangers of the world, for which they were wholly unfit. Many a one is sick of home, and fancies he would do better in a wider sphere, while he is failing in every relation of life in the place assigned him by Providence. Be content where you are; few lads have a better or more cheerful home, though all may not be as you desire."

"I know that indeed," said Jack eagerly. "I should be a villain to cherish discontent, while I have my father and dear good Cousin Cicely to make much of me. I am rather afraid my way will be made too soft and easy."

"Never fear," said Master Fleming. "That is a misfortune which I venture to say never yet happened to one who was honestly trying to serve God with all his heart. Our Father loves to see His children happy, but He is sure to send them all the crosses they need. Enjoy your peaceful sunshiny home while it is yours, for these are threatening times, and we may not long be left in peace. The sun shines just now, you see," he added, looking toward the vest where was piled up a gorgeous mass of thunder-clouds, "but it will soon set, and I hear already the growling of the coming storm. The sun will rise again, we know, but before that time many a fair barque may be wrecked, and gallant sailor drowned. Let us pray that we may be able to endure all these things, and to stand at last before the Son of man."

Awed and yet comforted, Jack turned his steps homeward. He found nobody in the shop but Simon the journeyman.

"Where is my father, Simon?" he asked.

"Your father and Dame Cicely have gone to see poor Dame Higby in her trouble," replied Simon, "and they did talk of stopping to supper with your cousin Master Luttrell. Madam Barbara is in the other room, waiting supper for you, and Mistress Anne is above."

"I did not think it so late," said Jack. "I am sorry I have kept the lady waiting. I will be with her as soon as I wash my hands."

"Your sister is ill at ease and keeps her chamber," said Madam Barbara, in reply to Jack's somewhat timid question. "I did not like to leave her, but she begged me to do so, and I thought perhaps she would be best alone."

Jack felt himself somewhat ill at ease at the prospect of a tête-à-tête with Madam Barbara; but the lady chatted on as usual about all sorts of matters. Jack could not help thinking, however, that there was something peculiar in her tone, and once or twice fancied that her eyes rested on him with unusual tenderness.

When the meal was finished and cleared away, Sister Barbara went up to Anne, and Jack sat down to occupy himself with his books. He did not find Horace very congenial to his present feelings, and was just wishing that he dared take out his Bible, when Sister Barbara again entered the room, closing the door after her, and came toward him.

Jack rose, but she made him a sign to be seated, and sat down near him. Jack's heart beat, for he felt that something was coming; but he kept silence and waited to be spoken to.

"Jack," said Sister Barbara, in a low tone, "will you forgive me? I listened to what you said to your sister this afternoon. I came into my room while you were talking, and I could not help listening. Will you forgive me?"

"There is nothing to forgive, dear lady," said Jack, recovering himself, for he was considerably startled. "I said nothing wrong to Anne, nothing I would take back. I know they were dangerous words, but they were true, and I am sure you will never betray me."

"I would not betray you unless I betrayed myself," said Dame Barbara, in a still lower tone. "Jack, I have so longed to hear words like those once more. I have heard them before from the lips of one who paid clearly for them."

Jack felt fairly giddy with astonishment. A new light seemed all at once to dawn upon him, which made clear a hundred little things which had puzzled him.

"Do you mean, from Agnes Harland?" he asked. "Did you hear them from her?"

"Hush!" whispered the lady. "Yes. However you heard the tale, it is true. It was from that poor child, that I learned to know the truth of what you said to Anne this afternoon. After she was secluded from the family, she was very ill and the heart of our prioress was moved with pity for her. She had always a pitiful heart, dear lady, and would fain have saved the poor girl, and got her away to her friends before the matter came out; but it could not be. However, she pitied her as I said, and at last got her moved from the prison cell to a more comfortable place where she could at least see the light of day. Father Barnaby consented on condition that she should see none of the family, and that I alone should attend upon her; for he thought I had grown up in the house, as indeed I had, and that I was too steadfast to be moved. Agnes did not live many weeks; but she lived long enough to tell me wonderful things, and to convince me that she was right; and when she died, she gave me this book, one of those which she had brought from home, and which, being small, she had managed to conceal about her person."

Madam Barbara drew from her bosom a small, thin, and much-worn book, and put it into Jack's hand. Feeling as if he were in a dream, Jack opened it and looked at the titlepage. It was an English translation of Luther's commentary on Galatians, with the text. On the margin was traced in trembling characters, "Fear not them which kill the body," and again, still fainter, "My peace I do give unto you."

"That is all of Scripture I have ever seen," continued Dame Barbara. "Agnes had the Gospels also, but they were discovered and taken from her when she was imprisoned. I have read and read this book again and again, and I prize it more than life; but I do so long to read the whole Gospel, the words of our Lord himself. When I heard your speech this afternoon, I was sure you had read them, and I determined at all hazards to ask you. Have I done wrong?"

"No, indeed, madam," replied Jack, recovering himself. "You have done well, and right thankful am I that I can bring you to a sight of the Gospel. I will lend you the book at once, and it may be that I can procure a Testament for you from the same friend who gave me mine. But you know it is a dangerous possession."

"I know that," said Sister Barbara. "Have I not jealously guarded this treasure of mine for two long years? But I am growing tired of secrecy, and I should like to speak out before I die."

"I am often troubled myself about this same secrecy," said Jack. "It seems a kind of denial of the Master; and yet, for the present I see no other way."

"Hush!" said Madam Barbara, "Here comes your father."

"So! I find you in good company, son," cried Master Lucas with his usual jolly laugh. "I have been thinking you would be lonely. But where is poor Anne? Not at the church or chapel in this storm, I trust?"

"Anne is not well, and is lying down, dear father, and Madam Barbara was kind enough to come and sit with me," said Jack. "How you find Dame Higby?"

"Why, poorly—but poorly," replied Master Lucas, his sunny face clouding at remembrance of the grief he had witnessed. "You see, her poor man died suddenly and without the sacrament—some say he refused them, but that I do not believe; and he hath left her but poorly off. I doubt when all the expenses of the funeral are paid, she will have little left to live upon. We must remember her, Cicely, and not let her want."

That night Jack put his Testament into Madam Barbara's hands, and the next day, he brought her a small copy from Master Fleming's store, now getting low.

CHAPTER XIV.

ANNE AT HOME.

Jack had hoped his explanation with Anne would have cleared up matters between them; but to his sorrow, he found their intercourse was more constrained, and on a more uncomfortable footing, than ever. Anne's treatment of him had heretofore been rather negative than positive. She had avoided all private conversation with her brother, and had kept him at a distance; but that was all. Now, however, she was absolutely unkind and harsh, and that in a very vexatious way. She treated him with that sort of contempt so hard for young persons to bear.

Jack was naturally fond of talking about his life and experiences in the country, and his father and Cicely liked to hear him; but Anne took special pains to show that she felt no interest in the matter. She constantly contradicted him, put wrong constructions on all he said and did, and seemed to find special pleasure in speaking slightingly of his most revered friends, Master Fleming and Sir William Leavett.

Jack turned the tables on her one day by remarking on her inconsistency: "You are shocked at my father for finding fault with the pride and luxury of the prior, and the rapacity of Father Joseph, because, forsooth, you say we ought to reverence the clergy and not to criticise them; but I do not see why you are not just as bad yourself. Sir William is a priest, and an old priest as well; and one whom every one allows to be a man of most saintly life and conversation. Why is it not as irreverent in you to find fault with Sir William as it is in my father to laugh at the prior?"

Anne had no answer ready, but she was not the more amiable on that account. In general, it must be confessed that considering his naturally hasty temper, Jack bore his sister's treatment with wonderful patience. Sometimes, indeed, he would show a flash of the old fire, and turn on Anne sharply enough: but he was always sorry when he was tempted to do so, for it did Anne no good and only burdened his own conscience. Both Master Fleming and Madam Barbara counselled him to patience and forbearance.

"You cannot tell what is working in Anne's mind," said Madam Barbara. "The poor girl is very unhappy, of that I am sure; and it is her unhappiness which makes her so fretful."

"She need not visit her unhappiness on my poor father," said Jack. "That does not make her feel any better."

"No, it is the last way in which to find comfort," replied Madam Barbara; "but it is very common conduct nevertheless."

In truth Anne was very unhappy, and that for more reasons than one. She would have repudiated the charge with indignation, if any one had told her she was jealous and envious of her brother; but such was nevertheless the case. Anne had, in fact, a great conceit of herself. Whether consciously or not, she cherished the idea that she was altogether superior to the other members of her family.

The childish fancy for playing at nun, had been considered as a wonderful instance of a vocation for a religious life in so young a child, and she was praised and petted for it accordingly, not only by her mother and her gossips, but by the nuns in the convent where she was sent to be educated at her mother's express desire. Anne found her convent life exactly suited to her taste. She had a good voice and a fine taste in music. She was naturally religious and had an especial bent toward ceremonial observances; and she was constantly held up as an example to the other pupils in the convent. Her opinion was already appealed to and considered of weight in the matters of decorations and music for festival occasions, and she was always put forward to sing at public services. She was constantly spoken of in her own hearing, as a young person of singular piety and talent, and one likely to rise to a high place in the sisterhood; for her taking the veil was considered by herself and others as a settled matter.

At home, she was only little Anne Lucas, petted, indeed, by her father and Cicely (who came to rule the house after Dame Lucas' death), and indulged in all reasonable matters; but not considered as of any great weight in the family, and now and then set down very gently indeed, but decidedly, by her father, when she transgressed the rules considered proper for the guidance of young women at home. It was no great wonder that with her disposition, she liked the convent best, and quite decided to make a profession when she was old enough.

Then came the death of the old confessor, who loved ease and comfort himself and had no disposition to deny it to other people, and the advent of Father Barnaby, who never spared himself, nor anybody else. The old nuns grumbled, and the prioress now and then rebelled, and successfully too, for she was a woman of spirit and ability and had no notion of being made a cipher in her own house; but the younger sisters, with only few exceptions, were enthusiastic partisans of Father Barnaby, and none more so than Anne. No service was too long for her, no penance too severe. She was bent upon becoming a saint on Father Barnaby's pattern, and the confessor encouraged her in the idea. All this helped to keep alive in her mind the idea of her own superiority. She was a good deal shaken indeed by the incident of her friend's disgrace and disappearance, and for a little time she was thoroughly humbled in her own eyes; but the penances she enjoined upon herself with a view of expiating her own offence and that of her friend, seemed to build her up once more in her own self-esteem. These penances she continued, as we have seen, in her father's house when she was sent home to remain for a year before taking the veil.

Her father with his bustling business habits, his love of moderate good cheer, and his perhaps too outspoken contempt and dislike for the monks and the religious houses generally, was a mere worldly-minded scoffer in her eyes; Cousin Cicely, whose whole life had been one long self-abnegation, but who could hardly read, and write not at all, was a mere housewife fit for nothing but her kitchen and her store-rooms; and Jack was but an insignificant chit of a boy, to be patronized and brought into the right way by his sister's influence. Jack was to become a priest, and perhaps be a bishop, while she was abbess of some great religious house (for already her ambitions soared far beyond the little sisterhood at Nunwood), and he was to owe all to her influence and direction.

It was a great shock to this fine castle in the air, when Jack utterly refused to leave Sir William Leavett's church and teachings for the spiritual guide she had selected for him. Jack declared that Sir William was a good man and kind to him; that he loved him dearly, and would not leave him for any of the fathers at the convent; and his father sustained him in his refusal, adding that in his opinion, Anne would do well to consult Sir William herself.

Anne had performed many "humbling" penances to perfect her in humility, but, strange to say, when it came to a real contradiction, these penances did not seem to help her in the least. She was as angry at Jack for presuming to have an opinion of his own, as if she had never kissed the feet of the sisters or knelt on the floor while they were at dinner.

But the vexation she had felt at Jack for refusing to be governed by her in the matter of a confessor was nothing to the anger which she felt against him at present. Jack presuming to read and decide for himself; pretending to have a higher standard than her own, and above all attempting to instruct her; Jack telling her that all her penances, her enforced works of charity, her bed of boards and ashes, her fasts and vigils, were all worthless and worse than worthless, and that he—he, a schoolboy, and three years younger than herself—had discovered a better and safer way! Anne had always found it hard to have any charity or toleration for those who differed from her, but this was the worst of all.

But this was not all. There was a deeper cause for her disquiet than wounded self-love. Anne had told the truth when she said that she had found it hard to forget the words she had heard from Agnes Harland. They had indeed rung in her ears for days, and a voice in her heart constantly made answer to them, "These things are true! They are no delusion—no modern invention. They are true, and if so all my belief hitherto has been false, all my sanctity wherein I have trusted and for which I have received honor of men is built on a false foundation."

For days and weeks these and such like thoughts tormented her. She confessed them to Father Barnaby; she performed with punctilious accuracy the penances he laid upon her; she tried with all her might to overcome her affection for poor Agnes, and to believe what Father Barnaby told her, that her betrayal of her friend's confidence to him had been a virtue and not a piece of base treachery. She did in some measure quiet her conscience and mind, and recover her self-complacency, by such means; but there yet lingered in the depths of her heart, an uneasy feeling that all was not right with her; that Agnes might after all have been a martyr for truth instead of a stubborn heretic.

She had not intended to tell Father Barnaby of what Jack had said about wanting to read the Bible; but, as Thomas Sprat had once said, she was as wax in the hands of her confessor. The clergy had begun to be exceedingly jealous on the subject of the Scriptures, already spreading among the common people, and to watch on all sides for the least indication of heretical opinions. Anne came away from her confession trying to think that she had done her duty to her brother, though she well knew to what her confession might lead. She felt that she had betrayed her brother's confidence, and it was this which made her so shy of him when he came home from Holford. Still, she said to herself she had done her duty, she had disregarded the ties of the flesh, as she had been told she was bound to do; and if she was made wretched thereby, why, there was only so much the more merit in the action, and that was some comfort.

Just as she had succeeded in attaining some degree of quietness, came Jack, determined to arrive at an explanation, full of the earnestness of a thorough religious conviction, and roused in her heart again all the old rebellious misgivings. In vain, did she strive to forget what he had said. It rung in her ears by night and day. The ghost, which had never been quite laid, came back to haunt her more constantly than ever, with the old whisper, "It is true. It is all true; and with all your efforts you have not made one step toward true holiness; because you have been walking in the wrong direction. You are a miserable sinner, not one whit better, not so good as these people you have been looking down upon all your life."

If Anne had yielded to these convictions, if she had listened to the voice speaking within her, she might indeed have been unhappy for a time; but her sorrow would not have been bitter, and she would soon have found peace. But she would not yield—not one inch. To do her justice, it was no fear of consequences which kept her back. She would have gone to the stake as cheerfully as any martyr that ever died. But her pride rose in arms, that pride which was her strongest characteristic, and which waxed stronger and stronger, because she never acknowledged its existence to herself. Was she to confess that all her life had hitherto been wrong and mistaken? Was she, the pattern to the pupils, and even to the elder sisters, the prospective prioress, the future abbess, perhaps, to own that she had no title to all these honors, that she was no saint, but a miserable sinner, that instead of doing anything to purchase the salvation of others, she could only sue as a beggar for her own?

There is no passion of the human heart harder to deal with than pride, even when we have all the helps which grace can give. It is hard to descend into the valley of humiliation and to catch no slips by the way; if we do chance to fall, our enemy is always ready to take advantage of our fall to disturb our rest; yet, when we are summoned to descend into this valley, there is no peace to be found but in obedience to the call. Anne heard the summons, and in her heart of hearts she felt that it came from God; but she was determined not to obey. She fought against conviction with all her might, but as yet the voice would not be silenced nor leave her, and the combat had to be fought out anew every day. Her life was made wretched by the discord in herself, and in her desperate distress, she visited her own wretchedness on all around her, especially on Jack, whom she looked upon as the cause of all her trouble. She knew that he prayed for her, and tried to be kind and patient with her, and that provoked her worst of all. She redoubled her devotions and penances, but she had lost all comfort in them. She would have eased her mind by confession, but, angry as she was at Jack, she hesitated at putting his life into the hands of Father Barnaby. Besides, the father was very busy preparing for his journey to London, and had no time to hear confessions at present, so she must even bear her burdens alone.

"Here is Father Barnaby asking for you, Jack," said Master Lucas, coming into the sitting-room where Jack was at work with his books. "He is just about to set out on his journey, and wants a word with you at the door."

"With Jack, father?" said Anne, in a tone of uneasiness. "Are you sure?"

"I know only what he said, sweetheart. He asked for Jack. Hurry, my son, and do not keep the father waiting."

Anne would have liked to listen, but she dared not do so, though she came into the shop. She saw the father give Jack a couple of books which Jack received with all due reverence, exchange two or three remarks with her father, and apparently decline politely an invitation to take some refreshment. Then, bestowing his blessing, Father Barnaby rode away as it seemed, in a very good humor; and Master Lucas and his son came back into the shop.

"What did Father Barnaby say?" asked Anne.

"He gave me the books he promised me, and advised me to study them," replied Jack. "I am sure I shall do so with pleasure, for he knows a great deal more about Horace than Master Crabtree does."

"Horace," said Anne in a disappointed tone. "You must be mistaken, Jack. I am sure Father Barnaby does not concern himself about such heathen and secular learning."

"Look for yourself," said Jack, smiling. "Here are the two volumes both of his own writing, one upon the Eleventh Ode of Horace, and the other on the Latin metres. Father Barnaby is a great student of the Latin poets."

Anne was convinced against her will, but she looked very much discomposed.

"Did he leave no message for me?" she asked.

"None," replied Jack. "He asked if all were well, and if Sister Barbara kept on with her school; that was all. Then he bade good-morning and rode away."

And was that all? Anne had much ado to keep back her tears of mortification and disappointment. After all her efforts to please him, he had gone away to be gone for weeks or months without a word. He had distinguished Jack with special favor, notwithstanding what she had told him about her brother, and had apparently forgotten her existence. It was very hard, and it did not tend to make her feel more kindly toward her brother. She went up to her room and cried till she was weary, and then imposed a new penance upon herself, because she had failed in humility. Poor Anne!

CHAPTER XV.

MARY BRENT'S LODGER.

"I am glad he is gone," said Sister Barbara to Jack, when she heard of the afternoon's visitor. "I could not be easy so long as he was about. He is a terrible man."

"And I am glad as well, and that for more reasons than one," answered Jack; "one of which is that poor old Father John will be left in peace. I have no fears of his disturbing other folks for heresy or anything else, so long as he is left to himself. But there is that sacristan, who is a prying, eavesdropping fellow, and men say a spy of Father Barnaby's."

"I grow very weary of all this concealment," said Sister Barbara. "I sometimes feel as if I must speak, come what may."

"Father William says the same, and I suppose it must come to that shortly," said Jack. "He has scruples about celebrating masses for the dead, and I think he will declare himself before long. He is not the man to act against his conscience. Do you think, madam, the time will ever come when the people of this realm will dare to speak out, and when the Scripture will be read in the churches?"

"It may come in your time, but I fear not in mine," said Sister Barbara, sighing, "and there will be terrible times first. The bishops and priests will not give up their claims on the people without a fierce struggle, and nobody can guess the side the King will take. You heard the sermon the priest of St. Mary's preached last Sunday about those who presume to read the new Gospel?"

"Yes, madam," said Jack laughingly. "He is a learned man. He said that Greek was a heathen tongue, and asked if it were likely that the Scripture would be written in the language of heathens, while Latin was the tongue of our Holy Father the Pope. He said Hebrew was the speech of unbelieving Jews, and therefore not fit even to be named by Christians.[2] I could hardly forbear laughing."

"Laugh while you can," said Sister Barbara sadly. "I greatly fear we shall all laugh out of the other side of our mouths ere long. Just think what a <u>power this man</u> and others like him hold in their hands; how they penetrate

2   This is a fair sample of the eloquence of the preaching friars.

the inmost secrets of families and individuals. Jack, there are hard, troublous times before us, and we do well to be sober, wary, and sad."

"Sober and wary if you please, but by your leave, dear lady, not sad," said Jack. "Since all our fate standeth not in the hands of these men, but in the power and will of our Lord who can overrule all their designs for the good of His children, and make, as the Psalm says, even the very wrath of man to praise Him. He says to His disciples, 'In the world ye shall have tribulation,' but He adds in the same breath, 'Be ye of good cheer, I have overcome the world.'"

"You are right, and I am wrong and faithless," said Madam Barbara; "but oh, dear brother, you are young, and you have never seen what I have seen. You have lived under the pure and peaceful shelter of your father's roof, and your priest, Sir William, is one of a thousand. But I have grown up in a convent; I have been behind the scenes and have been trusted. I saw the condemnation and punishment of Agnes Harland, who was murdered, if ever a sweet saint was murdered in this world for her boldness in speaking the truth."

"Murdered!" said Jack, starting. "I thought she died a natural death."

"And so she did in one sense, that is to say, she was not killed by any regular execution. No, it was by slow, hard, unrelenting tyranny, by exclusion from light and air and nourishing food, ay, often even from sleep itself for days together. Father Barnaby persuaded the prioress that such severity would overcome her obstinacy and bring her back to her duty; but he did not know with whom he had to deal. I have seen the prioress weep bitter tears after she had, at his instigation, given orders for some new hardship to the poor prisoner; and I believe she would never have consented to what was done, had she not verily believed she was acting for the good of Agnes herself. At last Agnes fell ill, so ill that all thought she must die. Then the reverend mother could bear it no longer. She was a spirited lady and used to rule, and she had her own way in spite of the confessor. She had Agnes removed to a more comfortable place, and appointed me to attend on her, because she said she knew I would be kind to her and that I was in no danger of being perverted. She little knew what was going on. But Agnes died at last. They persecuted her almost to the last minute to recant, but she was firm as a rock, and died peacefully, with the name of our Lord on her lips."

"They blamed me much for weeping for an obstinate heretic," continued Sister Barbara, wiping her eyes. "They buried her in an obscure corner of the graveyard, all overgrown with nettles, and without any sacred rites. The sisters were always afraid to approach the place, because others had been buried there before, nuns who had broken their vows, and one who was an heretic like Agnes. They said the place was haunted; but to me it seemed like holy ground."

"You will hardly wish to return to a convent to live, madam," said Jack, after a pause.

Sister Barbara shuddered. "I will never do so unless I am compelled by force," said she. "I had not been three weeks under this roof, before I felt that it would break my heart to leave it; but now that I know more of the matter, my mind is made up. I will remain in your good father's family and teach my little school as long as I am allowed to do so. I love my children, and they love me, and I hope I am doing some good in the world."

"And if they require you to return to the convent?" said Jack.

"Then I shall refuse; and if I am pressed I shall tell my reasons," said Sister Barbara; "and after that, things must be as they will, or rather, as the Lord pleases. Each day's trouble is sufficient for the same day. I shall always be thankful that I was allowed to learn what a Christian home was like."

"I am sure it was a blessed day that brought you here, madam," said Master Lucas, who had entered the room in time to hear the last words. "You have been like sunshine in the house ever since you came into it. I would all religious persons were like you, and above all that you could put some of your own bright spirit into my poor Anne. I know not what to do with her. I do not like to find fault, and besides it does no good; but it hardly seems fair that she should spoil the comfort of the whole family as she does. But as for you I do trust, madam, that you will never think of lodging elsewhere, so long as you can be content with such accommodations as simple folk like us have to offer."

"There is no fear of that, Master Lucas; I am only too happy here," replied Sister Barbara, smiling and sighing. "I never knew there were such kind people in the world as yourself and Dame Cicely. I only wish I could do aught to requite your kindness."

"And so you do, madam, so you do. To say nought of anything else, you have added much to my profit the last six months, by your skill in confectionery. But I am forgetting my errand. Son Jack, can you leave your books long enough for a walk this fine evening?"

"Surely, and with great pleasure, dear father," replied Jack. "It is not often you find time to walk with me."

"Nor have I the time now, for Simon has gone to Master Mayor's with the manchets and cold baked meats for the feast to-night; and I must be at home to send off the other matters. But here is little Peter come from Mary Brent to ask you to come down and see her lodger who lies very ill. Peter says he hath no infectious disease, but suffers from the effects of hardship and famine. It seems Davy's captain took him off a wreck on which he was floating, a few days before they came to port. He was very ill and all but starved; and Davy, like the good fellow he is, brought the poor man home to his mother's house."

"Has Davy returned, then? I am right glad to hear it," said Jack. "He was always a good lad, though he would go to sea in spite of the prior."

"I think none the worse of him for preferring to work and help his mother," observed the master baker. "But Mary would like you to come down and see the poor man; and hark ye, lad, you might as well carry a little basket with you, just some biscuits and manchets, and a jellied fowl. I had reserved two or three for ourselves, but we can well spare one, and it is just the meat for a sick man."

"And a pot of my spiced confection of cherries," added Madam Barbara. "They are very cordial to a weak stomach. But mayhap Master Jack is too fine a gentleman to carry such a large basket through the streets."

"I would cuff his ears soundly, if I caught him in any such foppery," said Master Lucas.

"And I give you full leave to do so," returned Jack, laughing. "Do but have the matters ready, and I will set out without delay."

As I have said before, Mary Brent's circumstances had greatly improved of late. She had repaired her house, which had once been a good one, and frequently took lodgers. These were generally of a very profitable kind, being ship-masters and mates, who spent their money freely, ate and drank of the best, and made many a valuable present to the gentle retiring widow and her pretty little daughter. She was standing on her own doorstep as Jack came up, talking with a neighbor who seemed to be rather out of humor.

"Oh, very well! Mighty well, Neighbor Brent!" she said, as Jack came up. "If you can afford to take a penniless stranger into your best room and keep him for goodness knows how long without the least hope of any pay, why, 'tis no concern of mine."

Mary looked as though she were decidedly of the same opinion, but she answered gently—

"It is no more than I should like to have some woman do for my boy, if he were wrecked and landed in a strange place, neighbor."

"All that is mighty fine," said Dame Higgins, tossing her head. "What I say is, 'let every herring hang by its own head.' If you don't look out for yourself, nobody will look out for you. Take care of number one, is my motto; and it has served me well so far. Take my advice, let this man be carried and laid where he belongs, at the convent door, and let the monks take care of him."

"I shall do no such thing," said Mary Dean. "Much beholden to you for your advice, neighbor; but I am not yet so poor as to turn a poor ship-wrecked sailor out of my house. I wonder you dare think of such a thing after the sermon Sir William preached to us only yesterday about the poor man that fell among the thieves."

"Oh, Sir William, Sir William," returned the woman, scornfully. "Sir William had better look out for himself. He is an arrant Gospeller and Lutheran, unless he is much miscalled; and we all know what that comes to. Just as you like, but you are a fool for your pains. The next time your children want bread, don't come to me, that's all."

"I am not likely to do so, since the only time I ever asked you for anything you gave me a flat refusal," said Mary Brent. "I trust my children will never be the poorer for my kindness to this poor lad, but if they are, I can't help it."

"And if they should be, you have enough of warm friends who will not let them or you want, my good Mary," said Jack, who had stood quietly listening to this conversation.

Dame Higgins started violently, as did Mary herself, for in the heat of discussion and the gathering twilight, they had not noticed Jack's approach.

"Is that you, Master Jack? I am right glad to see you," said Mary. "I felt sure you would come, or I should not have been so bold as to send."

"You did quite right," said Jack. "The folks at home have sent some delicacies for the sick man, and also something for your own table. Let me carry it in for you, the basket is heavy."

"Good lack, so it is," said Dame Higgins, casting an envious eye on the contents of the basket, as Jack lifted the clean white cloth which covered it. "What luck some folks have, to be sure! Such baskets never come to our house."

"But I thought your motto was that every herring should hang by its own head," said Jack, as he entered the house.

Dame Higgins only replied by a prodigious sniff, and some remarks; apparently spoken to the air, concerning folk who knew which side their bread was buttered, and how to turn their charities to good account.

"Dame Higgins is out of humor," observed Jack.

"She is seldom anything else, save when she has made an uncommonly good bargain, or some unexpected gain hath come to her," replied Mary Brent. "She and her husband seem to care for nothing but saving and making money. I have been poor enough, as you know; but I never saw the day I would exchange lots with Joan Higgins; with all her wealth, she is poorer this day, than ever I was in my worst times."

"She would always be poor, if she had the revenues of the cardinal himself," said Jack. "But what is this about your lodger?"

"Oh, poor young man, he is in a sad case enough," replied Mary Brent. "They found him floating on a kind of raft pinned together with bits of wreck, and took him off. He says the ship foundered, as nearly as he can tell, about twelve days before he was rescued, that there were two men and a young boy on the raft with him at first, but they died one after the other, till there was no one left but himself. He is a well-made but slender youth, and does not look like a regular sailor; indeed, I think he hath all the air of a gentleman born; but he is not willing to give any account of himself, and there is no use in teasing him till he gets stronger. He wanders a deal at times, but more from weakness than from fever, I think, and then his talk is always about Holford; and Davy and I thought that as you had been so long at Holford of late, you might perhaps find out something from him. He may have friends, perhaps a mother who is wearying for news of him."

"I will see what I can do," said Jack. "I had almost forgot to wish you joy of Davy's return. I hear he has done very well."

"Yes, indeed, Davy is second mate, which is great promotion for one so young," said Mary. "He earns good wages besides what he can make by trading on his own account, and he has brought me home a good sum of money, besides presents of foreign stuffs far too fine for me to wear, and many curious outlandish toys for the children. I know you will be glad to hear as much, for your folks have always taken his part," added Mary, wiping the glad and proud tears from her eyes; "but thank God, nobody can call my Davy a scapegrace any more."

"He is a brave good lad, and I always thought so," said Jack, "and to my mind has shown himself a far better Christian by going to work to help you and the children than he would have done by becoming a monk and leaving you to shift for yourselves or live on charity. But it grows late. Shall I go up and see this stranger?"

"If you will," said Mary. "He lies in my best room."

The stranger was as Mary had described him, a dark slender young man, sunburnt and emaciated, yet having the air of a gentleman. He was comfortably accommodated in his hostess's best bed, and Mary had combed his dark curling locks and trimmed his beard, evidently wishing to set him off to the best advantage.

The moment Jack's eyes fell upon him, he was puzzled by a resemblance to some very familiar face, but whose he could not tell.

"If I have never seen you before, I have certainly seen somebody very like you," was his first thought.

"See here, Master Paul," said Mary in a tone which was both affectionate and respectful. "Here is young Master Lucas come to see you."

"He is very kind," said the invalid faintly smiling. "I am no great sight, I am afraid, but any friend of yours is welcome, my kind nurse."

"I did not come to stare at you, but to see what I could do for you," said Jack, seating himself by the bed. "My father has sent you some nourishing food, and bid me ask what else we could do for you. You seem very ill and weak."

"I have gained a little, I think, since I came here," said the invalid. "It is such a wonderful blessing to be among kindly English folk once more and to lie still in a clean and decent bed."

"I am sure you are heartily welcome," said Mary Brent. "But I will leave Master Jack to sit by you if he will be so kind, for I have matters to attend to below stairs."

Mary went away, and Jack remained quietly sitting by the side of the invalid, who seemed to have fallen into a doze. The more Jack looked at him, the more certain he became that he had seen him or some one like him before.

Presently the stranger opened his eyes and asked for drink. Jack supplied his wants and arranged his pillow comfortably.

"Do you live in this place?" asked the stranger whom Mary Brent had called Paul. "You do not look like a town-bred lad."

"I am so nevertheless," replied Jack; "but I have been keeping sheep all the summer with my good uncle at Holford."

"At Holford!" repeated Paul with a little start.

"Yes, my uncle is shepherd to the good knight of Holford."

"What, old Thomas Sprat! Is he alive still?" asked Paul with interest.

"He is alive and well," said Jack more puzzled than ever. "Do you then know my uncle and the family at the Hall?"

"Yes—that is, I was once in the family of Sir John for a time," said Paul with evident embarrassment. "Is the good knight well?"

"He is well, or was so last week," said Jack. "I saw him in the market-place a few days since. He hath grown very gray of late years, but still holds his own."

Paul sighed. "And my—I would say, my lady—have you ever seen her?"

"Oh, yes, often while I was at Holford," replied Jack. "She goes about among the poor people a great deal, but rarely visits among the gentry since her son's death."

"She believes him dead then," murmured the stranger so low that Jack could but just catch the words.

He answered them as if they had been addressed to him quietly, but with his heart beating fast as a wild idea occurred to his mind.

"My lady thinks him dead, and has caused many masses to be sung for him; but the knight will not believe it. They say he keeps his son's room in the same order in which the poor young gentleman left it, when he went to college, and he will not suffer his son's old dog to be killed, though the poor old beast can hardly crawl from the hearth to the hall door. I have of-ten marvelled much how the young master could leave such a kind father."

"Because he was a fool," said Paul vehemently, "a gull, a thrice-sodden ass; an ape who must needs mimic what others did, and ruffle it in silk and gold with the sons of court favorites and noblemen."

"Then you knew the heir of Holford?" said Jack, his first idea growing stronger the more he heard.

"Yes—that is, I knew him at college," replied Paul, making an evident effort to control his agitation. "He was a foolish boy, and unworthy of so good a home."

"I have heard that the men blamed the knight for having been over-strict with him, and that the young gentleman himself laid his wrong-doing to the same cause."

"That is not true," said Paul almost fiercely. "He never sunk so low as that. He would have been the basest hound that ever lived, had he done so."

"I am glad to hear that," said Jack. "I can never think much of those who strive to excuse themselves by laying all their faults on the shoulders of others. I wish he would come back to his home. I am sure the good knight would receive him joyfully—even as the prodigal in the parable was received by his father. But you are talking too much for one in your weak state," he added. "Let me give you some food or a cordial, and then do you try to sleep."

"I am indeed weary," said Paul. "But must you go away?"

"Not if you need me," replied Jack. "I will stay all night if you desire it. I can easily send word to my father, and I am sure he will make no objec-tion to my doing so."

Paul said something about it being too much to ask of a stranger, but he was so evidently pleased by the proposition, that Jack at once decided to stay, and went down-stairs to seek a messenger.

Davy willingly undertook the office.

"And what do you make of him?" he asked.

"Very little as yet," replied Jack, unwilling to mention his suspicions. "He has been at Holford at some time, I dare say in the train of some gentle-man who came to visit at the Hall—and his mind runs on it. He is very fee-ble, and his mind is disturbed, but he seems to like to have me beside him."

"I am sure you are very kind," said Davy. "What shall I say to your father for you?"

"Only that I am going to watch by the stranger's bedside, with his good leave," said Jack; "and you may, if you please, ask Dame Cicely for my warm doublet, for the nights are growing chill."

"And that reminds me that I may as well kindle a little fire in the room," said Mary. "A blaze is a cheerful companion, and, as you say, the nights are growing chill. But, Master Jack," said she, detaining Jack for a moment, after Davy had gone on his errand, "I want to consult you about a certain matter, and that is, as to whether I should send for a priest?"

"Has the young man asked for a priest?" inquired Jack.

"No, that he has not," replied Mary. "He shook his head when I asked him at his first coming whether he would have one; and when I did but hint at it again, he said right sharply, 'No, no! No priest,' and Davy bid me not trouble him about the matter. But maybe he should have one for all that."

"I would not trouble him at present," said Jack. "If he grows worse we can send for Sir William, who will come any hour of the night, you know."

"That he will, the good man," returned Mary. "Better man never lived, for all they call him a Lutheran. But you know, Master Jack, my poor husband died without the sacraments, and I would ill like to have such a thing happen again in my house."

Jack quieted the good woman with renewed assurances that he would send for Sir William if it became necessary. He reminded her that the stranger was very weak, and it was not worth while to oppose his wishes when a little thing might set him back and perhaps throw him into a fever.

"I dare say you are right," said Mary. "I will get you some supper and make ready a comfortable morsel to eat during the night, for you must take care of your own health, you know, and you have been delicate of late."

Jack was too much excited with the discovery he supposed himself to have made, to feel hungry; but he was one who could put his own feelings aside for the sake of other people. He consented to eat some supper to satisfy Mary's hospitable thought, and found, as young people are apt to, that he was hungry enough to do full justice to the savory fare she had provided.

He then stole back to the sick man's chamber, where a cheerful little fire was already burning, while a pile of wood and fagots offered the means of replenishing it during the night. Mary Brent moved about gently putting matters in order, and covering a little table in one corner with refreshments for the watcher as well as the invalid. Finally she beckoned Jack aside and, with rather a mysterious air, opened a little cupboard, hidden by a piece of tapestry:

"Here are some books which belonged to my poor husband," said she. "I found them when I was putting the house to rights, and hid them away that the children might not see them, for I cannot read, and know not whether they be good books or no. But I dare say they will not hurt you, and they may serve to help you keep awake."

Jack looked over the books, which were partly written and partly printed. They formed an odd collection of Canterbury tales, lives of saints, and one or two old romances. He turned them over and at last discovered, hidden under the disguise of a volume of ballads, a manuscript book carefully written out. He took it to the fire to examine it, and read on the title—

> "This boke ys the boke of the prophet Isiach, written out by me from a boke of the Scripture which a man had in Antwerp, and ys doubtless ye trew word of ye livinge God."

Underneath was written in the same hand—

> "O Lord, how long."

Jack was overjoyed at the discovery. He had never seen any part of the Old Testament except the Psalms, and could hardly believe in his good fortune. He looked the books over once more, and found a part of St. John's Gospel, evidently copied by the same hand.

Both books had been carefully studied, as was evident from the marks and marginal notes they contained. Jack understood at once the secret of David Brent's refusal to see the priest, and his dying, as his wife said, without the sacraments, yet as peaceful and calm as a babe. He felt, as he looked at the books written out with so much care by a hand evidently unused to holding a pen, like one who comes unexpectedly on the writing of a dear friend long dead; and he vowed that as long as he lived, David Brent's children should never want anything that he could do for them.

He trimmed the shaded lamp and sat down to read, but even the interest of his new discovery could not divert his attention from the sick man. Was he really Sir John Brydges's long-lost son? And if so, what was to be done to restore him to his parents? Could he be persuaded to return to his father's house? That would be best for all.

"But if he will not, the knight must come to him," Jack said to himself. "I must bring the father and son face to face, and then I am sure all will be well. I remember what the knight said on the terrace at Holford the day I went to speak with Master Fleming. Oh, how I wish he were here. But there is no use in speculating. I must wait and see how matters will turn out."

Jack once more addressed himself to his book, and read till he was aroused by the voice of the invalid. He rose and went to the bedside. Paul had been sleeping quietly for some time, but he now began to talk, though without opening his eyes; and Jack perceived that he was wandering, between sleeping and waking. He held his breath not to lose a word.

"Mother, mother," murmured the sick man. "Mother, I am not dead. I need no masses, even if they were worth anything. Only take me home, and lay me on my own bed, and let my father sit by me as he used to do in old times. Father will forgive me for disgracing him when he knows I am sorry for what I have done. 'While he was yet a great way off, his father saw him.' Master Firth bade me return to my father and seek his forgiveness. But a heretic!"

Jack started and drew nearer to the bedside.

"A heretic!" repeated Paul.

And then looking up, and seeing Jack bending over him, he added eagerly, but yet with a certain wildness which showed his mind was still wandering—"You have seen my father of late. Do you think he would receive and forgive me if he knew that I had heard the Lutherans preach—that I was of the new religion?"

"I am sure he would—quite sure," said Jack. "Some men say he is a favorer of the new religion himself."

"But my mother—what would she say? She is a proud and devout lady, you know."

"She is your mother," said Jack briefly, as though that were enough.

"But if she should refuse me when she knows the truth, if she should turn her back upon me after all, it would go near to break my heart. And you know I must needs speak the truth. 'He that loveth father or mother more than Me, is not worthy of Me.'"

Jack saw that his patient was becoming over-excited, and was likely to do himself harm.

"Hush!" said he, with kindly authority. "You will do yourself a mischief by talking so much, and I am sure your mother will not be pleased with that. Let me give you some refreshment, and then I will read to you, and you must try to sleep."

"But what will you read? Will you read from the Scriptures?" asked Paul, looking eagerly into Jack's face. "But no, you must not do so, or they will put you in prison and on the rack as they did me. See here," and he pushed up his sleeves and showed his emaciated wrists covered with terrible scars, the sight of which made Jack's blood boil and his fingers clinch involuntarily. "You must not read the Scripture, and besides you do not know it."

"I do both know the Scripture, and will read it to you, dearest brother," said Jack, striving to speak calmly, though he was thrilling all over with excitement. "Do but lie down and be quiet, and I will read as much as you will."

"But are you then a Lutheran?" asked Paul, looking wistfully into his face, "Or are you laying a trap for me, as they did in Flanders? There be no Lutherans in England."

"May God so deal with me as I am dealing truly with you," said Jack, solemnly. "There are some—yes many, in this place—who love the Gospel and read it, but as yet secretly, for fear of the oppressors. Have no fear, but down and rest, and I will read the holy Scripture to you as long as you will."

Seemingly reassured, Paul lay down, and Jack began reading from the book he had discovered. There was much of course that he did not in the least understand, but he found enough which was plain to make him long for more.

Paul now and then spoke a few words, but more and more dreamily, and Jack had at last the satisfaction of seeing him fall into a sound quiet sleep. He sat reading and thinking by the bedside till the gray dawn began to steal in at the window. As he rose to replenish the fire, Paul was roused and opened his eyes.

"Are you still here, my kind nurse?" said he, speaking faintly, but with no appearance of wandering or bewilderment. "Is it not very late? It seems as though I had been sleeping for a long time."

"It is very late, or rather very early. It is just growing daylight. You have slept soundly for several hours. How do you feel?"

"Much better," replied Paul. "My dreams have been very sweet. Did I dream it, or were you reading to me before I went to sleep?"

"You were not dreaming, dear brother," said Jack. "Have you any recollection of what read?"

"Why do you call me brother?" asked Paul, with a wondering look. "It is a dear name, but I never knew I had a brother."

"I call you so because I cannot but think that in one sense we are brothers," said Jack. "But tell me, do you remember what I read?"

"It could hardly be so," said Paul; "and yet—it seems to me as if you had read to me from the Scripture. You are not a priest, are you?" he asked, starting. "I fear I have been saying more than I ought."

"Have no fears," returned Jack. "I am no priest, or priest's tool, of that you may be sure, and you have betrayed nothing. I did read from the Scripture to you last night, because you desired it, and because I myself love the Book. I could not betray you if I would, for I should myself stand in the same peril."

"It is well," said Paul. "I am most thankful to have fallen into such good hands. I do think I may trust you," he added, looking wistfully into Jack's face. "But I have been so betrayed by those in whom I have confided, that it has sometimes seemed to me that I could never trust man again."

"Have you no family friends near here?" asked Jack gently. "I should think you a Somerset man by your speech."

"No—yes—indeed, I know not what to say on that matter," replied Paul, in an embarrassed tone. "I had once as kind friends as ever lived, but I know not whether they would own me now."

"Never mind," said Jack, who did not wish to agitate or alarm his patient. "We will talk of that when you are stronger, if you are disposed to give me your confidence. At present, be sure you are among friends who will do all in their power for you."

"I must think of it," said Paul, sinking back. "It is no mere question of a shipwrecked sailor coming home in rags and poverty, you know. I may tell you this: that my family are gentlefolk of condition, and that they have good reason to be angry with me since I have brought upon an ancient and honorable house not only trouble but disgrace. There are more interests than mine to be considered, you see, and therefore I must weigh the matter well. I would gladly die, if die I must, with my head on my father's breast; but not even for that dear privilege would I bring a new pang to rend his bosom."

"Think then, dear brother, think, but pray also," said Jack, deeply moved. "You know the Apostle bids us, when we lack wisdom, to ask it of God, nothing doubting, and it shall be given us."

"I will indeed do so," replied Paul. "Nobody knows more than I the value of prayer. But do you go home now, and go to rest. I hear the good people of the house stirring."

Jack went home, but not to rest. He walked through the quiet street in the crisp morning air, thinking what he had better do. He did not know a great deal about sickness, but he could see that Paul's state was critical. A very little might turn the scale, so that there could be no recovery; and how sad if he should die without being reconciled to his father! From what he knew and guessed, Jack felt sure that there would be no trouble between Paul and his father, on the subject of religion. He walked three or four times up and down the street, but at last he made up his mind.

"I will do it," said he. "I will do what lies in my power to bring the father and son together. I will talk to my father, and if he is willing I will borrow Master Felton's pony and set out without delay."

CHAPTER XVI.

JACK'S ERRAND.

"Is my father up, Simon?" asked Jack, as he entered the shop, which the journeyman was just putting to rights.

"I think not, Master Jack. I have not heard him stirring, and he usually calls me to come truss his points for him."

"I will myself go up and help him to dress," said Jack, and he went softly up-stairs to his father's room. Master Lucas was just awake.

"So you have come home betimes," said he, rubbing his eyes. "You have had a long watch and will be for taking a good nap, I dare say, though you do not look very sleepy either," he added, looking in his son's face. "You seem as if you had heard some good news."

"And so I trust I have," said Jack. "I want to consult you, dear father, about a matter of moment."

"Give me my gown, then," said his father. "It is time I was up. Now let me hear the story."

Jack sat down on the side of the bed, and told his father of the discovery he supposed himself to have made, with the grounds of his belief. Master Lucas listened with attention.

"But supposing this young man to be the heir of Holford," said he, "do you think his father would receive him again?"

"I have good grounds for thinking so, which you shall hear," said Jack, and he repeated his reasons, which we already know.

"Poor gentleman! My heart aches for him," said Master Lucas. "But what is it you propose to do? You cannot take Master Arthur to his home, weak as he is, even if he were quite willing to go."

"No; and, therefore, I propose to bring his home to him," said Jack. "I propose to ride to Holford, see the knight, and tell him all that I have told you. Then he can act as he pleases."

"Have you said aught of your intention to Master Arthur—or Paul, as he calls himself?"

"Not a word, dear father. I thought it best to be silent. Paul—his name is Paul as well as Arthur—Paul is in doubt as to his reception at home. He says he has brought shame and disgrace on his honorable house, and he knows not whether he ought to return—"

"So had the youth Father William preached about yesterday, brought shame and disgrace on his family," interrupted the baker. "Yet he returned, and his father received him gladly."

"And if the poor prodigal had been ill and starving, repentant, and longing above all things for a sight of his father's face, yet too weak and too fearful to go to him," said Jack, eagerly, "do you not think that he and his father both would have been thankful to that man who had brought them face to face, who had carried news to the father that the son was languishing, perhaps dying, within his reach? Make the case your own, dear father, and tell me."

Master Lucas turned and looked at his son with tears in his honest blue eyes. "Jack, you are a strange lad for your years. I cannot understand what has made a man of you so suddenly. Even do as you will, and manage the matter your own way, my son. I cannot see what harm can come of it. If the knight should refuse to see his son, the poor young gentleman will at least be prevented from a bootless journey."

"He will not refuse," said Jack. "Then, with your leave, dear father, I will set out directly."

"As soon as you have rested a little and taken a good meal, my son. Nay, I must insist upon that much, or we shall have you ill again. Remember you are all the son, I had well-nigh said all the child, I have in the world. Get you down and send Simon to engage for your neighbor Fulford's pony. It is an easy beast to ride, and faster than my mule. It is a market-day, and the roads will be full of people, so you will have nothing to fear from robbers, or I would send Simon with you."

"I do not need him," said Jack. "Nobody would think of robbing a lad like me; and besides I doubt Simon would be no great safeguard. He has not the heart of a chicken. Father," added Jack, earnestly, "I do heartily thank you for trusting me so fully."

"When I see aught to distrust in you, it will be time to begin," said Master Lucas. "My blessing upon thee, dear lad. Thou hast never yet wilfully given thy father a heart-ache."

A pang shot through Jack's own breast, as he remembered how soon he might be called upon to do and suffer that which would wring his father's heart with anguish through no fault of his own. "Oh, if it were only myself," he reflected, as he sought his own chamber, "how easy it would all be to endure." And, dearly as he loved his father, Jack almost felt like praying that the good old man might be taken away from the evil to come, before the storm burst which Master Fleming had foretold.

Calmed and refreshed by his morning reading and prayers, Jack came down to his breakfast dressed for his journey, his sober, resolute face showing that his determination was unshaken.

Cicely exclaimed against his setting out on such a ride after he had been watching all night.

But Master Lucas made her a sign, and she said no more, except to entreat her darling to eat and drink heartily, and to put a comfortable morsel in his pocket, that he need not be faint by the way.

She was dying with curiosity to learn the object of his journey undertaken so suddenly, but she knew of old, that unless Master Lucas chose to tell there was no use in asking.

Anne was not so discreet. She came in when breakfast was half over, from the priory church, where she had been praying since four o'clock. Kneeling on cold stones for three hours on a stretch without one's breakfast is not likely to improve the temper, whatever other spiritual graces it may impart. Anne felt weak, exhausted, and wretched, and all ready, as her father said, to take the poker by the hot end.

"What is Simon doing, walking that horse up and down before the door?" she asked, as she sat down. "Have some of Jack's grand friends come to visit him so early?"

"I did not know that I had any grand friends," said Jack.

"I thought it might be Master Fleming," pursued Anne. "He seems to use our house as his own at all times."

"If he does, he is no more free than welcome," said her father. "I ever esteem his visits an honor as well as a pleasure. But you are wrong this time. The pony is for no less a person than our Jack, who is about to ride into the country for some miles."

"Indeed!" said Anne. "And what takes him into the country?"

"Business," replied her father briefly. "Business of importance, which no one can well do but himself. Ask no questions, sweetheart, for more I cannot tell you."

"I do not mean to ask any questions," said Anne, flushing. "I know well that I am the last person to be trusted, especially by Jack."

"Do you say so, Anne?" asked Jack, turning full upon her, as his father left the room. "Methinks I have trusted you already farther than you were willing to have me, farther than I had reason to do, considering all things. But I do not mean to reproach you, dear sister," he added, repenting, the next moment, as he saw how Anne winced. "The business I go upon is not mine, or you should know all about it."

"Nay, I have no desire to penetrate it," said Anne, coldly, but with eyes that flashed an angry fire. "I desire to enter into none of your secrets. I can guess its nature well, and will not even presume to warn you, though I know the terrible risk you are running. You are working to bring down ruin upon yourself and your father's house, fancying that you are having your own wilful way, while all the time you are being made a tool and a cat's-paw of, by craftier heads than your own."

No lad of sixteen likes to be called a tool and a cat's-paw. Jack had his share of pride as well as Anne, and he had to bite his lip hard to repress an angry answer. He did repress it, however, and after a moment of silence answered quietly, "Anne, would you like to have anyone speak to you in that manner? Would you like it, for instance, if I were to call you a cat's-paw and spy of Father Barnaby?"

"You have no right to call me so," said Anne. "I am no spy, and I will not submit to be called one."

"You have no need to submit, for I have no intention of calling you a spy or any other disagreeable name," said Jack, smiling. "I only put the case for your consideration. As to my business, all this secrecy which nevertheless is needful at present, is just making a mountain out of a very small molehill. Come, Anne, do not let us quarrel just as I am going away. Why should we not be loving and gentle to one another as brother and sister should be?"

"Because you are a heretic," replied Anne. "It is my duty to try to bring you back to the faith, and failing that to treat you as—"

"As Agnes Harland was treated, perhaps," said Jack, interrupting her. Then repenting the next moment, "Dear Anne, forgive me; I am wrong. I should not have said so much."

He would have taken Anne's hand, but she repulsed him.

"Yes, as Agnes Harland was treated," said she sternly. "Even so. You have no right to expect any thing else at my hands. I have had many regrets, many misgivings, as to this matter, but I will allow them to influence me no more. The Church is more to me than father or brother or friend. I am the vowed bride of Christ, and I will be faithful to my vow—ay, though I had to walk over the dead body of every friend I have in the world. I will be faithful to my vows and to my conscience. Now you know what you have to expect."

"Very well," said Jack. "My life is in your hands. But, Anne," he added, looking fixedly at her, "are you sure that you are faithful to your conscience? Are you sure your conscience is not telling you this minute, that what you have heard from Agnes and from me is true, every word true? Are you not at this very moment resisting the Spirit which tells you that you have been mistaken and wrong hitherto; that shows, you all your built-up righteousness to be more worthless than rags and dust, and pleads with you to forsake your errors and turn to the truth; to leave the broken cisterns hewed by man, and seek the fountain of living waters? I believe it is so.

Anne, Anne, beware! For me, I am in God's hand, and no real harm can chance to me, but I tremble for you. Anne, Anne, beware how you grieve the Spirit by resisting your convictions of truth!"

"Time is wearing away, my son, and it were well you were on your road," said Master Lucas, entering the room. "The days are shorter than they were. Shall you return to-night?"

"Yes, father, if I can finish my business," replied Jack; and then desirous of diverting his attention from Anne, he said hastily, "I was thinking whether there was any token I could carry to the old priest at Holford. He is a good-natured old man and was kind to me, and I should like to show that I remembered him."

"That is well thought on, my son. Do you get my saddle-bags, and I will put up some sweetmeats and comfits for Father John's sweet tooth, and also something for Uncle Thomas. We must not forget old friends."

Jack went for the bags, and while his father was filling them, he found opportunity for another word with his sister.

"Anne, I am sorry if I have grieved you."

"Words cost very little," said Anne coldly. "Let me see you confess and abjure your errors, and I shall know how to believe you."

"My errors, as you call them, shall be confessed with my latest breath, if God gives me grace to hold fast to Him," returned Jack. "You would not have known them, had it not been for my earnest desire to comfort you in your trouble. Nor do I regret having spoken them, though by so doing I have put a weapon in your hands to slay me withal. It seemed to me that I must speak, whatever came of it. The Gospel says, 'Whosoever shall be ashamed of me and of my words, of him shall the Son of man be ashamed when he shall come in the glory of his father and of the holy angels.' And again, 'If we deny him, he also will deny us.' Dear Anne, only listen to the Word and to the Spirit, only take up the cross and follow the Lord, and all will be well."

Anne compressed her lips and made no reply, and her father coming in at that moment, she escaped to her own room.

"Is all ready?" asked Jack. "Then give me your blessing, dear father, and I will set out."

"Thou hast it, thou hast it, my son," said Master Lucas, laying his hand on his son's head as he bent his knee before him. "May our Lord and the saints prosper thy journey and bring thee safe home again!"

Jack's mind was at first hardly in a state to enjoy his ride. He had a sharp battle with himself before he could subdue the anger and wounded pride which stirred within him; and his conscience told him that he had not been without blame. He had spoken harshly and scornfully to his sister, and made an ungenerous use of the secret she had confided to him.

Anne was deeply angered at him, that was plain; and he had, by offending her, lessened his chance of influencing her for good. He had another cause of disturbance. It seemed to him that much as he had thought on the subject, he had never realized before, the trouble he was likely to bring on his friends, especially on his father, by accepting the new doctrines, as they were called. He said to himself, as he rode along, that he might be taken up and thrown into jail any day, and that there would be probably no release from prison for him, save by the ignominious death of the stake, or the still more shameful and fatal way of recantation.

He pictured to himself the stake and chain, the crowd of scornful gazers and the blazing torch, or the scaffold set up in the market-place where the apostate must stand bearing his fagot while a monk preached from the pulpit over his head.

"It would kill my father in either case," said he to himself. "He would never recover the grief and the disgrace. And if it should prove a delusion after all! If Anne should be right and Master Fleming and the others wrong!"

It was a fearful combat that Jack fought out with the Tempter that sunny autumn day, as he rode over the heath and along the still green hedgerows. The travellers he met saw in him some youth going out on a holiday excursion, and marvelled at his sombre face and compressed lip.

It rarely happens in these days that any young person is called to really give up all for Christ, to choose between His love and service and the love and respect of all nearest and dearest friends; and when it does so chance, there is usually everything in the sympathy of Christians to make the task as easy as it can be made. Moreover such a choice, though it may bring grief and estrangement, involves no actual loss or disgrace.

But in the time whereof I am writing, the case was very different. The man or woman who embraced the new doctrines, as they were called, not only came out from all the dear old customs and sanctities of the familiar home life, not only broke up "the old sweet habit of confidence," but he brought shame and public disgrace into his own family circle, if he did not entail upon his friends absolute pecuniary loss and serious danger to life and liberty.

I have sometimes heard it said, that those martyrs by the stake and the rack had an easier work to do, and deserved less credit therefore, than those have who bear with the trials and vexations of every-day life. I think those who say so forget one thing; namely, that the martyrs who perished on the stake or rack, had just the same wearying, worrying, every-day trials and cares that we have, in addition to the one great trial.

Anne Ascue had her household vexations, and those no small ones; her trials with husband and children and servants, lack of money, and uncertainty as to the future. Tyndale and Frith had to contend with misprints and misunderstandings, the stupidity and dulness of printers and proof-readers unused to the language in which they worked, with pirated editions, and all the other manifold annoyances which beset authors and publishers nowadays. Were these, think you, any easier to bear for the great trial which was always in the background? Were the clouds any the more transparent because of the total eclipse which was impending? I think not. How then were they borne?

I think the answer is to be found in this—that these men and women who thus took their lives in their hands, and went forth to witness for their Lord in the midst of an adulterous and perverse generation, lived daily very near to God. They realized in a wonderful way God's love for them, His constant care for them, His superintending providence which would let nothing happen which was not for their good.

Master Garrett, at Oxford, when he was in danger of being apprehend-ed, kneeled down weeping in his chamber and read the tenth chapter of St. Matthew, and the words were to him a living reality. These men literally, and in no figurative or exaggerated sense, gave up all for Christ. They liter-ally left all and followed Him; and to them was fulfilled in all its fulness the promise, "Ye shall have tenfold more in this life, with persecutions, and in the world to come life everlasting."

With many, the conflict was sharp and the victory sometimes doubtful; but sooner or later the word was fulfilled and the strength given according to the day.[3]

So Jack Lucas found it, riding that soft autumnal day along the quiet lanes and over the barn heath. For a time the conflict was fierce, and the enemy strong—so strong that the young warrior more than once groaned aloud in the bitterness of his soul, and was ready to cry out:

"I sink in deep waters; Lord, why hidest thou thy face in the needful time of trouble?"

But by degrees, his mind grew calmer. He could not trust himself to argue with the Tempter, or even to fight with him but, like Christian in the dark valley, "he was forced to put up his sword and betake himself to another weapon called All-prayer—so he cried, 'O Lord, I beseech Thee, deliver my soul!'"

And so it was, that the Master he served was pleased to give him the victory for that time. A wonderful calm and peace descended upon his spir-

---

3   I think any one will be convinced of the truth of this statement who will read for himself the letters of the martyrs, especially those written in prison.

it, and he was able to enjoy the beauty around him, and to take pleasure at being once more in the country.

He arrived at Holford in good time, and rode direct to the Hall. To his great disappointment, he found that both the knight and his lady were away. They had gone to visit a sick friend in the neighboring parish.

"But they will be home before evening," said the porter, as Jack expressed his disappointment; "so, if your business is urgent, you might as well wait for their return."

"I think I will do so," said Jack; "and meantime I will go to visit my uncle and the good father at the village."

"Ay, the old man will be glad to see you, and his reverence as well," said the butler, who had come out to speak with Jack. "I promise you, the father gave our knight a good character of you, for I heard him myself. He said you had given him great help at a pinch, and had much to say of your scholarship, especially of your Latin."

"It was no very great help I gave him," said Jack; "but he is a good-natured old gentleman. Well, Master Butler, I will go down to the hamlet and see the priest and my uncle, and return about the time the knight is expected."

CHAPTER XVII.

HOLFORD AGAIN.

Jack's first visit was to his uncle. He found the old man in his accustomed seat on the turfy hill, with Bevis sitting by his side. He could not but think that Thomas had grown visibly older and more infirm during the few weeks of his absence.

"I have been quite well," he said, in reply to Jack's anxious inquiries; "but either because I have missed your good company or because I am so many weeks older, I do not feel quite my usual strength. But then, I am an old man, dear son. I am fourscore and four years old, and cannot expect to use my limbs as lightly as when I followed our old knight to the wars more than sixty years ago. But what brings you to Holford so soon again?"

"I had an errand to the knight, from one of his friends in Bridgewater," said Jack, hesitating; "at least—Uncle Thomas, I should like to tell you the whole story, but I suppose the knight should know my errand before any one. Only, uncle, will you pray that I may have wisdom to guide me? For my mission is something delicate."

"Surely, surely, dear son, thou hast my prayers at all times. The knight has been very kind to me of late. He has ever been so, but there seems now to be a new bond of union, if I may so say, between us. I have also had more than one visit from our good friend Master Fleming, who, as you doubtless know, has been several times at the Hall, and never without seeking me out. I have been greatly blessed in mine old age in being allowed to see again the light which shone upon my youth. But how has it fared with you, my dear lad? Methinks you, too, have grown older since I saw you."

"I almost feel as though I had never been young," said Jack, sighing. "I have so much to think of. Uncle Thomas, I do feel guilty in keeping this matter secret from my father. He has ever been the best and kindest of fathers to me, and I cannot bear to feel as if I were deceiving him. I feel as if I must tell him all."

"I am not sure but you are right, my clear lad," said the old shepherd, thoughtfully. "I like not concealments more than you do, and, as you say, your father hath every right to your confidence."

"If the secret had been mine alone, he should have heard it long ago," said Jack. "But there was yourself, and Master Fleming."

"Think not of me, my son," said Thomas Sprat; "I am, as I think, already suspected and watched, and at best my time is short. You had best consult Master Fleming, however, before moving in the matter. He may see reasons for secrecy which I do not, and you know that the secret, once told, can never be got back again."

"I have told one who will, I fear, have less mercy on me than my dear father," remarked Jack. "Anne knows all about my share in the secret, and I cannot tell how she will use her knowledge."

"How happened it that you told her?" asked the shepherd.

Jack repeated the story, adding, "I do not know but I was wrong, but I could not see her so unhappy without striving to comfort her. It seems to have done no good, however, but rather harm, for I am sure she has been more miserable than she was before, and she grows more and more hard and cold toward me every day. She told me this morning that she would keep no terms with heretics, and that she would be true to her vow and to the Church, if she walked over the dead body of every friend she had in the world. I know not what she would do, but I would fain anticipate her, at least with my father."

"It is a hard strait," said the old man, sighing; "yet I suppose Anne feels as you do, that she must follow the dictates of her own conscience."

"If she were only doing that," replied Jack; "but I cannot help fearing that she is acting not against her own conscience, and trying to stifle its voice."

"If so, she is indeed in evil case, and needs all our prayers," said Thomas Sprat. "Be very gentle and patient with her, dear son, and seek you wisdom of God, doubting not that it shall be given."

"Have you seen Father John of late?" asked Jack, after a short silence.

"Only twice since you went away. I have not been to the church in service time, but I have met him in the village, and once at the Hall. His reverence has always an inquiry and a good word for you. He seems more easy and jovial, more like his old self, since Father Barnaby went away."

"Yes, I dare say. He is afraid of Father Barnaby, and I must say I am glad he is gone, for all our sakes. He is a hard, dangerous man. I must go see the old gentleman, for he has been very kind to me, and I have a token for him from my father, of a kind he will like right well."

Jack found Father John looking much as usual, seated at his ease in his great chair with his dinner before him, flanked by a mighty tankard of ale on one side and a flask of wine on the other. He gave Jack a warm and affectionate welcome, and would have him sit down to dinner with him.

"I am late to-day," said he; "I have been out visiting the sick, and have taken a long ride, for me—quite to the other end of the parish. But I have great news for you, my son," he continued, piling Jack's plate with good things while he spoke. "The bishop's sumner was here yesterday, and he tells me Father Barnaby is expected to go to Rome on a mission of weight for the king and the cardinals. I am sure I hope he may have a pleasant journey, and that his Holiness will like him so well that he will make him a cardinal, or, at least, a bishop of some good bishopric on the other side of the world."

Jack smiled. "Perhaps his Holiness will keep him in his own family," said he.

"So much the better—so much the better," said Father John, hastily. "I bear no ill-will to Father Barnaby, but his merits are too great for such an obscure station, and we are a deal more comfortable without him."

Jack could hardly forbear laughing. He brought forward the sweetmeats and other matters which his father had sent, and had the satisfaction of seeing them received with great delight. Then excusing himself, he hastened once more to the Hall, and found that Sir John and his lady had been at home for an hour.

"I told the knight you had been here, asking for him, and he bid me show you to him as soon as ever you came back," said Master Butler. "He waits you in the library."

Jack felt somewhat abashed, not to say frightened, when he found himself alone with Sir John, and hardly knew how to begin his tale.

"You come a messenger from Master Fleming?" said Sir John, kindly, seeing the youth's evident embarrassment. "Speak freely; we are quite by ourselves."

"It is not upon any business of Master Fleming's that I have come, Sir John," said Jack, gathering courage. "I know not but you will think me very forward and presumptuous when I open the matter to you. In that case, my only excuse must be that I have done as I would be done by under the like circumstances."

"It is a good excuse, if any be needed," returned the knight gravely. "Of that I can judge better when I hear what you have to say to me."

"Your worship has a son," said Jack, determined to go to the root of the matter at once.

Sir John started and turned pale. "I have—or had," said he, trying to speak calmly. "I know not if he be living or no. Have you heard any news of him?"

"I believe that I have—nay, I am sure of it," replied Jack. "It was that which brought me here this day."

Sir John paused a moment, and then asked, "Is the news good or bad?"

"Altogether good, as I think."

"Tell me at once what you have to say," said Sir John. "I can bear anything better than suspense. My son is then alive?"

"He is alive, and likely, as I trust, to live, though he has been ill and is still very weak," replied Jack.

He then went on and told his tale in as few words as possible, adding, "I am come to you, Sir John, wholly on mine own motion, and without authority from Master Arthur. But it seemed to me no more than right that you should know the truth."

"Does not my son then desire to see me?" asked Sir John.

"He does, indeed," said Jack eagerly. "He said last night that his only remaining wish was, to ask your forgiveness and to die in your arms. But he cannot come to seek you. He is very weak and low, unable so much as to rise from his bed, and besides, I can see he is full of fear and doubt. He says he has brought disgrace and shame on an honorable house, and he knows not whether his friends would not rather think him dead. I do not think he even guesses that I know his secret, for I gathered it from his wanderings last night, whereof he remembered nothing this morning. I most humbly crave your pardon, if I have done wrong," said Jack, not knowing how to interpret the knight's face.

Sir John rose, and walked to the door of the ante-room, where a servant was in waiting.

"Tell David to put my saddle on gray Hastings," said he sharply and briefly. "Bid him also saddle a fresh horse for young Lucas, and take care of the one he rode, that it may be returned tomorrow; and let David make himself and Hugh ready to ride with us. Make haste and then return hither."

Sir John shut the door, and returned to where Jack was standing.

"My young brother," said he, "for brother you are in the bonds of the gospel—you have done for me what I can never repay. However this matter may turn, I shall never forget your service. I had, heretofore, taken you for a boy of promise and grace, indeed, but yet a boy. You have shown yourself a wise and discreet man, as well as a good Christian. Tell me, does any one know of this matter besides ourselves?"

"Nobody but my father, sir," answered Jack. "I was obliged to consult him before taking so much upon myself; but I am sure he will never mention the matter."

"That is well. I would have nothing said here till the matter is settled. Not that I shall be ashamed to own my son before all the world; but I would not have his mother disturbed while there is the least doubt. Now I must order refreshment for you, while I apprise my lady of my sudden journey."

"I have but lately dined with the good priest at the village," said Jack. "I shall be ready to ride so soon as your worship is ready."

"Ay, you are very far in Father John's good books," said the knight, smiling. "Poor old man, he would fain be at peace with all the world, I believe. But you must eat and drink for the honor of my house. I will but seek my lady and be with you again."

Lady Brydges was much surprised to hear of her husband's sudden journey, but offered no opposition.

"I had hoped you were done with public affairs," said she. "At our age, the chimney corner is the best chair of state."

"I am wholly of your mind, sweetheart," replied her husband. "This is no matter of public business, however, but a private concern of mine own. I shall, I trust, be with you or else send you word of my progress tomorrow; and I would have you say a word of kindness to young Lucas, who has done me a great service, and, as I think, saved me from losing what I could ill spare."

My lady was always disposed to be gracious, at least, to her acknowledged inferiors. She asked Jack about his studies and his school, told him of a sovereign remedy for the headache, to which he was subject, and ended by giving him a plum-cake, and a silver piece.

At another time, Jack might have resented being treated like a schoolboy, but just now he was too full of interest and compassion to harbor any such feeling.

In the course of half an hour, the party were on the road, and riding at the best speed of the knight's good horses; the pony being left behind to rest and regale himself in Sir John's stable.

"You say my son was very weak and low," remarked Sir John after riding some time in silence. "Has any physician or priest been to see him?"

"Davy Brent sent for old Doctor Berton directly," answered Jack; "and he hath been to Master Arthur every day, but Master Arthur did not desire to see a priest."

"Did he say aught to show you the state of his mind?"

Jack had been hesitating as to whether he ought to say anything about Arthur's religious condition; but now that the way seemed so clearly opened, he hesitated no longer.

"Master Arthur begged me to read the Scripture to him, and I did so," said he. "He seemed, at first, to fear that he had betrayed himself to a spy of the priests, and when I reassured him, he showed me the scars which had been made on his wrists by the rack as he said, whereby I supposed he had been in the hands of the Inquisition somewhere in the Low Countries or in France. He seemed to fear that your worship would not receive him because he had heard the Lutheran preachers, and said it was Master Frith who told him he ought to return to his father."

"My poor boy!" said Sir John, and then followed another long silence, which was hardly broken till they reached Bridgewater.

The horses and man-servant were left at the inn, and Sir John walked down to Mary Brent's house attended by Jack, and followed by the wondering looks and respectful salutes of all he met, for Sir John was almost as well-known in Bridgewater as the tower of St. Mary's.

"You had better go up first and see how my son is," said the knight, as they reached the door. "But what shall we say to the good woman of the house?"

"I will manage that," said Jack, marvelling at his own confidence. "I can easily content her."

Mary Brent in her neat widow's weeds was always fit to be seen, and welcomed Sir John with all due humility.

"The dear young gentleman has been much better to-day," said she in answer to his inquiries. "He said he felt as though Master Jack had put new life into him. I hope your worship will see no harm in him," she added somewhat uneasily. "I could do nothing else than take him in when my son brought him home."

"You have done quite right, and I thank you, dame," said Sir John graciously. "If the young man proves, as I think he may, a kinsman of mine, you shall be no loser by your kindness."

Jack found his new friend sitting up in bed, supported by pillows, and looking eagerly toward the door. He seemed a little disappointed as Jack entered alone.

"Is it you, my kind nurse?" said he. "Are you alone? I fancied I heard another voice."

"A familiar voice?" asked Jack, smiling. "A voice you have heard before?"

"It did seem so," replied Paul, sinking wearily back again on his pillows. "But it could have been but a sick man's fancy. I doubt I shall never live to hear that voice again."

"Whose voice did you think you heard?" asked Jack; then, as Paul did not answer, "Was it your father's?"

"It did, indeed, seem like his," returned Paul. "But I know it could not be. Oh, could I but once fall at his feet like the poor prodigal!"

"The prodigal did not fall at his father's feet, though he might have meant to do so," said Jack, softly. "When he was yet a great way off, his father saw him, and ran and fell on his neck and kissed him."

Paul started up with more energy than one would have thought possible. "Have you brought my father to me?" he cried. "Is he here?"

"Hush hush!" said Jack, gently laying him back on the pillow. "Do but be quiet and composed, and all shall be well. There is, indeed, a worthy gentleman below stairs, and when I see you yourself again, I will bring him to your bedside."

Great was the amazement and delight of Mary Brent when Sir John, coming down-stairs from his long interview with her lodger, took her by the hand, and, in fitting and formal phrase, thanked her for the kindness she had shown to his only son and heir.

She could hardly comprehend the matter, and looked from Sir John to Jack in evident bewilderment.

"Do you not understand?" said Jack. "The young gentleman above is Mr. Arthur Paul Brydges, Sir John Brydges's son, long in captivity in foreign parts and supposed to be dead. He was on his way home when he was wrecked and saved by your son Davy."

No happier or prouder woman than Mary Brent could be found in all Bridgewater and Somersetshire to boot. It was plain that Paul, or Arthur, as we must now call him, could not be moved at present; so fitting furniture and garnishing was procured for Mary's empty rooms, and the next day Lady Brydges and her waiting gentlewoman came in from the Hall and took up their lodging with the shipmaster's widow.

After all Jack's care in preparing the way, the shock of the meeting told severely on Arthur's enfeebled frame, and for many days, he hovered between life and death. At last, however, youth and good nursing carried him through, and he was able to be taken home to his father's house.

It may easily be guessed that the knight and his lady were not wanting in thanks and in more solid tokens of esteem toward the kind little widow and her family. All the furniture which had been bought for Lady Brydges's use was given to Mary. Davy was advanced by Sir John's interest to be commander of a coasting vessel, and her younger children rejoiced in the new clothes, the toys, and sweetmeats, which made them the envy of all the school-children.

"'Tis a fine thing to have grand friends," said Dame Higgins, who had made an errand to Mary Brent's house expressly to see the new furniture. "You were in luck, after all."

"I should not have been in luck, if I had taken your advice and left poor Mr. Arthur to take his chance at the convent gate," returned Mary, unable to resist the temptation of triumphing a little. "But he should have been welcome to my best bed all the same, as long as he needed it, if he had been the poor sailor we all thought him."

"Some folks have all the luck," grumbled Dame Higgins. "If I had taken in all the poor vagabonds in the port, they would never have turned out anything but vagabonds."

"When you take in a poor vagabond sailor, he will turn out a prince of the Indies at least," said Davy Brent bluntly. "My mother did what she did from pure love and kindness, and she would not have failed of her reward, however it had turned out."

"Well, well, I don't want to quarrel," said Dame Higgins. "You are sure to be rising folks, now that you have obliged such great people; and I only hope you won't forget old friends in your prosperity, that is all."

CHAPTER XVIII.

CONFIDENCES.

Some four or five weeks had passed quietly over the heads of our friends since the events recorded in our last chapter.

Master Fleming had returned to London, carrying with him the thanks and blessings of all the poor in Bridgewater, and of all whom he had led into the knowledge of the Scriptures and the way of life. Dame Barbara continued her school, now as large as she could manage.

Jack had made more than one journey to Holford to visit his uncle and Arthur, between whom and himself had grown up a warm and intimate friendship. This friendship, though approved by Sir John, was not viewed with altogether favorable eyes either by my lady or Master Lucas. My lady, though she acknowledged the obligations of the family to Jack, nevertheless thought it rather beneath her son's dignity to be so familiar with the son of a citizen; and Master Lucas, who was fully as proud in his way as my lady was in hers, did not like to have Jack visit at a house where he was likely to be looked upon as a presumptuous intruder.

However, Arthur's mother was inclined to treat her son with every indulgence, so long as he continued in his present weak state, and, though she gently mourned over the degeneracy of the times which made such a friendship possible, and was sometimes more condescending in her kindness to Jack than was altogether pleasant, still she was kind, and, moreover, acknowledged that the young man had parts and breeding which would not disgrace any station.

It may be guessed that Jack and Arthur never wanted for topics of conversation. Arthur had lived a roving and somewhat wild life for two or three years after he went abroad, till he at last fell dangerously ill at Antwerp. Alone in a strange place, without money and without friends, he was likely to fare badly; when he was found out by those two eminent saints and confessors, Frith and Lambert, then engaged in distributing and preaching the Word of God among their own countrymen abroad. By them Arthur was fed and nursed and cared for till he recovered his health, and by them was he led to see what was the root of all his troubles, to renounce the errors in which he had been brought up, and to profess the truth.

Arthur had naturally a quick and strong mind and a warm heart. He studied eagerly and earnestly, and by the time he was able to be about again, he was fully grounded in the new doctrines. He was desirous of undertaking some useful work to show his thankfulness and sincerity, and taking with him a package of Testaments and tracts, he travelled from city to city and from village to village distributing the seed of truth, especially among his own countrymen.

Moved by the arguments and solicitations of his friend Frith, he at last became convinced that it was his duty to return and make his submission to his father; and he determined to do so, though sorely in doubt about his reception, for his father was a proud man, and it was a boast of the Brydges that no heir of the family had ever brought disgrace upon it.

It was at Brussels, on his way home, that Arthur Brydges was betrayed by one who had come to him pretending to be in want of an English Testament. This man had been in trouble, himself, as a Lutheran, had abjured his so-called errors, and was now endeavoring to atone for them by making himself serviceable as a spy. His former connection with English Protestants enabled him to assume the character to perfection, and perhaps Arthur in his zeal was not so careful as he should have been.

At any rate, he fell into the trap, went as he supposed with his new friend to a secret assembly of Protestants, and found himself in a dungeon of the Inquisition, from which he hardly escaped with life, by the connivance of an English priest who was not yet lost to all feeling of humanity or patriotism.

"The base hound—the infamous, cowardly traitor!" exclaimed Master Lucas when he heard the story. "Did he betray his own countryman to death, and that under the guise of friendship? I would go all the way to Bristol on foot to see him hanged."

"There have been worse cases than this," said Arthur; "cases in which the brother has literally betrayed the brother to death, and the father the son. Nay, I knew of one in which a brother informed against his own twin sister, and believed he was doing God service."

"Such things seem impossible," said Master Lucas. "I wonder what his parents said."

"They may have approved," said Anne, bending closely over her work as she spoke. "If the sister were an heretic and a blasphemer, the brother's duty to the Church—"

"Tell me not of duty to the Church!" interrupted the baker. "I say the man was a villain, unfit to live, not worthy of the name of hound, since even brutes know the ties of affection and friendship. Why, the very old cat there, thief that she is, would fight to the death for her kittens. But here I am growing as hot as one of mine own ovens," said he, wiping his forehead and smiling at his own vehemence. "Only, Anne, thou shouldst not vex thine old father by taking the contrary side."

After Arthur had gone, the story of his adventures was talked over at the table, and Master Lucas again vented his indignation against the cowardly spy who had betrayed Arthur, and against spies and traitors in general.

"If it had been my son who had done such a thing, I would never see him more."

"Suppose it were your own son who was a heretic?" said Anne.

"That is a different matter," replied the baker. "It would be a great misfortune, and much to be deplored, but it would not be a base and traitorous action like the other. Nay, I could forgive heresy—the wildest heresy—in a man, sooner than treachery."

"I do not see the treachery," said Anne. "If he warned his sister beforehand what he was going to do, in case she persisted in her error as you call it, she had no cause of complaint. His duty as a Christian stood before his duty to his family, or any other carnal and fleshly ties. I think he did right," said Anne, flushing as she spoke. "I do not see how he could do otherwise."

"Would you, then, do so?" asked Sister Barbara.

"I would," replied Anne. "I should think it my duty."

"Then wouldst thou never again enter thy father's door or receive his blessing!" exclaimed Master Lucas, striking the table with his fist so that the dishes jingled. "Never would I see again a child capable of playing such a villainous part. My curse—"

"Dear father!" exclaimed Jack, laying his hand entreatingly on his father's arm. "My dear good father, do not be angry with Anne. She would never do anything to forfeit your blessing, I am sure."

"I beg, Jack, that you will not interfere," said Anne, who seemed bent upon raising a storm. "It does not become you to meddle. Let my father say his will."

"My will is to bid thee hold thy tongue, for a malapert contrary wench as thou art, and not provoke thy old father to make a fool of himself, or bring on a fit of apoplexy," said Master Lucas, making an effort to control himself and speak in his usual pleasant tone. "Reach me a cup of cool water, my son. It was an evil day that I sent my daughter to a nunnery to learn to despise the honest and natural ties of blood and childly duty among a parcel of fantastic and bigoted old maids—craving your pardon, madam," he added, turning to Sister Barbara. "But it is enough to make a man a heretic in spite of himself, to hear one's own child upholding such notions to one's face. I verily believe more heretics are made by the priests than by any one else."

"I wonder what my lady says to Arthur's new notions," said Sister Barbara. "She used to be very strict lady about such matters."

"She was greatly grieved and shocked at first," said Jack; "but she is becoming more reconciled of late, and, I believe, she has never shown Arthur any unkindness in respect of them."

"Well, I don't wish Master Arthur any ill, but I wish he and our Jack were not so intimate," remarked Cicely. "The next thing we shall have Jack, himself, infected with Lutheran notions. They say Father William has come round to be an out-and-out Gospeller, and is all for having folk read the Scripture for themselves. Not that I see why the Gospellers are to be blamed for that," added Cicely simply. "Because, of course, if it were the true Bible, the more they read it, the more devout Catholics they would be."

Jack and Sister Barbara both smiled.

"Father William has been nothing else but a heretic this long time," said Anne angrily. "I am glad if he has at last had honesty enough to confess it."

"Heretic or not, he is one of the best men that ever breathed," said Master Lucas. "One cannot but think there must be something in these new doctrines, since such men as he are carried away by them. Jack, are you for riding out to the Priory Mills with me? I have some business with the miller there, and the afternoon is fine."

Jack accepted the invitation with alacrity, thinking he saw an opening for the confidential conversation he had been longing to hold with his father for some days past. The burden of secrecy had been troubling him more and more, of late, and he had determined at last, that, come of it what would, he would bear it no longer. He hastened to make himself ready, and, as he was descending the stairs, he was beckoned by Sister Barbara.

"Jack," said she, "I cannot but think I am playing a deceitful part by your good father. I cannot think it is right to go on so. I shall grieve to leave the shelter of this roof where I have been so happy—where I have first learned the meaning of the word home," said the good lady, her eyes filling with tears; "but it is not right to expose your father to the dangers which may arise from harboring a heretic. I must leave you, though I know not whither I can go."

"Do nothing hastily, dearest sister," said Jack. "I myself shall open my heart to my father this afternoon, and we will see what is to be done. I trust all may yet be well."

"All will yet be well," returned Sister Barbara. "It cannot but be well if we are only faithful; but I doubt we shall see terrible times first. Let us pray for one another that our faith fail not in the fiery trial."

In the course of their ride, Jack opened his heart to his father, as he proposed. He found Master Lucas not unprepared for the disclosure, and though much disturbed yet not inclined to be angry.

"I have been suspecting as much, this long time," said he. "Ever since your return from Holford, I could not but see that you were greatly changed and improved—yes, I will say improved. But to think that you should have heard all this from Uncle Thomas. Truly, one never knows where danger lies. Had I been told to select a safe place for a lad, I could not have thought of a better one."

"Did you not, then, know the story of his father?" asked Jack.

"I do remember hearing something of it, but the matter happened long before my time, and was hushed up as much as might be. And then, who would think that Uncle Thomas, who could not have been more than fifteen at the time, would have remembered and held fast his father's teachings all these years, and after all he has gone through? It is truly wonderful!"

"It is, indeed," said Jack. "You would be astonished to see how much he remembers of what he learned when he was a little lad. But, dear father, I am so glad you are not angry with me. I feared you would be so, but yet I felt that I could not keep a secret from you any longer. You have been so good and kind to me, that it made me feel like a traitor to know that I had any concealment from you."

"Your secret has not been so well kept but I have had a shrewd guess at it," said his father, smiling somewhat sadly; "but I waited till you should tell it me yourself, as I felt quite sure you would do, sooner or later. But, my son, have you counted the cost? You know to what all this may lead."

"Yes, father, I know it well, and have thought it over many times. If it were only myself on whom the danger and the disgrace were like to fall, I should care less; but that I should bring this trouble upon you, who have ever been the best and kindest—" Jack's voice was choked, and he turned his head away.

"Nay, dear son, be not grieved for that," said his father kindly. "I see not but a man must follow his conscience wherever it leads. Neither can I see why the priests should so angrily oppose the reading of the Scripture."

"If you should read it yourself, you would see," replied Jack. "There is not one word in the whole New Testament about the worship of the Holy Virgin, nor of purgatory, nor vows of chastity, nor a hundred other things which the priests teach us to believe. St. Peter himself was married, and so were St. James, and St. Philip."

"But the priests say this Lutheran Gospel is not the true Scripture," remarked his father.

"I know they do, and for that reason they discourage with all their might the Greek learning that is spreading so much at the universities. But, father, the Greek Testament is the very same."

"And nothing about purgatory or about the masses for the dead, either?" asked his father. "Art sure, Jack?"

"Not a word, father."

"Then a deal of good money has been thrown away," was the next reflection of the business-like master baker. "I myself paid more than three hundred marks for masses for your mother, who was as good a woman as ever lived, barring her little peevish tempers; and twice as much for my father and mother. And the priests have robbed poor Dame Higby of almost the last penny to sing for the soul of her husband. But how have we been befooled if these things are true!"

"Only read for yourself, dear sir, and you see," said Jack.

"Nay, I am no scholar, as you know," returned his father. "But how as to Madam Barbara? I have sometimes suspected that she was in the same boat. If so, it is like to go hard with her, having been a nun."

Jack told his father, as she had desired him, the story of Sister Barbara. Perturbed in mind as he was, Master Lucas was considerably amused.

"Poor Anne! She little thought what a wolf in sheep's clothing she was bringing into the fold when she spent such a time in trimming up her altar in Madam Barbara's room. I have seen, this long time, that there was no great confidence between them. But what we are to do, I cannot guess; for the outcry against heresy grows louder every day. I think, Jack, you had best go abroad for a time."

"But, dear father, how can I leave you?"

"It would be very hard," said Master Lucas sadly; "hard to lose both my children, for I doubt I shall have no more comfort with Anne. But it were better for me to know you safe in Germany or the Low Countries than to see you in prison or worse. Truly, I am fallen on evil times in, mine old age which I thought to spend so quietly."

"I think I could bear all, if I had it to bear alone," said Jack. "It is that which has made the cross so heavy to me. But, father, you would not have me false to my conscience, and traitor to my friends, like the man Arthur told us of?"

"God forbid!" returned his father solemnly. "Better a thousand deaths than that. But we will not anticipate evil," he added. "Some say our gracious prince favors the new gospel."

"I fear there is not much to be expected in that quarter," returned Jack; "but as you say, we will not borrow trouble. I have breathed more freely ever since Father Barnaby went away. I think him a most dangerous man. He has gone to Rome, as they tell me, where I hope, as Father John of Holford says, they will make him bishop of some place on the other side of the world."

"But as to Madam Barbara," said Master Lucas after they had gone on a little way in silence.

"Well, dear father."

"My son, I cannot help having great fears for her. I would she were in some place of safety. I should miss her sorely from the house, that is the truth, for she is like sunshine itself."

"I have sometimes thought," said Jack slyly, "that if Madam Barbara were not a nun—"

"That you might have a step-dame some of these fine days, you rogue," returned his father, laughing. "What would you say to that?"

"I should rejoice heartily," said Jack eagerly; "for I am sure she would make a good wife, and I love her dearly already. Besides, I should be pleased with anything which made you happy."

"Well, well! There is no question of that matter now," said his father, who was obviously not displeased with the idea. "We must not forget that madam is a born lady, though she condescends so kindly to become one of ourselves. But the question is now not of marriage, but of saving from hanging."

"I will talk to Father William about the matter," said Jack. "I will go to him this very evening. Dear father, I am so glad I have told you all, and that you are not angry with me."

"I could not be angry, son Jack, though I do not deny that I am greatly grieved. I would fain spend the remnant of my days in peace. Not but I would gladly see the Church reformed, and especially some order taken with all these lazy monks and begging friars, who eat honest, industrious folks out of house and home, and carry off silly girls to convents; but I fear your friends are too sweeping. I cannot bring myself to believe that so much we have been taught to receive as Gospel truth is no more than men's invention."

"Only read for yourself, father, and you will see."

"Well, well, perhaps I may, if only to put my head in the same halter with yours. One word more, Jack, because we may have company home and no chance to speak further. How much of all this does Anne know?"

Jack repeated to his father what the reader has heard already.

"I cannot think that Anne would betray me, for all she says," he added.

"I do not know," said Master Lucas, shaking his head. "Anne is a true nun. She thinks all family affections are carnal and fleshly ties, and to be trampled under foot. I cannot—I will not think of your mother's daughter, that she would do such a deed, but I hope she may not be tried. But after all, we may be borrowing trouble. Father William makes no secret of his new ideas, nor does Arthur Brydges of his, and I hear my Lord Harland is as open, and he is very great with the bishop. Anyhow, I wish we were well out of the scrape."

CHAPTER XIX.

A SORROWFUL PARTING.

That evening Jack went, as he had proposed, to consult Father William about Sister Barbara.

Father William had lately made full profession of his faith, and preached the reformed doctrines openly in his church by the waterside, whither hundreds flocked to hear him—some urged by personal affection, for Father William was by far the most popular priest in Bridgewater; some from curiosity, to hear what was beginning to make such a noise and stir; and a few moved by earnest desire to hear and understand the truth. As yet, no disturbance had arisen in consequence of his preaching.

The other priests, indeed, were furious, and the preaching friars thundered unsparing denunciations against the heretic and all who heard demonstrating to their own satisfaction, at least, that he was possessed with ten devils, and would certainly be torn in pieces by them some day. The priest of St. Mary's was an infirm, easy-going old man, of the same school as Father John of Holford, and the prior of the convent was engaged in an active warfare with another convent concerning certain tan-yards and mills which they owned in common. Moreover, it was pretty well-known that the bishop of the diocese was, if not in reality a favorer of the gospel, yet nowise inclined to interfere with those who were.

Under all these favoring circumstances, Father William remained unmolested for the present, and he improved the time by preaching every day in his own church, and instructing in the truth those persons—and they were many—who came to unburden their minds and consciences to him.

Jack found him sitting at his frugal supper table, not eating, but leaning back in his chair; and he could not but remark how worn and thin the good man looked.

"You are killing yourself with this constant labor, dear father," said he; "you must take some rest."

"I must work the work to which I am sent, while it is yet day," said Father William. "The night cometh apace, in which no man can work. Unless I am greatly mistaken, this calm which we now enjoy is like to be of short duration, and I must use it diligently to win souls to my Master, and plant seed which may spring and grow when I am laid low. Besides," he added, with a sorrowful smile, "why should I save the body for the hangman or the stake? I should esteem myself blessed, indeed, if I might but die at my work. But what can I do for you, my dear son?"

Jack briefly opened his business.

"The danger is imminent, as you say," said priest when he had heard the story. "It would be certain death for the lady to return to the convent, and she may be called to do so any day—especially if she be suspected of heresy."

He mused a little while, and Jack almost thought he had forgotten the subject of conversation, when he roused himself from his abstraction.

"I think I see my way," said he. "I know a gentleman's family among the hills, yonder, where I think she would be welcome, both for her own sake and the gospel's. It is a wild and rocky nook—they say the sun is scarce seen there in winter, for the height of the hills which surround it— and there are abundance of places where, if need were, an army might be concealed. I shall be going that way tomorrow, and will see the lady and break the matter to her."

Sir William was as good as his word, and in two or three days, he told Jack the result of his mission. The lady was overjoyed at the thought of having such a companion in her solitude and such a teacher for her daughters, and the squire was ready to afford succor to any one who came to him in the name of the gospel.

"They are but rustic folk," said the priest, "and, though of gentle blood, far behind our town burghers in refinement and luxury. Sister Barbara must be content to rough it not a little, but that is a small matter. Any home, however rude, is better than a prison."

The result of these negotiations was communicated to Sister Barbara. At first she was distressed at the thought of leaving her school and her new friends, but a little consideration showed her that flight was the best course.

"I care nothing for roughing it," she said; "the good father well says that any home is better than a prison, and doubtless I can find ways to make myself useful to the lady and her daughters."

"And if this storm blows over, as I still hope it may, you will return to us, dear madam," said Master Lucas. "Truly the house will seem empty and dreary without you. Meantime, let no word of this matter be dropped in the household—before Anne, least of all."

"I cannot make up my mind to distrust Anne," said Jack.

"No person is to be trusted whose mind and conscience are wholly in the keeping of another," said Master Lucas. "I pray you, let me manage the matter my own way."

"So Madam Barbara is going to leave us," said Cicely, a few days afterward. "Father William has discovered some friends of hers off among the hills who desire a visit from her, and she is to go to them. We shall miss her more than a little."

"I hope to return, one of these days," said Madam Barbara. "I am sure I shall never find a happier home than this or a kinder friend than you are, dear Cicely, if I go over the world to look for them; but this lady is very lonely, and she has daughters to educate, and, moreover, there are other reasons which make my going desirable."

"Well, well; every one knows his own business best, and blood is blood—I don't deny that," said Cicely, "and I can't but think one's own relations were meant to be nearer than other folks, for all Anne says about it. But it must be a wild, dreary place—especially in winter."

"The more need for sunshine in the house, and I am sure Madam Barbara carries that with her wherever she goes," said Jack.

Anne heard of the intended departure of Sister Barbara with little regret. There had, of late, been no sympathy between them. Anne felt that Sister Barbara wholly disapproved of her conduct to her father and brother; and dead as she believed herself to be to all earthly things, she could not endure even an intimation of that blame she was so ready at all times to bestow on others. Moreover, she was jealous. It was impossible to live with Sister Barbara and not love her, and though Anne did not and would not take any pains to make herself agreeable or beloved, yet it angered her to the soul, to see another taking the place which belonged of right to herself.

Anne's life, at this time, was one of sheer inconsistency. She was fighting in behalf of a faith in which she, in her heart, scarcely preserved a shadow of belief; she was determined to crush out all earthly ties, and at the same time she was able to endure the thought of not being first in her father's house; and though she had told her brother that she should feel perfectly justified in betraying him, she was yet fiercely indignant at him for withholding his confidence from her. All this inward conflict did not tend to make her the more amiable, and while she revenged upon herself by renewed penances any failure in "holy humility," she was deeply hurt and indignant if any one in the least degree reproved or resented her bursts of temper.

She asked no questions as to Sister Barbara's plans, and hardly returned her expressions of affection at parting, yet she stood at the door watching the party as far as she could see them, and then, going up to her room, she wept long and bitterly—partly over the parting, partly over the disappointment of the hopes with which she had welcomed her former friend, and a good deal, it must be confessed, from mere hysterical fatigue consequent upon fasting and watching for sixteen or eighteen hours.

Jack and his father rode with Madam Barbara to within some ten miles of her destination, when they were met by Mr. Hendley, who gave the lady a hearty welcome, and to her friends an equally hearty invitation to come and see him and his wife, and stay any number of days or months.

Then, seeing the lady mounted on a pillion behind her protector, they took their leave of her, and turned their faces homeward. Taking advantage of a late moon, they had set out long before day to avoid any prying observations or questions from the neighbors, and it was still early when they returned home. As they turned into their own street, Jack uttered a vehement exclamation of surprise, at the sight of a stout elderly gentleman, in a cassock, descending with apparent pain and difficulty from his mule.

"What now?" asked his father.

"It is Father John, from Holford, as sure as you live, father!" exclaimed Jack. "What miracle or earthquake can have brought him so far from home?"

"We shall soon hear," replied his father.

"Yes, if the poor man have any breath left to speak," said Jack, as he threw himself hastily from his own beast. "I should think that doubtful."

"Well, we must give him all the welcome and refreshment in our power," said the master baker, dismounting more leisurely. "Your reverence is heartily welcome to my poor dwelling," he added, addressing the poor old priest, who had dropped exhausted on the first seat. "I would we had been at home to receive you in more fitting form. I pray you to walk into the parlor."

The old man rose with some difficulty, and, accepting the support of Master Lucas's arm, he made out to walk into the sitting-room. Jack ran before to bring forward the easiest seat and place a footstool before it, and then to bring a cup of ale, which Father John drank without a word.

Then turning a lack-lustre and piteous eye upon his cupbearer, he ejaculated—

"Alack, my dear son!"

"I trust nothing unpleasant has chanced to bring you so far from home, father," said Jack, fearing he knew not what. "It must have been a toilsome journey for your reverence."

"Alack, you may well say so. I did not believe I should ever ride so far again—and it is all for your sake. I would I were safe home again, that is all. These vile footpads would as soon rob a priest as a layman, I believe, and I am shaken to a very jelly."

"Your reverence must not think of returning to Holford to-night," said Jack.

He was dying to learn the good man's business, but he knew by experience that to try to hurry him was only to throw his brains into a hopeless confusion.

"I am sure my father will not be willing to have you leave us so suddenly, now that you have honored us with a visit."

"No, indeed, good father!" said Master Lucas heartily. "You must sup with us, and give me time to thank you for all your kindness to my boy."

"Tut, tut! That was nothing," returned Father John. "The young rogue! I could find it in my heart to wish I had never seen him, for he hath so wound himself round my heart as I could not have believed possible."

"Is my good uncle well, sir?" asked Jack.

"Well—why, yes, for aught I know," replied the priest, rather hesitatingly; "and yet—Is any one within hearing? I must speak to you in private."

Jack went out of the room and presently returned to say that Cicely and Anne had gone to evensong, that Simon was busy in the bakehouse, and he had set little Peter, the 'prentice, to watch the shop door.

"It is well," said Father John; "but yet we will speak low. My business is this: Father Barnaby has returned from his travels somewhat suddenly, and, it is said, with extraordinary powers from the Cardinal, to search out heretical books, and apprehend the owners thereof."

Jack looked at his father in dismay.

"Now I know not that this concerns you, my dear son," continued the priest, laying his hand on Jack's arm, and looking earnestly at him. "I hope, with all my heart, that it does not, and that for many reasons; but I know you are intimate with Arthur Brydges who makes no secret of his opinions, and there are other reasons: Father Barnaby is a hard man, and especially bitter against heresy; and I would not, to be made Abbot of Glastonbury, have any harm happen to you."

"And you have taken this long journey to give me warning," said Jack, much affected, and kissing the old man's hand. "Truly, I know not how to thank you, dear father."

"But you must not say so, for the world, my dear son," said Father John hastily. "Remember, I am not supposed to know anything of this matter, and have come to consult your father on the investing of certain moneys left me by my brother, lately dead. I would not hear a word—supposing there were any such thing to hear—lest I should be called on to testify. Do you understand?"

"We both understand, reverend sir, and feel your kindness," said Master Lucas. "Believe me, I shall never forget it—"

"Tilly-vally, tilly-vally!" interrupted the priest. "It is naught! I have lived, I fear, a selfish life, and I would fain do some good before I die. I love not these new-fangled ways better than Father Barnaby himself. I am sure a parish priest's life is hard enough as it is, and they say the Lutherans are for having sermons every Sunday, and Scripture readings, and what not. No, I love no new fancies in religion, but I do not hold with all these burnings and imprisonments and the like. I think kindness and good treatment far more likely to bring men back to the truth."

"Why, there was Father Thomas, the librarian at Glastonbury; in his youth he was greatly taken with such of these new notions as were current—Lollardism, men called it then—and some of the brethren were for having him hardly dealt by."

"'Let him alone, let him alone!' said the abbot—that was Abbot John, not the present Abbot Sylvester—'Let him alone,' says the abbot. 'Let me deal with him.'"

"So he calls Brother Thomas, and after some talk, he makes him his secretary, and custodian of all the books."

"'And, Brother Thomas,' says he, 'I would have you take especial care of the Latin authors, and cause some new copies to be made of Cicero his Offices, and of Virgil and Horace, and spare no expense upon them.'"

"Well, that was the end of Brother Thomas's hankering after heresy."

Jack could not help smiling at the story, though it was, in some respects, a sad one.

"And now I have discharged my errand, and you must make what use of it you will," said Father John; "only, if you love me, let no word of the matter go abroad. I have given them warning at the Hall, also—and, if I have done wrong, the saints forgive me. Alack, my poor bones!"

"If your reverence will take some brief repose, we will have supper ready directly," said Master Lucas; "here comes my good housekeeper. Cicely, let our meal be prepared directly; and, let every thing be of the best, since this good father is to be of our company."

"Nay, I know not if I ought to remain here," said Father John, who had been solacing himself all through his long and, to him, arduous journey, with the thought of the master baker's good cheer. "I ought, perhaps, to go to the convent—"

"I am a villain, if you leave us this night," said Master Lucas sturdily. "It were foul shame to me to let such a reverend father, and my son's benefactor to boot, depart from my roof fasting. Make haste, good Cicely, and do your best; and you, son Jack, attend me with the lantern, that I may draw some good wine for our honored guest."

"What is to be done now, son?" asked Master Lucas, so soon as they were alone in the cellar.

"Indeed, father, I cannot say," returned Jack. "I see not but I must abide the storm."

"By our Lady, that shall you not!" said his father. "This good old man has given us warning, and it were a mere tempting of Providence, not to profit thereby. When will Davy Brent be sailing again?"

"Not under two weeks, he told me yesterday. But, father, how can I leave you?"

"Better lose you for a little time, than altogether," said Master Lucas sadly. "Son, son! It was an evil day when I sent you from me."

"Nay, my dear father, say not so," replied Jack earnestly. "Truly, this cross is a heavy one, and hard for flesh to bear; yet I cannot regret that I have taken it up. The truth as I have learned it, first from Uncle Thomas, and afterward from the Scripture itself, is worth more to me than all the world hath to offer. I only pray that I may have grace to hold it to the end."

"Well, well! It skills not, arguing that matter now," said his father rather impatiently. "The question now is, how are we to use the good man's warning. You might go to Harrowdale where Madam Barbara is. I am sure the squire would give you welcome—or you might go out to Holford."

"I doubt that would be stepping from the frying-pan into the fire, as matters are at present," said Jack; "and yet I would fain see my uncle."

"Well, well, we will talk farther, presently, when the folks are abed," returned his father; "we must not remain longer here, or Anne will suspect something. I would she were away."

"Father," said Jack earnestly, "I beg of you, and it were the last favor I should ever ask of you, as it well may be—I pray you, be kind and patient with Anne. She is very unhappy, and at times, I think, she is hardly herself."

"If she be honest and true, I will be a kind father to her, as I have ever been, I think," said the baker; "but if she prove a traitor, and do aught to betray her brother—"

"She may not be able to help it," said Jack. "Do you not see, dear father, that she must answer any questions the priest chooses to ask her? With that engine of confession in their hands, the churchmen hold the inmost keys of every man's house and family."

"A plague take the whole of them!" exclaimed Master Lucas.

"A plague is like to take them, and that before long, if all we hear about the breaking up of the religious houses be true," said Jack. "It is because they know how it will take the power out of their hands, that the priests so oppose the spread of the true gospel. But I pray you, father, be kind to Anne, for my sake."

"Are you and Jack going to stay in the cellar all night and catch your deaths with the damp?" called Cicely from the top of the stairs. "Here is supper all but ready, and you would but draw the wine and ale, and I am sure you must need your food, as well as the good father yonder. Marry,

I was fain to give him a dish of cakes to stay his appetite till supper was ready."

At supper, Father John was the merriest of the party. Like many easy-going people he had the gift of putting far-off the evil day, and persuading himself that what he wished not to happen, never would happen. He had made what was for one of his habits a great sacrifice of ease and comfort to warn his young friend, and he was inclined to take the reward of his good deed. He praised Cicely's cooking, paid Anne various old-fashioned compliments, and made her very angry by telling her she was a foolish girl to wear out her youth in a nunnery. She had far better marry some stout young fellow and bring up a dozen of sturdy lads and maids to comfort her in her old age.

"I would you could persuade her to do so," said the baker.

"I have already told you, father, that I look upon myself as the vowed bride of the Church," said Anne with more asperity of tone and manner than altogether suited the character she avowed. "If I am to hear more such discourse, I shall retire from the table."

"Hoity-toity!" said Father John; "Since when hath it been the fashion for maidens to threaten their fathers either natural or ghostly in such wise? But, come, I meant no offence. I did but say what I truly think. I am an old man, my daughter, and, though I am a priest, I have seen much more of life than you have, both in the cloister and out of it; and I tell you, in all seriousness, that a woman who brings up her children in honor and in the fear of God, does a more acceptable work in His eyes—ay, and bears more pains and penances, too—than any cloistered nun since the days of St. Bridget herself. Think you the vigil is not as acceptable which is passed in soothing and tending a sickly, suffering babe, as that which is spent in kneeling on a chapel floor?"

"I should say so," said Cicely, much edified. "And yet nobody thinks of there being any merit in a wife's or mother's care of her family, because it just comes along in the course of life."

"That is to say, it comes in the course of God's providence," said Jack. "The one state of life is God's appointment, and the other is man's invention."

"I say not so much as that," said Father John hastily. "Doubtless the cloister is His appointment for some, as the family is for others. But come, Mistress Anne, since that is your name, be not displeased with me, who am a man old enough to be your father, and a priest beside, but pledge me in a cup of this sweet wine which is just fit for a maiden's drinking."

"I thank you, but I drink no wine," said Anne coldly.

"Anne, you are scarce civil," said her father. "I pray your reverence to pardon her ill manners."

"Oh, let her have her way," said the old priest. "Caprice is the privilege of women, poor things, and it were hard to deprive them of it. Young maids love to say No. Eh, daughter?" he added, with his jolly laugh. "We all know what that means. The 'I will not' of a bishop-elect and that of a maiden come to much the same thing in the end."

Good reason as they had for gravity, neither Jack nor his father could forbear laughing at Anne's discomfiture.

"Come, come, never mind it, child, and do not spoil the evening by peevishness," said her father. "Who knows how many more happy evenings we may spend together? Father John, will your reverence take another cup of wine?"

"No more, no more," replied the old man. "I am no toss-pot, my good Master Lucas, though I love a social cup now and then. I would fain go to rest, since you are so kind as to afford me a bed, for I am weary after my ride."

"When did you and Anne go to church?" asked Jack as he returned, after lighting the father to bed, to help Cicely put away the wine.

"Anne was not at church with me," replied Cicely, surprised. "I left her at her prayers, in the little cabinet yonder, while I went to carry some broth to Dame Higby."

Jack started.

Then Anne had, after all, heard the whole. What use would she make of her knowledge? He could not guess. He went at once to his father's room, and told him what he had heard from Cicely. Their conference lasted long, but with no very satisfactory result, and at last it was decided to wait till morning, and consult Sir William.

"The morrow is the feast of St. Michael's," said the baker. "They are not likely to do anything on that day, and we shall have time to think a little. But, Jack, if you have any of these books, I pray you hide or destroy them this very night."

"I will do so," said Jack. "Give me your blessing and your forgiveness, dearest father, before I leave you."

"Forgiveness is none when there has been no fault," said Master Lucas. "From thy cradle to this time, thou hast ever been to me a dutiful and good son. My blessing thou hast and wilt ever have, let this matter end how it will."

CHAPTER XX.

THE BREAKING OF THE STORM.

Jack went to his room, where his lamp was already lighted, and taking his beloved books from their usual hiding-place, he began to think what he should do with them. They were not many. There was first and dearest of all, the New Testament with Tyndale's notes, which had been given him by Master Fleming; then his Greek Testament; the Prophecy of Isaiah which he had brought from Mary Brent's house, and two or three small tracts and treatises. These last he read carefully through, once more, and then burned; but he could not bring his mind to burn his Bible.

There was a certain little cupboard in the wall, concealed by a sliding panel, which Jack had discovered by accident some few years before, and of the existence of which he had never heard any one speak. He had concealed his discovery with a boy's fancy for mystery, and now it was to serve a good purpose. He opened it and placed his books therein, all but his Greek Testament, which he thought he might safely reserve. He then closed the panel, and pushed his desk against it, and he had just finished these arrangements when he heard some one open his door.

He looked hastily and angrily round.

There stood Anne with a lamp in her hand.

"What now?" said he, trying to speak indifferently. "What brings you here so late?"

"I might ask what keeps you up so late," returned Anne. "You seem to have little regard to the repose of your guest, that you make such a noise."

"No fear of disturbing him, honest man," said Jack. "He is snoring like a porpoise, this minute, and I dare say he sleeps all the better for his unwonted exercise. He is a kind, good-natured man, though he may have his little infirmities, like the rest of us."

"It skills not talking of him," said Anne, entering the room, and closing the door. "Jack, what have you been doing, this night?"

"I have been burning some papers, if it imports you to know," replied Jack, not altogether pleased with the tone Anne assumed.

"Jack, have you destroyed your vile, heretical books?"

"I have no vile, heretical books, Sister Anne; therefore I have no opportunity to destroy them. Let me ask you in turn, since questions are the fashion, what has brought you to my room at this time of night?"

"It is, indeed, a time of night for all honest folks to be abed, unless they watch, as a duty," said Anne; "but if I had been inclined to sleep, I could not do so. What were you and my father talking about, so long?"

"You had better ask my father, if you desire to know," replied Jack. "If he sees fit to tell you his business, I can have no objection, but I do not think he would thank me for repeating it."

Anne stood silent, a moment. Then she said, "Jack, where has Sister Barbara gone?"

"She has gone to her friends, as she told you."

"That is not answering my question. I ask you to whither she has gone."

"And I reply, Sister Anne, that even if I knew, I would not tell you."

"You mean to say that I am not to be trusted."

"Even so."

"Jack," said Anne, setting down the lamp, and coming nearer to her brother, "do you know that Father Barnaby is returned, and is, even now, in Bridgewater?"

"I knew he had returned, but not that he was here," replied Jack. "How do you know that he is here? Have you already seen him?"

"No; that is—Jack, do you mean still to persist in your heresy? Do you mean to draw down disgrace and ruin on your father's house, to break his heart and mine, all that you may follow your own wicked and headstrong fancies? Are you so much wiser than all the world? What chance have you had to learn so much more than I, that you are so confident in your own opinion?"

"To your first question," replied Jack, "I answer that I do mean, God helping me, to hold fast even to the death, to His truth which you call heresy. I do not pretend to be wiser than all the world, but if I see all the world wrong, that does not excuse me for being wrong also. I am not following my own will or conceit, but the Word of God, and I must go whither it leads me, though it be to prison and death as it led Agnes Harland, and has led many another."

"And when you are brought—I mean, if you are brought before Father Barnaby, you will say these same things. Oh, brother, brother!" she exclaimed, falling on her knees at Jack's side. "Do not be obstinate! Do not throw away your life for nothing. You are young; you have been misled by others. They will be merciful to you if you do but recant your errors, and tell the names of those who have misled you. Oh, brother, brother! Do not be stiff-necked; do but confess, and all will be well."

A sudden light broke in upon Jack's mind. He cast off his sister's hand and drew back, as if from a snake.

"Anne!" said he sternly. "You have betrayed me."

Anne did not answer. She covered her face with her hands.

"You have acted the traitor's part a second time," continued Jack. "It was not enough to give over your friend to death, but you have stained your soul with this new treason. I believe you have already seen Father Barnaby."

Anne did not deny it. She sunk her head still lower, but said not a word.

"You have, then, done the mischief already," said Jack. "When did you see the priest?"

"It does not become you to question me or to speak to me thus," said Anne, striving to assume her usual tone. "I have but done that which was right, and my duty. No man is bound to keep faith with heretics. You speak of acting according to your conscience. Why should I not act according to mine?"

"You know that you have not done so," said Jack, fixing a penetrating look on his sister's face. "You have belied your own conscience, and betrayed me to death, for the sake of what, in your heart, you know to be a lie. Yes, Anne, in your heart, you believe that what I have told you, and what you heard from Agnes, is true—God's own truth. If this may be heresy, you are at heart as much a heretic as I am."

"I will not hear this!" said Anne hastily. "No one shall call me a heretic. You have no right to complain. I gave you fair warning. I come to you, to-night, not because I repent of what I have done, but to warn you—to give you a last chance."

"Many thanks to you!" said Jack, with a bitterness he could not altogether restrain. "Pray, what is to be the price of this piece of villainy? Are you to be made a prioress, or are you to found a new order? But I not speak so," he added hastily. "God give me grace to forgive you."

He walked up and down the room two or three, times, and then threw himself on his knees, by the bedside.

Anne stood, stiff and silent.

At last, Jack rose and turned to her.

"Anne," said he, "you have done a base and cowardly deed, and you will one day see it so, however you may regard it at present. I know not what has prompted you, and I desire not to judge you. Only remember this, when your day of remorse and repentance comes—as come it will—remember, there was forgiveness even for them who crucified our dear Lord, and the same forgiveness will be granted to you if you truly repent, and accept the offer of mercy. For my own part, I freely pardon you, and if I do not do so wholly, now, I believe the grace will be given me. But I warn you, that you are placing yourself in imminent danger of eternal perdition, by your present resisting of the Spirit and of your own conscience. 'He who denieth me before men, him will I deny before the angels of God,' says our Lord Himself. He now holds out His pitiful arms even to you, but there may come a day when He will hold them out no more—when you may long to confess what you now deny, and it may be forever too late."

Anne still stood silent, but her face showed the storm within.

"But I must not throw away my life," said Jack hastily. "It may be that I can yet escape."

"There is no chance. The house has been watched ever since your return," said Anne, in a hoarse voice. "You will but make matters worse."

"Be it so, then. I will bide the storm which you have brought upon me," said Jack. "I pray you to leave me, sister. I have need of time and solitude to collect my thoughts and prepare for that which is coming."

Without a word Anne turned and left the room, and Jack fastened the door.

Then, drawing his Bible from its hiding-place and trimming his lamp, he knelt down and read, again and again, the tenth chapter of St. Matthew's Gospel.[4] He passed several hours in reading and prayer, and then, as the gray morning began to creep in, he rose and dressed himself as for a festival, and when it was fully day, he went down to his father's room, to help him dress, as usual. He was met at the door by Simon, with a face full of terror and dismay.

"Oh, Master Jack, Master Jack! What can have happened? The constable with his men are at the door and demand entrance, and Father—I cannot think of his name—"

"Father Barnaby," said Jack gently. "Go down, Simon, and say I will be with them directly. I will but see my father."

"What means all this disturbance?" asked Master Lucas, opening his door. "Who are those men without?"

"Let me come in, dear father, and I will tell you all," said Jack. "Go down, Simon. Dear Cicely, do but be quiet, and dress yourself."

Jack entered his father's room, and, shutting the door, told him what had happened.

"Then it is too late!" exclaimed Master Lucas, wringing his hands in anguish. "My son, my dear son! Fool that I was! Why did I not insist on your leaving me last night?"

"It would have been useless," said Jack. "I have reason to know that we were watched from the moment of our return. But let us go down and face these men quietly and manfully."

---

4   I request every reader of these pages to do the same.

They descended accordingly, and found the shop filled with men. Father Barnaby occupied the sitting-room, and was attended by Brother Joseph, the sacristan from Holford, who favored Jack, on his entrance, with a glance of triumphant malignity, from beneath his down-dropped eyelids. Father John occupied the easy-chair, sitting upright and grave, and as Jack and his father entered the room, he arose, and with a tone of marked kindness, bestowed his blessing upon them.

"I thank you heartily," said the baker; and then, turning to Father Barnaby, he said, "Your reverence is an early visitor. May I ask what has brought you to my poor house at this hour?"

"My business is far from pleasant, Master Lucas," returned the priest austerely. "It is simply to search your house for heretical books, and to arrest this youth, your son, that he may be examined concerning certain errors which he has received and also endeavored to spread abroad among the faithful children of the Church. I must ask you to call all your family together."

"Jack, call your sister and cousin," said the baker briefly.

"With your leave, the young man abides here," said Father Barnaby.

"As you please," returned Master Lucas; "here comes one, to speak for herself. This is my cousin, Cicely Annan, a widow, who hath kept my house since I lost my wife. My daughter is, I suppose, in her room. Peter, call your young mistress."

Anne presently made her appearance. She was very pale, and evidently greatly agitated.

"This is the whole of my family," said Master Lucas. "This reverend gentleman is from Holford, and did us the honor to sup and sleep with us."

"I know Father John of Holford, well," said Father Barnaby dryly. "Methinks he might be better found in his own parish, on this holy day."

"Good brother—or son, as I may well call you, since I am old enough to be your father—I have yet to learn on what ground I am to ask your leave as to when and how I shall leave my parish," said Father John, with more dignity than Jack had thought he could assume. "If your commission extends to my private affairs, I would fain see your warrant."

Father Barnaby looked somewhat disconcerted, for a moment. "I crave your pardon, good brother," he said, recovering himself. "Doubtless it was business of moment which brought you to this house. But, Master Lucas, have you not a lady abiding with you—a lady formerly a nun in the convent where your daughter was bred?"

"She has been with us, but she left us yesterday, to go to friends in the country," replied Master Lucas.

"Where did she go?" was the next question.

"I know not," replied Master Lucas. "It is somewhere among the hills, but I know not the name of the place nor of the family whither she has gone."

This was true, for both Master Lucas and Jack had carefully abstained from informing themselves on these points.

"Umph! Well, that matters not now," said Father Barnaby. "Master Lucas, I regret to say that I have certain information that this your son (who is a youth of parts and understanding beyond his years) entertains the most heretical and false opinions concerning the sacraments, the adoration of saints, and other matters of the last importance. Do you know aught of this matter?"

"Your reverence can hardly expect me to bear witness against my own son—at least till I am obliged to do so," replied Master Lucas. "He hath ever been a good and dutiful son—that I can say for him."

"Have you any heretical books in your possession?" asked the priest, turning to Jack.

"I have a copy of the New Testament in Greek," replied Jack, "if you call that heretical; also, I have two treatises which your reverence gave me, one concerning the eleventh ode of Horace, and the other on the Metamorphoses of Ovid. Your reverence knows best what they are. Also I have Virgil and Horace, and certain other Latin books."

"Play not with me, young sir," said the priest, frowning. "I have certain intelligence from one who has seen it, that you have in your possession a copy of the Lutheran New Testament. I require you to put it into my hands."

Jack was silent, and did not move.

"Come, my son," said Father Barnaby, assuming a more friendly tone, "I pray you, be not obstinate. Do but give me up your books, and promise me to confess openly your errors, and all may yet be well. Unless you will do so I must search your father's house, and commit you to prison, where it may go hard with you."

"I am a prisoner in your hands, and you must needs do your pleasure," said Jack briefly. "I have nothing more to say, except that, whatever I may be, my father knows naught of these matters."

Jack and the rest of the family were in the sitting-room, while the house was thoroughly searched, but in vain. The hiding-place the books remained undiscovered, to the great chagrin of Brother Joseph, who showed himself an adept in the business, and who had to report his ill success to his principal.

"It matters not, we can take another way. Daughter," said Father Barnaby, turning to. Anne, who had hitherto stood quite silent, "you, at least, are a faithful child of the Church, as you have already shown. Can you tell me where these books are likely to be hidden?"

"I believe them to be in a small cupboard in the wall, behind my brother's desk," answered Anne, in a husky tone.

"Vile wretch that thou art, wouldst thou betray thy brother?" exclaimed her father, thrown off his guard.

"Your daughter, Master Lucas, does but do her duty in discovering her brother's guilt," said Father Barnaby. "It is the greatest kindness she could show him. Rejoice that you have one faithful child left."

"She is no child of mine from this day," said Master Lucas. "I wholly disown and cast her off. I would she had died at her birth, rather than she should have lived to be what she is."

"Father, remember your promise," said Jack; "I pray you do nothing hastily."

Brother Joseph now returned with the books. "Is this all you have?" asked the priest, examining them.

"That is all."

"You and your uncle had other books when you were at Holford, I know," said the priest. "What were they, and whence did you obtain them?"

Jack was silent.

"You will do the old man no service by this silence, if that be your thought," said Father Barnaby. "You had best be frank with me, since I mean you naught but good."

"No doubt," answered Jack dryly. "I thank your reverence for your good intentions."

"There is enough of this," said Father Barnaby angrily. "Since you are obstinate, matters must take their course. Constable, lead this youth to jail, and lodge him like the others. Master Lucas, I advise you to remain quiet and be amenable, and no harm shall befall you."

"Farewell, dear father," said Jack. "I pray you heartily to be of good comfort and put your trust in God. Have no fears for me, I am in His hands who did never fail them that trust in Him, and no real harm can befall me. Farewell, dear Cicely, you have been like a mother to me. Father John, I thank you heartily for all your kindness and good counsel."

"Have you no word for your sister, dear son?" asked Father Barnaby.

"I have already said my farewell to my sister," replied Jack gravely and sadly. "I have no more to add, save to beg her for her soul's salvation to remember my parting words. I am ready to go, Master Constable."

"My blessing go with thee, my son!" said his father. "I trust we may yet see you here again."

"And mine, also," added Father John, rising "and if my interest in your behalf is of any you shall have it with all my heart, as well as my prayers to our Lord and all the saints for your good deliverance."

Master Lucas stood gazing after his son till he could be seen no longer. Then, turning away, his eye fell on Anne, who remained standing.

"Do you stand there in my presence, after what you have done?" he asked, in sternly measured tones, as if he would not express the wrath which stirred him at sight of his daughter. "Think you the sight of you can be grateful to my eyes? I would you had died at your birth ere I had lived to see this day!"

"Nay, my good, my kind friend," said Father John. "Be not over hasty. I trust that this maiden had nothing to do with her brother's misfortune. Is it not so, daughter?"

"I did what was right," said Anne, striving to speak calmly. "My brother is an heretic, and a blasphemer of Holy Church and the sacraments, and not only so, but he was ever striving to prevent me. I delivered him to justice for the sake of his soul and mine own."

"I verily wonder whether thou art my own daughter," said the master baker slowly, "or whether my child died in the convent yonder, and some devil entered into her body! Surely, thy mother and I never had such a monster! I will not curse thee, for the sake of him who has gone; but get thee from my sight, or I cannot answer for what I may do! Get to thy chamber— dost hear me?" he repeated, stamping his foot.

"Yes, go, daughter," said the old priest. "You do but enrage your father the more by your carriage, which I must say is neither maidenly nor Christian. Get you to your chamber, and repent if you can, for, in sooth, you have been guilty of a great sin. My poor, dear friend!" he added, as Anne withdrew. "Let us forbear harsh words. They can do no good. Let us kneel down and pray, not only for our dear young brother, but for this misguided girl. I do trust all may yet be well. The bishop is a kind-hearted man, and averse to all harsh measures, and I have some interest with him which I shall not spare to use. I hope all may yet be well."

CHAPTER XXI.

ANNE.

Anne retired to her room and locked herself in, a precaution which she might have spared, for nobody came near her except one of the maids to bring her some food. The girl, though she did not speak, looked at Anne with an expression of wonder and reproach, which went to her heart.

"Where is my father, Dorothy?" she asked, feeling as if she must say something.

"Your father has gone out with the old priest who was here last night, Mistress Anne," was the short reply.

And Dorothy, who was usually disposed for a gossip at the smallest encouragement, retired and shut the door without another word.

Wicked and base as was the action she had committed, in itself, Anne was very much to be pitied. Her mind had for weeks been utterly unsettled.

As Jack had said, she was, in her heart, almost entirely convinced that her brother was right, and that she was wrong. In spite of herself, as it were, she could not help recalling all that she had heard and read with Agnes Harland, which was a great deal more than she had told Jack. In spite of herself, when she was listening to the harangues of the preaching friars against heresy, her mind would persist in bringing up and arranging arguments on the other side. When she repeated, as she did daily, her long litany of invocations to the saints and the Virgin Mary, something kept constantly telling her that it was a useless labor, and making such suggestions as these:

"How do you know that these saints can hear you? They were, and are, but finite beings like yourself, and cannot possibly be present in all places and at all times at once."

These were but a few of the distractions which beset her night and day, destroying her peace of mind, humbling her pride, and undermining her faith in those things wherein she had made her boast.

But Anne would not listen. She said to herself that they were but temptations of the enemy, such as had beset all eminent saints, and were to be banished by the proper means. So she fasted and scourged herself, and lay on the bare floor, and repeated ten times more prayers than ever. She had been fed upon "Lives of the Saints" from the time she could read, and for years, her cherished ambition had been to become a saint, on the model of Elizabeth of Hungary, or St. Bridget: to be looked up to as a pattern of holiness and austerity; to found a new order of nuns, more self-denying even than the "poor Clares," more contemplative than the Carmelites; to rule them while she lived, to be made a saint, and have miracles worked at her grave, when she was dead and buried.

Father Barnaby had cultivated these notions, seeing in the girl material which might encouraged her to believe made useful, and had believe that in the course of a few years she might be placed at the head of a sisterhood of her own founding. Anne had plenty of imagination, and hundreds of times she had gone over the whole matter in her own mind, arranging the rules and services of her house, and the very dress of the sisters. She fancied herself like St. Hilda, giving counsel and advice to abbots and priests, even to bishops and heads of the Church; as helping to stay the tide of heresy by her prayers and writings; as educating girls to perpetuate the doctrines and ways of her new order.

And was all this to be given up? Was she to abandon all her cherished ambitions and be content with the life of a daughter at home or a mere commonplace mother of a family? Or, still worse, was she to run the risk of open shame and disgrace and punishment, of being despised and held up as a warning, instead of an example, by those over whom she had hoped and expected to rule? Was she to confess that all her righteousness, her prayers and penances and sufferings, were worse than worthless in God's sight, and receive the gift of salvation as a free, wholly undeserved alms? Was her only title to heaven to consist in the fact, not that she was a saint, but a sinner? It could not be true—it should not be true! It was a work of the devil tempting her to abandon her vocation and all the great things she had planned.

And then came the thought—was it not her own fault after all? Had she not by weakly yielding to family affection—those fleshly ties from which she had been told again and again she must tear herself loose—had she not given the Tempter a handle against her? Ought she not to do all in her power to prevent the spread of heresy, and had she not, by yielding to her regard for her only brother, and concealing his fault, made herself a partaker therein? Would not her peace of mind return, if she were once to make the sacrifice? Would not that sacrifice be an additional and most precious jewel in the crown of martyrdom she coveted?

Yes, it must be so, and the sacrifice must be made. Once done, the deed could never be recalled. She would be held up as a bright example of piety, and she should again find her former peace, and satisfaction in prayer and penance and saintly reveries, and the doubts which disturbed her would depart forever.

Then there was Sister Barbara—Sister Barbara whose coming she had expected and prepared for, with so much pleasure, who had been one of the elders of the order, and a pattern of sanctity. There had long existed not even the semblance of confidence between them, but Anne had no doubt she was as bad as Jack, every whit. She had seen a book in her hands which was no prayer-book—she was sure of that—and she was always reading it while her "Hours" and her rosary lay neglected day after day. Sister Barbara and Jack were always talking quietly together and exchanging smiles and glances. Besides, did she not go to hear Father William preach even after he had refused to celebrate masses for the dead, and declared his opinion that it was lawful for priests to marry if they saw fit?

These and other indications convinced Anne that Sister Barbara was as bad as Jack—nay, worse, for was she not a nun, and had she not been a person in authority? Then there was her school! Was she to be allowed to pervert the children under her charge?

The morning that Sister Barbara went away, Anne went to the Priory church, determined, as she said, to decide the matter one way or the other before she came home. The first person she met was Father Barnaby. In her excited state of mind, this encounter seemed a supernatural sign sent for the confirmation of her wavering resolution, and she did not rest till she had told him all. She could not indeed tell the place where Sister Barbara had taken refuge, for she did not know it, but she told all she did know about the matter.

Father Barnaby was well pleased. He had come down, as Father John said, armed with a special commission for the searching out and destruction of heretical books and the suppression of heresy, and he was determined to carry through his work with an unsparing hand. It was a good omen to be thus met at the beginning, and served in some degree to counterbalance the chagrin he had felt at discovering that his chief prey had escaped him.

Father William had set out only the day before his return, on a visit to London, and there was too much reason to fear that by the connivance of friends, he might escape to Germany. But here was a notable prey to be taken at once, and he was not the man to let the grass grow under his feet. He commended Anne for her faithfulness, though he gave her less praise and paid less attention to the rest of her confession than she thought she deserved. However, he told her she had taken the best means to get rid of her trouble of mind, and confirmed her in the idea that it had all been owing to her having wickedly concealed her brother's errors. A watch was at once set upon Jack's movements, and he was apprehended, as we have seen.

Anne returned to her home with a strange feeling of exultation. She had done the deed. She had sacrificed what was nearest to her, and shown plainly that nothing was so dear to her as the cause of the Church and true religion. Surely, surely all must now be right with her. There would be an end forever of these haunting doubts, these wild temptations to go to Jack, own herself convinced, and beg for instruction. This feeling lasted her all day and till she saw her brother finally carried away to a fate which she knew too well, and heard her father's voice commanding her to her chamber. Thus she went to her room.

Lo! Her enemy was there awaiting her, armed with tenfold power.

She had done the deed. She had betrayed her brother to shame and death, she had incurred her father's hatred and curse, which was withheld only for the sake of his son; and all for what? Was she any nearer to the quiet of mind she had so ardently desired? She did not find it so. Instead thereof, her doubts returned with tenfold power. They were no longer doubts, they were certainties—demonstrated truths. She did not reason upon them; she could not.

She felt, rather than knew, that it was Jack who was the martyr for the truth, and she was the Judas who had betrayed him. She had denied her Lord, belied her own conscience, and sacrificed her family to a monstrous lie. What would she not have given to recall the events of the last few hours? But it was too late—forever too late; and the thought filled her with inexpressible anguish and despair.

Anne rose at last from the floor, where she had thrown herself at the foot of the crucifix, and in the sheer restlessness of misery wandered into Jack's room. There were all his treasures; his strings of birds' eggs, his shells and other foreign curiosities derived from traders and sailors, his Latin books and exercises. The blackbird and squirrel he had brought from the country were hopping about their cages, and seemed to wonder why they were neglected. Anne took down the cages and ministered to the wants of the occupants. The action, simple as it was, seemed to bring her some relief, and as the blackbird tuned up its mellow whistle, she leaned her head beside the cage, and wept long and bitterly.

The little cupboard where Jack had hidden his precious books stood open. Anne bent down, and looking into it she saw something in a far dark corner, for the recess extended deep into the wall beside the chimney. She drew it out, and looked at it. It was a small copy of the New Testament. Arthur had received from London a number of these new books, and had given one to Jack. Jack had put it away with the rest, but it had been overlooked by the searchers in their haste and triumph at finding their great prize. Anne stood looking at it for a few minutes, and then returning to her room and once more fastening her door, she sat herself down to read, nor did she move from her place till it was too dark for her to see.

At dark, Cicely herself brought her a light.

"Where is my father?" Anne ventured to ask.

"He is below, poor dear man!" returned Cicely sobbing. "He has been to the prison to see—" here her voice was lost in tears. "Your brother is better lodged than we had hoped," she continued presently, "along with old Thomas Sprat and some of the townspeople, and we are permitted to send him bedding and refreshment. Your father says you are to use your pleasure as to staying in your room or coming down to supper. He does not desire to make a prisoner of you!" added Cicely, with emphasis.

"Return my thanks to my father," said Anne sorrowfully but calmly, "and say to him that, with his good leave, I will remain here. Tell him I thank him for his goodness, and if he will but add this much, to pray for me, I can ask nothing more."

Cicely repeated the message, adding that she hoped Anne was not going out of her mind, or meditating anything desperate, for she looked as if she had seen a ghost.

CHAPTER XXII.

THE TRIAL.

When Jack arrived at the jail where he was to be confined, he found a great crowd gathered round the door, and was greeted from the midst of it with more than one cry of, "God speed thee, dear lad!" "Be of good courage, brother, and God bless thee! Our prayers are with thee!" And he read in most of the faces surrounding him only pity and sympathy.

Father Barnaby frowned ominously on the assemblage, and hurried his prisoner as soon as possible into the jail.

"Let this young man be shut up by himself," said he to the jailer.

"Your reverence must needs build him a cell, then," returned the jailer, who seemed to have no special pleasure in his task. "Every place is full and overflowing, except the dungeon, where there are only two. Shall I put him therein? I think he were best out of sight of this crowd."

"Do so, then," replied the father. "Youth, I advise thee to take the time of thy imprisonment to consider and repent of thine errors. Thou art but young, and thou hast been misled by more crafty heads than thine own. Thou hast also good parts, and I would fain serve thee, and make thee an instrument of good in the Church."

"I thank your reverence," replied Jack, in a steady tone, and then raising his voice he said, "Good people, pray for me and mine, and be steadfast in the truth, you who own it."

"We will! We will!" shouted several voices in return; and one man added, "Let the Jack Priest look to it. If old Harry quarrels with the Pope, we will pull down their crow's nest about their ears ere long."

Jack was hurried into the jail and the doors shut upon him, so he heard no more, but he noted even then the look of furious wrath mingled with confusion on Father Barnaby's face. He had no time for further observations before he found himself pushed into the cell of which the jailer had spoken, and the door locked upon him.

It was some minutes before his dazzled eyes could distinguish anything in the dim dungeon, which was lighted only by a small grated aperture near the ceiling. As he grew more accustomed to the place, however, he saw that it was a small room about twelve feet square, with stone walls and floor.

The furniture consisted of a stool or two, a rude table, and two pallet beds, on one of which lay stretched a sleeping man. Another man, apparently just aroused from slumber, rose to his feet and advanced a step to meet him.

"I cannot say thou art welcome, friend, to this dungeon," said a voice Jack knew right well; "but to such slight entertainment as we have, I do bid thee welcome."

"Dear uncle," exclaimed Jack, recovering his dazed senses and springing forward, "dearest uncle, do you not know me?"

"My son, my son!" cried the old man. "Is it indeed my son? I feared this, but hoped you might have timely warning. And is it to this I have brought thy youth?"

"Nay, dearest uncle," returned Jack; "not you, but the malice of our enemies, and the enemies of the truth of God. You brought me to the knowledge of that truth and goodness, which shall make all their wrath to praise Him. But who is our companion?"

"It is Master James Dennett, a ship-owner and merchant here in Bridgewater. Disturb him not, for he hath been sorely tried in spirit, and unable to sleep the whole night. Truly, I am glad to be eased of his lamentations. But sit you down here on the bedside, and tell me how all this has chanced. I had hoped you would have had timely warning."

Jack told the story of his betrayal and arrest.

"Alas! Poor maid, was she so far left to herself?" said the shepherd, when he heard of Anne's part in the transaction. "We must put up many prayers for her. And how is your father disposed?"

"He gave me his blessing ere I left him, and do not think he is angry with me. I left him with old Father John, who rode all the way from Holford to give me warning, but he was too late. But how were you taken, dear uncle?"

"Even as I would have desired—on my knees," replied the old man smiling. "I was in the little thicket whither I have long resorted for prayer and reading, as my father did before me, when a band of men, headed by Brother Joseph the sacristan, broke in on me. I told them it was paying a fair compliment to an old man-at-arms, that at nearly ninety, he should need six men to secure him."

"But surely Sir John Brydges will take your part?" said Jack.

"I believe he can do nothing," replied Thomas Sprat. "They have raked up the old matter of Lollardie, and Father Barnaby assures me that as a relapsed heretic, I have no chance of being admitted to mercy, though if I will recant my errors I may perhaps, in time, be delivered from purgatory."

"Many thanks to him," said Jack. "He hath been profuse in his promises to me if I will recant, even to promising me church advancement. But do you know aught of Arthur?"

"They have not apprehended him, but more than that I do not know," replied the shepherd.

"But here comes the jailer with our bread and water."

"Methinks on a feast day they might offer us better fare," said Jack. "It is scarce canonical to fast upon St. Michael's day."

"Don't cry out before you are hurt, young sir," said the jailer, depositing a jug of broth on the table. "I have so far stretched my orders as to bring you the same breakfast as the other prisoners who are only confined for highway robbery, murder, and the like."

"Many thanks for your courtesy, Master Davis," said Jack. "When I am again at liberty, I will do as much for you."

"I would you were at liberty to do it," said the jailer bluntly. "This turning the key on old friends and neighbors is no pleasure to me, I can tell you. What then? A man must do his duty, be he jailer or mayor; but he need not have a heart as hard as the nether millstone. I judged you and the old man would like to be together, so I clapped you in here; but do not you tell yonder monk so."

"Never fear," said Jack. "I do not love him so well as all that. Again I thank you, Master Davis, and so will my father. Be assured you shall be no loser. Come, we are better than we might be," said he after the man had closed the door. "I am heartily glad we have fallen into such good hands. Shall we awaken our companion? He sleeps soundly."

"He has not slept all night," said Thomas Sprat. "I fear much he will not stand the trial. The goods and ties of this world are over-near his heart, poor man. What, brother! Will you awake and break your fast?"

"Where am I?" said Master Dennett, sitting up and gazing round him with a bewildered expression. "What has happened? Alas, I know too well!" he added, sinking back again. "That I should ever live to find myself here in Bridgewater jail! And who is this new companion in misery? Surely, it is Master Lucas's son. Alas, young man, what has brought you hither?"

"The fear of God and the love of His Word," said Jack. "But come, sir, arise and eat, that you may be strengthened for the day's trial."

"And what will strength avail?" asked the ship-owner somewhat peevishly. "Can we break out of the dungeon by dint of strength? Or can we bend the hard hearts of our enemies?"

"The God we serve can do both, brother," said the old shepherd; "or, failing that, He can give us strength to confess that truth which shall minister to us an entrance into His Eternal Kingdom. But come, arise, and eat at all events. There is no use in refusing such good things as we have."

Master Dennett essayed to eat, but desisted after a few mouthfuls, and threw himself upon his pallet again.

Jack made a tolerable meal, and then bestirred himself to render the place as comfortable as might be. The rest of the day passed quietly enough.

Master Dennett lay on his pallet and wept over his hard fate.

Jack and his uncle talked quietly together, recalling many passages of Scripture, and encouraging each other to steadfastness in the trial which they knew was awaiting them. Towards night, the jailer brought in their evening meal, and a large bundle.

"Here are some matters sent you from home," said he to Jack, "bedding and such like, as I guess. Your father hath been here, and has begged me to be kind to you, as why should I not? You never harmed me, I trow."

Jack warmly thanked the jailer, who, surly as he was, seemed disposed, indeed, to be as kind as his duty allowed.

The bundle contained bedding and linen, and artfully concealed in the centre of a great loaf, some paper, a pencil, and the means of striking a light, together with two wax tapers. There was also a Psalter, in which Jack perceived a leaf doubled down. He opened the book, and found underlined the passage, "Be of good courage;" "Fear not," and others of similar import, and doubly underscored the word "Wait." He turned to the first page and read the name of Father John. There were glad tears in the boy's eyes as he showed the book to his uncle.

"The good, kind, old man!" said Thomas Sprat. "I know not what he can do, and yet I thank him with all my heart. I would not have believed anything would lead him to make such an exertion. For myself, I hope nothing in this world save a speedy passage out of it, and that my age gives me warrant to expect: but I would gladly have you, my son, saved from the fiery trial, if it might be done without your denying the faith."

"Better death an hundred times than that!" said Jack.

"Be not confident, young man," said Master Dennett, apparently somewhat displeased. "Better bethink yourself how you will answer when you are brought before the council."

"I am not over-confident, I trust," replied Jack; "but I trust in Him who says, 'I will never leave thee nor forsake thee,' and therefore I am bold to say, 'The Lord is my helper: I will not fear what man may do unto me.' As to meditating how I shall answer, I make bold to refer you to the words of our Lord: 'When they take you up, take no thought how or what ye shall speak: for it shall be given you in that same hour what ye shall say. For it is not you that speak, but the Spirit of your Father which speaketh in you.'"

"Ay, but those words were not spoken to men like us," said Master Dennett. "They were spoken to apostles and saints."

"And what were the apostles and saints but common simple men like to us?" asked Thomas Sprat. "Are not all God's children called to be saints, and does He not promise the same grace freely to all if we are but faithful?"

"Alas, my faith is not like yours," said Master Dennett. "You are, besides, an old man, and must soon die at any rate; but I cannot but bethink me of my young wife and her babes, and the happy fireside I left but yesterday, with my old mother sitting in the chimney corner with my youngest-born on her knees. Little did I think as I bade them farewell and went out to my business, that the evening would find me here."

And the poor man threw himself on the pallet again in an agony of grief.

"It is indeed hard for flesh and blood," said the old man. "The spirit is willing, but the flesh is weak. We will pray for and with you, brother, that you may have strength in the evil day."

The night passed without disturbance, and in the morning came another basket of provisions from home.

"Your father has sent meat and alms to all the prisoners—debtors and all," said the jailer; "and a handsome present to my wife as well. He might have spared that, but he is a kind and liberal man. Truly, you have no cause to thank them who brought you into this scrape."

"Nobody led me into it, good Master Davis," said Jack. "I thank you heartily for bringing me these things. Have you heard whether we are to be brought to trial this day?"

"Nay, I am in none of their secrets," growled the jailer, and withdrew.

Jack made haste to examine the provisions. In one loaf, he found a short letter from his father, full of affection. In the other, he discovered what astonished him beyond measure. It was a small book carefully wrapped up, which, on being opened, proved to be the Testament lately given him by Arthur Brydges. In the envelope was written in Anne's hand, "Forgive and pray for me! A. L."

Master Dennett had also received a missive from his wife, and while he was reading it, Jack took the opportunity to show Anne's gift and note to his uncle. "I know not what to think," said he. "It is Anne's hand, I am sure. I cannot wonder so much at what she hath written, but that she should send me the Testament passes my comprehension."

"It is indeed strange," said Thomas. "Can she have repented of what she has done?"

"I cannot but hope so," replied Jack, "if only for her own sake. I have all the time thought she was fighting against her inward convictions. Poor maiden! I forgive her with all my heart. I suppose I had better destroy this writing, though I should love to keep it."

"Destroy it by all means," said the shepherd hastily, "lest it bring the poor girl into trouble."

With the next morning came Brother Joseph and a summons to the prisoners.

"Nay, not so fast, my young scholar," said the sacristan, with a sneering laugh, as Jack rose to accompany his uncle. "Your time will come soon enough."

"Am I not then to go with my uncle?" asked Jack. "You are to stay where you are till you are called, when, mayhap, you may wish yourself back again."

"Farewell, then, dearest son of my love!" said the old shepherd, embracing and kissing Jack. "Fear nothing, but remain in prayer and meditation of that goodness and faithfulness which will fail neither of us. Master Dennett, let us this day play the man for our Master. Once more, farewell, my dear lad. Pray earnestly for me, but have no fears. I am not alone in this matter, but One goes hence with me who will not suffer me to fall."

"Enough of these blasphemies!" said Brother Joseph harshly. "And spare your breath for your own porridge. It will be hot enough to need it all. As for you, young sir, bethink you well, for I tell you unless you wholly recant and confess who were your movers in this thing, not all your Greek and Latin can save you from the fire, here or hereafter."

"You do but throw away your words," returned Jack. "I would rather be in my place than yours."

The whole of that day Jack was left alone. It was the longest day of his life. The little book which Anne had so strangely sent him was his greatest comfort, and he read till his eyes ached with the dim light, striving to impress on his memory the words of the sacred text, lest the book should be found and taken from him.

When he could see no more, he found a bit of wood which had once formed a part of a rude bench, and busied himself in carving some crosses to be sent as farewell gifts to his father, sister, and other friends. He was still so engaged when the jailer came to pay his evening visit.

"Where are my uncle and Master Dennett?" was Jack's first question.

"Ask me no questions; you will know soon enough," was the gruff answer.

"I pray you, Master Davis," said Jack, in some agitation, "tell me how it has fared with mine uncle! Hath he been condemned?"

"Yes, then, if you must know," returned the jailer. "There was no chance for him. They said he had been respited once before—that his father was burned for a Lollard, while he was pardoned for his youth, and by the intercession of the old knight. Brother Joseph, as they call him, testified that he had overheard the old man instructing you in matters of heresy, and that you had both read from the Lutheran books. He was especially bitter against yourself. Then they went about with the old man to learn who had purveyed him the Testament, but they could get no satisfaction from him. I promise you he answered them roundly. Well, the end of it all is, the poor old father is to be burned tomorrow, and you are to be carried to see the show. So there! It is a shame. I care not who hears me say it, and he like a father to you."

"So said one of the priests. ''Tis like seething the kid in its mother's milk,' said he, and old Thomas, who disdained to say a word for himself, plead earnestly for you that you might be spared the sight, but they said it was for your soul's sake, and they would not hear him. What now! Keep up like a man! I have more for you to hear. See, drink this," said the jailer, with rough kindness, holding a cup to Jack's lips. "I have a message for you, and I promised to deliver it."

Jack made an effort to overcome the faintness which was stealing over him, and roused himself to hear the rest.

"The old man bade me tell you to be of good courage and care not for what was to happen to him; 'for,' says he, 'my pain will be but short and my happiness eternal, and so will yours be, so you be but faithful.' There, I had no business to tell it you, but I am not one to refuse a request to a dying man."

"Master Dennett?" asked Jack.

"Oh, he hath recanted and confessed all," answered the jailer, with a touch of scorn. "He was a cock of another sort, I promise you. He is to do penance tomorrow in face of the people, and suffer some fine. But I pray you consider well what you are about, for this monk is in fiery earnest, and it were pity of your father's son to suffer such a death."

"And will you not let me see my uncle again?" Jack asked.

"I could not, if I would," replied the jailer.

"The old man is not here, but confined in the room in the church tower yonder. Fare you well."

When Jack was left alone, he sat down on his bedside like one stunned. Burned! That good, innocent old man! That one whom he loved like a father—who had been truly, and not in mere name, a spiritual father to him. Burned alive! And he was to see it! There was no escape. He was in hands which knew not how to show mercy, and which would never spare him one pang.

He said to himself that he had expected this—that he had known all along that it would come at last; but none the less did it come on him with the suddenness of a hard blow. There are certain things for which no amount of preparation will prepare us. Then would come the old horrible thought—was it worth while after all? Was he not sacrificing life and reputation for a mere dream—a figment of the imagination? Was not one religious belief as good as another—were they not alike the inventions of men? Then, how many good men had believed that which he was about to die for denying! His father believed it still—so did Father John and my lady. Might it not be true, after all? And if it were not strictly so, was it not at any rate as true as the rest? Might he not profess his own belief, and so escape till better times—those times which Master Fleming believed would surely come, when the storm should have spent itself and passed away?

He might keep his Bible and read it in secret, or he might slip away and go abroad to Wittenburg, where he could confess the truth without fear.

But Jack had learned already that the devil is never to be conquered by listening to and arguing with him, but by taking refuge from his malice and sophistry in the presence of God.

He threw himself on his knees, and then on his face, and there poured out the bitterness of his soul. At first, he could say little more than "Lord help me! Lord deliver me!" over and over again, but by degrees he grew calmer, and the quieting and comforting influence of the Holy Spirit made itself felt in his soul.

Promise after promise came thronging to his mind, full of beauty and force as he had never known them before, and at last the full crowning work of Divine grace was wrought in his soul, and he was able to say for his friend as well as for himself, "Thy will be done on earth as it is in heaven." He had never felt any fear for his uncle's steadfastness, and he no longer had any as regarded his own. He felt sure that the Lord was faithful who had promised; and that strength would be given him according to the work he had to do.

He rose at last, and, lighting his candle, he took out the precious little book which had so strangely come to him, but he had read barely one chapter before he heard footsteps approaching, and hastily extinguishing his light, he thrust that and his book far into the straw of his bed. He had hardly done so before his door was unlocked and Father Barnaby entered his cell.

"You watch late, my son," was his first greeting; "methinks you should be glad to sleep."

Jack simply inclined his head.

The priest put down the lantern he carried, and sat himself down on the pallet opposite to Jack, as if prepared to enter into conversation. Jack quietly waited for him to begin.

"You have heard the result of the trial to-day, I suppose," said Father Barnaby, after some minutes silence.

Jack assented.

"I would willingly have saved the old man," he continued, "but the evidence was too plain against him. He was convicted on the witness of one who heard him not only reading and speaking heresy, but striving to corrupt you. There was nothing to be done."

Still Jack did not reply, though the priest paused as though expecting him to speak.

"For you, my son, I would fain save you from a like fate," continued Father Barnaby. "I trust to be able to do so, if only you will be conformable and docile as becomes your youth. You will be brought before us in the morning early, before the execution takes place, and I have come to see if any argument of mine can move you so that you shall then be ready to confess your errors."

"You are the jailer and I am the prisoner," said Jack, breaking silence for the first time; "therefore I must hear you whether I will or no; but I tell you plainly, I am not to be persuaded. If indeed you do mean kindly, I thank you for your kindness, but I would rather it displayed itself in leaving me alone that I may have space for thought and prayer."

"But you will not refuse to listen to me," said Father Barnaby gently. "I have not come to argue with you, my son. I know well that in such cases, arguments are of little avail. But I desire to set before you plainly the results of two different courses of action."

Father Barnaby then proceeded to set forth the consequences of Jack's persistence in heresy. He would die a disgraceful and horrible death. He would bring upon his family a lasting shame and probably a suspicion of having shared in his fault. Even if it could be so managed that he should escape with life, he could look for nothing but life-long ignominious imprisonment, secluded from books, from friends, and all that made life worth having.

On the other hand, he had but to abjure his errors to be set at liberty. He should not even be asked to do public penance. The worst penalty inflicted on him should be a short seclusion in some religious house, where he could have the use of such a library as he had never yet seen, and pursue those studies which he so dearly loved. After that he should go to Oxford, or to some college at Rome, and who could tell to what station he might arrive? The great cardinal himself was the son of a butcher, and other eminent men at Rome were of equally obscure origin.

Jack listened so quietly that Father Barnaby thought he was gaining the day, and waxed yet more eloquent. At last he stopped.

"You are very silent, my son. May I not hope that you are coming to a better mind? Upon what are you meditating so deeply?"

"Upon the temptation of our Lord," replied Jack. "The devil took Him up into a very high mountain and showed Him all the kingdoms of the world and the glory of them, and said, 'All these will I give thee if thou wilt fall down and worship me.' Do you think if our Lord had done so the devil would have kept his promise? Or if he had, do you think the kingdoms of the world would have been worth the price?"

Father Barnaby colored and bit his lip. "You are scarce civil, my son."

"I meant not to be uncivil," said Jack. "So far as you mean kindly, I thank you; but the things you propose have no charms for me at present. I am too near death not to see their true character. As a man would be a fool who should give away the inheritance of a kingdom for the sake of playing the king one day before the eyes of man, so do I hold him a million times a fool who barters his assured hope of a heavenly inheritance for aught this world has to give."

Father Barnaby sat silent for a moment. Then he said with energy—

"My son, every word you say makes me more anxious to save you, not only for your own sake, but for that of the Church. We cannot afford to lose you thus. I do not ask you to change your opinions all at once. I only ask you to recant them, and then take time to study under proper instruction. As a priest, you could study the Scripture without sin, and I will take care that you have every facility to learn not only the Greek but the Hebrew. The Church hath power to bind and loose, and even if you commit a sin in this matter, she can absolve you."

"Ay," said Jack; "but suppose I lie to the Church, how shall I know that the Church will not lie to me? Once more, father, I thank you. I do believe you are willing to save my life, but I tell you plainly that I have no mind to be saved in any such way. I know that the God I serve can yet deliver me out of your hands, if such be His will, and I am content that His will be done. In all courtesy, I pray you to trouble me no more, but to leave me to the rest I need."

"It is enough, ungrateful, obstinate lad," said Father Barnaby rising. "I leave you to your fate. I shall pray for you that you may open your eyes before it is forever too late."

"I shall also pray for you," returned Jack; "and so I bid you good-night."

CHAPTER XXIII.

A FRIEND IN NEED.

Early the next morning Jack was aroused by the entrance of the jailer and his men.

"You are to go before the priest," said the jailer shortly.

"I am ready to do so," returned Jack calmly, rising from his bed. "I should be glad of water to drink and to wash in, Master Davis, if it be your pleasure."

The jailer looked at Brother Joseph, who answered sharply, "What need of such fopperies? The reverend fathers cannot be kept waiting."

"As you will," returned Jack. "Master Davis, since it may well be that I see you no more, I thank you for all your courtesies to me, and beseech you to convey these little tokens to my father with my love."

"What are they?" asked Brother Joseph.

"You may see them if you will," Jack was beginning, but the jailer interrupted him—

"What then? I am captain of this jail, I trow, and not you, Master Joseph. Take your prisoner way as quickly as you will, but I will have none of your airs here. Marry come up! You are no such great man. Goods left by my prisoners belong to me, I would have you know. I will do your errand, Jack Lucas, and I wish heartily that you were well out of this scrape."

The sacristan deigned no reply, but hurried his charge away as quickly as possible. Early as it was, the street was already full, and in the short passage between the jail and the convent, Jack heard many words of encouragement and met many kindly glances. He was taken into a room in the Benedictine convent, where he found his judges already waiting and a secretary ready to take down his replies. He was asked the usual questions as to his belief, and warned to answer truly.

"I have no desire to answer otherwise," said Jack, with an expressive look at Father Barnaby.

He was then questioned as to his belief in the authority of the Pope, the sacraments and purgatory, to all of which questions he returned straightforward answers.

"Whence did you obtain your heretical books?" was the next question.

"I am not here to criminate others, neither do I own to having any heretical books," replied Jack.

"Call in the witnesses," said Father Barnaby.

Jack looked earnestly toward the door, and started as Anne entered supported by her father. Anne was pale and worn, but seemed quite calm.

She gave her brother a long look which he could not understand. It was full of love and supplication, and then brightened into a sort of triumph and joy.

"This maiden is the sister of the prisoner," said Father Barnaby. "With a degree of faith and piety rare in this age, she hath herself, by her own act, delivered him into the hands of the Church that his soul may be saved even by the destruction of the body. Speak, my daughter, without fear. How did you first suspect your brother's heresy?"

"He came to me to comfort me one day when I was in trouble," answered Anne clearly and readily. "He found me in tears, and strove to console me by telling me what he had learned from reading the Bible."

"Well—" said the prior, "and you refused to listen to him?"

"I did at that time," returned Anne.

"What did he say?"

"He told me that all my penances and exercises were of no avail; that—"

"That will do!" said Father Barnaby. "We have heard enough of these blasphemies without troubling you to repeat them. Is it your belief that your brother is wholly a heretic?"

"He is wholly a believer in the gospel as set forth by Master Tyndale," said Anne, "as—as I am also!" she added firmly. "I believe with him! I was blinded for a time—blinded and besotted by spiritual pride and selfishness, and I fought against my convictions with all my might. Tempted by the devil, I betrayed my brother into your hands; but God in infinite mercy hath given me the grace of repentance. I believe my brother is right—and I desire no more at your hands than leave to die with him."

All present stood as if stupefied for a moment, when Jack, wrenching himself from his detainers, sprang forward and clasped his sister in his arms.

"Your prayers have been heard, dearest brother," said Anne, kissing him. "I am not now afraid to speak the truth. A long time I fought against it, but it would not be withstood. I am come to confess it and to die by your side."

"The maid is frantic," said Father Barnaby, recovering himself. "This distress has driven her beside herself, and she knows not what she says. She hath ever been a faithful child of the Church."

"I know right well what I say," returned Anne. "It is no new thing. The work was began in the convent by Agnes Harland, and was finished by the reading of God's Word. I—" She stopped, strove to continue, raised her hands as if grasping for something, and then, slipping from Jack's arms, she sank senseless to the ground.

"So! Did I not tell you she was beside herself?" said Father Barnaby. "Master Lucas, has your daughter been ailing?"

"She hath not complained," replied Master Lucas, stooping and raising Anne in his arms; "but she has looked very ill ever since yesterday, when she came from visiting a family of children in our lane who are down with the sweating sickness."

"The sweating sickness!" exclaimed the prior, in alarm. "Let her be removed at once! It is as much as our lives are worth to be in the room with her. Master Lucas, will you take home your daughter?"

"Ay, that will I," replied Master Lucas, raising Anne in his arms. "My son, my dear son! How can I leave you here?"

"Think not of that now, dear father, but take care of Anne and of yourself," said Jack. "I trust we shall meet again in a better place where no malice of our enemies can separate us."

"Let us have no more of this," said Father Barnaby. "Master Lucas, take this poor maid home and let her have fitting attendance. I attach no weight to her words, spoken in the delirium of disease. Brother Joseph, secure the prisoner."

But Brother Joseph evidently shrank from the task. "He has just embraced and kissed this woman, your reverence," said he, "and—"

With a smile, Jack kissed his sister once more and walked back to his place. His bearing evidently made a strong impression on the prior, who whispered something to his fellow inquisitors, to which Father Barnaby replied with a frown. As soon as Anne was removed, Jack was again questioned as to the person from whom he had received his books. He resolutely declined to answer.

"Have a care," said Father Barnaby. "There are means for wrenching the truth from unwilling witnesses. We have no time to waste."

"Let them bring hither the old man," said the prior. "He will perhaps be more complying this morning. My lad, if you would save yourself and your uncle from sharp pain, you must answer freely. Did you receive your book from Sir William Leavett?"

"No," answered Jack decidedly. "So far I can satisfy you, but I shall answer no more questions."

There was a short pause, and the inquisitors seemed to be busily consulting together, while the messengers were despatched for the old shepherd.

Brother Joseph presently returned with a startled and awe-struck expression of countenance.

"Well! Why have you not brought him?" demanded Father Barnaby sharply.

"Please, your reverence," stammered the subordinate, "there is no—no use—the man is dead!"

"Dead!" exclaimed the two priests together.

"Yes, your reverence. He lies on the floor of his cell, his hands clasped and his limbs composed as if he had died in sleep. On the wall at his head these words are written: 'I know in whom I have believed.'"

"Thank God!" exclaimed Jack fervently. "He hath won his eternal crown of glory, and hath escaped the malice of his enemies! The Lord be praised, who hath not delivered him over as a prey to their teeth. The snare is broken, and he is delivered. Thank God!"

"He hath escaped an earthly only to sink into an eternal fire," said Father Barnaby sternly; "but we have you still. I am willing to show mercy, and I promise you your life shall be spared, if you will recant your errors, and confess the names of your seducers. Otherwise, in three hours' time, namely at noon, you shall burn at the pile prepared for your uncle."

"I am in God's power, not in yours," returned Jack steadily. "He can yet deliver me out of your hands, but if not, know that I will not bow down to your idols nor deny His truth."

At this moment there was a knock at the chamber door, and a monk entered.

"What now, brother?" asked the prior.

"Here is the bishop's sumner and two other men, who have ridden express with a letter from the bishop to Father Barnaby," returned the brother. "He will deliver it into the reverend father's own hands."

"Bid him come in," was the reply, and the sumner or summoner entered, a stout, good-natured looking man, whose air and complexion savored more of the alehouse than of the church. Father Barnaby opened the letter which was presented to him, and as he did so a look of intense vexation and annoyance passed over his face. He crushed the letter in his hand, and then as if recollecting himself, he smoothed it out once more and restored it to the cover. The prior cast an inquiring glance at him.

"It is from the bishop himself," said Father Barnaby, in a low tone. "The peevish old man hath taken great umbrage at my proceeding in this matter without consulting him, and requires me to send young Lucas at once to him, that he or his chaplain may examine him in person."

"Umph!" returned the prior, evidently not at all sorry to be rid of his own share in the business. "So much the better. We shall be well rid of him. But had you not consulted the bishop, brother?"

"Not I! I never thought of him. My powers were held from the cardinal, you know, and the bishop hath lately been so infirm and so careless of anything which went on—"

"Nevertheless, I think it was taking a good deal on yourself," said the prior, evidently not ill-pleased at Father Barnaby's discomfiture. "The bishop is the bishop, so long as he is alive, and we must not ignore him. What are your orders concerning the prisoner, Master Sumner?"

"My orders are to carry him back with me that his lordship may examine him," returned the sumner somewhat bluntly. "I would lose no time, so please you, for the days are short. We will but wait to refresh ourselves and our beasts and then ride forth without delay. I have a spare horse for the young man."

"It is well," said Father Barnaby. "The bishop's order shall be obeyed. How he will answer the matter to the cardinal, is his concern, not mine."

"Exactly so," returned the sumner, who seemed to have scant reverence for the monk. "In an hour, then, we set forth."

It was something more than an hour, however, before the sumner was ready to set forth, and then it was observed by some persons that his rubicund face was redder than ever, and that his speech was something thick. It was also said that the sumner was met at the tavern where he had stopped by a strange gentleman, who had professed an acquaintance with his brother in London, and who was very free in treating him and his attendants, to both ale and strong waters. There was quite a crowd around the convent gates as they issued forth, and Jack found himself jostled almost off his feet. In the press, he suddenly felt a hand laid heavily on his shoulder. Somebody pushed a well-filled purse into his hand, and whispered in his ear—

"Treat the men well, have your wits about you, and when you hear the owls hoot, keep a good lookout."

Jack pocketed the purse, and being at last mounted and placed between the sumner and one of his men, the party set off at a good pace and were soon clear of the town. Jack would fain have had news of his sister, but that was clearly out of the question. They had ridden some four or five miles in silence, when they passed a decent looking alehouse, and Jack remarked—

"If it were not against your orders, Master Sumner, I would ask leave to buy some refreshment. I have fasted from both meat and drink since yesterday even."

"Who says it is against my orders?" returned the sumner. "If men are hungry, I know no reason why they should not eat—always supposing they have wherewith to pay."

"That have I," answered Jack; "and I dare say you and these good fellows will not be the worse for a can of ale to wet your throats."

"Not a whit! Not a whit!" answered the sumner. "Here, good host! What! Are you all asleep there?"

The host presently appeared at the door, all deference to the great man, who was not an infrequent customer. The party alighted, and Jack soon had a good breakfast set before him, while his guards were accommodated with foaming pots of ale. Jack was not much disposed for food, but he made the best figure he was able, and the ale being discussed, he asked the landlord if he had no strong waters, remarking that cold ale was sometimes thought unwholesome to horsemen. The medicine was produced, and a goodly dose swallowed by each of the patients with little reluctance. Jack paid the reckoning liberally, and the party were again on their way.

They were approaching a thick wood on the borders of Lord Harland's estate, when Jack bethought himself of a grisly tale of murders and ghosts he had once heard of this same wood, and asked the sumner with an appearance of interest, whether the tale were true. The man had never heard it, and Jack repeated it at considerable length. This brought on another story of robbers relating to the same place, and then another.

The sun had now sunk pretty low, and the road bordered by woods on one side, and on the other by a desolate hillside, was in deep shadow. Jack remarked how dismal the wood looked, and how deep the shadows were. The sumner assented, and started nervously and crossed himself, as the hooting of an owl was heard among the trees, which was answered by another voice farther on.

"Avaunt Satan!" exclaimed the sumner, crossing himself once more. "Who ever heard owls so early in the day?"

"They are birds of ill-omen, and haunt places where foul deeds have been committed," said Jack, his heart beating fast. "I trust we shall meet with no evil creatures in this lonely place."

"Speak not of it," said the sumner in great agitation. "There again!" as the hooting of the owl sounded nearer. "Santa Maria, ora pro nobis! I would I could remember a psalm or a prayer!"

At this moment, and just as they were arrived at the darkest part of the road, three or four men well-armed and masked rushed from the wood and confronted them, seizing the bridle of Jack's horse and commanding them all to stand. The sumner and his men, confused, half drunk, and wholly frightened, did as they were bid.

"By what authority do you stop men on the highway?" asked the sumner in a quivering voice.

"By the authority of our Master!" answered the leader of the band in an extraordinary deep voice. "This youth is an heretic, and belongs to our Master as his rightful prize. Over you we have no power unless you resist us, but if you do so you are ours;" concluding with a deep growl, "Ride on, and look not back, and we shall do you no harm."

The sumner and his companions lost no time in obeying the command, nor did they once look backward till they had left the dreadful wood far behind them.

Arrived at home, they told fearful tale of a band of robbers, at least twenty in numbers, and of unheard-of height and appearance, who demanded the prisoner as an heretic in the name of their master. The sumner more than insinuated that the leader was no mortal man and that the heretic had been carried off by the devil whom he served.

Our readers will naturally desire an explanation of this sudden change of affairs. The day on which Thomas Sprat was condemned, Father John who seemed suddenly to have grown twenty years younger, rode over to visit his old friend and college companion, the bishop. After some gossip, Father John spoke of Father Barnaby's return and the clean work he was making of heresy over in Bridgewater.

The bishop was an old man, very infirm, and somewhat childish, but excessively jealous over his episcopal dignity, and very indignant at any infringement thereof, especially by the monks and preaching friars. He grew angry at once, wondered what that upstart was thinking of, and declared that he would not have his poor people hunted and imprisoned by any Jack in office of them all, and that Father Barnaby should know. Just at this juncture arrived Lord Harland, ostensibly with a present of rare and valuable foreign books, but really on the same errand as Father John. He understood the hint on the instant, and took pains to blow the coal already kindled, till the bishop was roused to the point of summoning his secretary and dictating a sharp letter to Father Barnaby, which he declared should be sent the first thing in the morning.

The next day the young Harlands contrived to fall in with the messengers, and by judicious and liberal treatment, secured all the information they wanted. The rest may easily be guessed.

When Father Barnaby heard the tale, he pronounced it an evident and gross case of rescue, and hinted that the sumner had made his account of the transaction. He tried to rouse the bishop to investigate the matter, but the bishop, satisfied with having vindicated his dignity and snubbed the monk, declared it was not his business to catch footpads, and that if Father Barnaby wanted the heretic back, he might go to the woods and look for him.

The sumner and his companions declared point blank that Jack had been carried off by the devil; and gave a fearful description of the giants who had stopped them in the road, and the fearful screams and yells they had heard while riding away. The preaching friars repeated the story with many and wonderful additions all over the country, till it was at last declared that the heretic had been torn to pieces on the spot and his bones scattered far and wide. Father Barnaby might, perhaps, have investigated the matter more fully, but a few days after he was gratified at receiving an appointment of dignity in the Cardinal's own splendid household. He left Bridgewater forever, and it may safely be said that nobody regretted his departure.

CHAPTER XXIV.

CONCLUSION.

Four or five days after the events recorded in the last chapter, Master Lucas came down into his shop while it was yet early, and sending little Peter, the 'prentice boy, out on an errand, began setting certain matters in order. Master Lucas, had, of course, heard the story of Jack's disappearance, and while he was as much at a loss as any one else to understand how it had come about, he could not help hoping that his son had escaped and was in safety. But the suspense was terribly trying; and the usually cheerful and equable spirit of the master baker was heavily oppressed.

He had another cause of anxiety. Anne had never spoken or shown signs of consciousness since the day she had sunk down in the council chamber of the convent. Excitement and grief had been too much for a constitution already enfeebled by watching and fasting. It was hard to say what was her disease, but whatever might be its nature, it yielded to no remedies, and the patient was evidently growing weaker every hour. Cicely was untiring in her attendance on the poor girl, and she found a faithful and wise assistant in Mary Brent, who left the care of her house and lodger to her sister, and came to help her old friends in their trouble.

Master Lucas finished his arrangements in the shop and sent Simon to eat his breakfast. He was thus left alone, and was sitting leaning his head on his hands, when a gentleman entered the shop, whom he recognized at a glance as one of the young Harlands, though the stranger had his hat pulled down and his face well muffled in his cloak.

"You are Master Lucas, if I mistake not, the owner of this place?" said the stranger, addressing him with marked courtesy.

"The same, at your service," returned the baker, rising. "Can I do aught for you?"

"I desire to purchase certain matters for my lady which you will find set down in this paper," said the stranger, giving him one with a meaning glance and a slight pressure of the hand. "I or my servant will call for them in an hour." So saying he turned and left the shop.

Master Lucas opened the paper and saw at a glance that it contained another on which was written, in a hand he well knew, "Read and burn quickly."

Putting it into his bosom, he called Simon into the shop, and locking himself into his own room, he read the following letter:

"I doubt not, dearest father, you have heard ere this of what chanced in Warton wood. I write now from the cabin of a vessel to tell you of my safety thus far, and that I have good hope of escaping to Germany along with Paul. I have had the kindest and most hospitable treatment at the house where I have been before I came on board this vessel, which waited for me at a place near at hand. I name no names for fear of trouble. Dear father, I pray you be very kind to Mary Brent's family, and, so far as may be, discharge the debt I owe to young Mr. Harland and his brother. Also, if it lies in your way, do something to pleasure the bishop's sumner, who treated me courteously and kindly while I was in his hands. I shall write again when I can do so safely. My love to all at home, especially dearest Anne, and also my duty to Father John, who exerted himself greatly in my behalf. I cannot now write more, for we are about to sail. Dear father and sister, pray for me."

The letter was not signed. Master Lucas read it again and again, and then going down to the bakehouse, he put it into the hottest fire. He then returned to the shop and busied himself in doing up the goods named in Lady Harland's list, and a little relieving his heart by adding thereto a large packet of sugar candy and some rare and precious spices and perfumes which he had obtained from London through the agency of Master Fleming. He had hardly finished when the stranger entered the shop once more.

"What, all these!" he exclaimed, as he saw the packages. "My mother must intend to set up a shop. And how much am I to pay?"

"Nothing," answered the baker. "Not one penny will I take from your father's son. I pray you present these matters to your lady mother with my humble duty, and if it were not presuming too far—"

"Well," said the stranger, laughing, "the younger son of a poor lord is no such great person, Master Lucas, that you should use so much ceremony, besides that we are, so to speak, in the same boat just now. In what can I pleasure you?"

"Only by breaking your fast with me," returned the baker, smiling in his turn. "My household is something disordered by these troubles, and by the serious illness of my daughter, but I will do what I can for your entertainment."

"Good faith, Master Lucas, that is a presumption easily pardoned by a hungry man as I am," returned the stranger good-humoredly; "but I fear I shall put you to inconvenience. I trust your daughter is not dangerously ill. She must be a brave maiden. I hear she confounded the priest finely the other day."

"She hath never spoken or known any of us since that time," said the baker mournfully. "I fear she will never speak again."

"You are indeed greatly afflicted," said the stranger, in a sympathizing tone; "but I hope all may yet be well, and that you may once more have your son in your arms, though perhaps not very soon. My father thinks that there are very great changes impending, both in Church and State. But these are dangerous matters to talk upon."

When they were by themselves and safe from eavesdroppers, Mr. Harland gave his host an account of Jack's escape. After the encounter in the woods, he had been taken under cover of night to the house of Lord Harland, where he had been concealed for two days. Here he was joined by Arthur Brydges, who brought him news that Davy Brent's vessel would be in waiting at Porlock quay at a certain time. The two young men were furnished with horses by Lord Harland, and riding by unfrequented roads, they reached Porlock without any accident or detention, and got on board the vessel in safety.

Davy Brent was going round to Plymouth, where he expected to find vessels bound for France and Germany. Arthur was well supplied with money by his father, and Sir John had also provided Jack with a well-filled purse. They proposed to travel in the guise of students, and to make for Wittenburg where they would be in safety.

Mr. Harland had scarcely taken his leave, when Cicely summoned Master Lucas to the sick-chamber.

"Anne hath opened her eyes and spoken," said she, weeping. "She is quite herself, but I fear—"

Master Lucas hastily obeyed the summons, and the moment he entered the room he saw the state of the case.

Anne's eyes were open and rational, but that awful shadow rested upon her face which once seen cannot be mistaken.

"My dearest daughter," was all her father could say, as he bent over her and took her hand.

"Jack?" whispered Anne, with a look of eager inquiry.

"I trust truly that he hath escaped and is in safety," whispered her father in return. "I have had a letter from him written on shipboard, and there is every reason to hope that both he and Arthur will make their way safely to Germany. He sent his love specially to you."

Anne smiled sweetly, and lay silent for a few minutes. Then she said faintly but clearly—

"Dear father, you have forgiven me?"

"As fully and truly as I hope myself to be forgiven, dear child."

"I have not been a good or dutiful daughter," said Anne slowly. "I have lived in a strange, foolish dream all my life, but I see all clearly now—how you have forgiven and borne with and pitied me all the time I was fancying myself so superior and learned and wise—so far above all the rest of you. But, father, I did try to serve God—"

"I know you did, daughter. I knew it all the time," said her father.

"You have been the best of fathers to me, and you will have your reward," continued Anne dreamily. "Father, what became of the little book I sent Jack?"

"I do not know, my love. I suppose he took it with him."

"That book finished the work which Agnes began," said Anne. "I fought against it—I fought against my own conscience, with all my might, but God would not let me be lost. Father, if you are ever able, I pray you, for my sake and Jack's, to read and study the Gospel. Never mind what men may say or how they may treat you. The truth is worth it all, and the truth shall make you free."

These were the last words she said. Cicely would have sent for a priest, but even while she was speaking of it, all was over. The weary overworked body and the wounded spirit found repose.

Toward the close of a pleasant day in the latter part of May, 1538, a gentleman rode through the street of Bridgewater, looking around him with great interest, not so much like a stranger as like one who, having been long away, takes cognizance of things which have happened in his absence. He was a scholarly-looking man of perhaps six or eight and twenty, well dressed and riding a good horse. He turned into Bridge Street and alighted at the door of "John Lucas, white and brown baker and dealer in sweetmeats and spices," as was set forth on a huge signboard decorated with a most ramping lion.

"I see no changes here, save that the old lion has been regilt and painted since my day," said the horseman, deliberately surveying the front of the house. "And as I live, I should say there was the very same old cat sitting on the end of the counter. But that can hardly be. I do not see my father, but he may be out."

A stout, respectable-looking journeyman came forward to attend to the stranger, who looked at him with attention, and then asked courteously—

"Are Master Lucas or any of his family within?"

"Not at present," was the reply. "My master and mistress have gone to hear the Bible reading, and Dame Cicely has gone out also. Will it please you to sit down and await their return?"

"To the church, to hear the Bible reading!" repeated the stranger with a smile. "That would have been a strange sound years ago, when I left this place. Do they then have regular Bible readings in the church?"

"Ay, sir, every afternoon."

"And do many people attend to hear?'

"Oh, yes, sir. My master hardly ever misses, and, beside that, he reads in the Bible to his family every morning. You may see the great book lying yonder beside his chair."

"Is your master well in health?"

"Ay, sir, extraordinary well and stout for a man of his age, specially since he married my mistress."

"So he is married!" exclaimed the visitor. "And who is the new dame?"

"I do not know her right name," returned the shopman. "She used to live here years ago, and then we called her Madam Barbara. She was a nun once in the same convent with poor Mistress Anne, or so I have heard. Anyhow, she is a good mistress and makes my master a very happy home. But will you not sit down, sir? They will soon be home."

"I thank you, but I will walk toward the church and meet them," said Jack Lucas; for as our readers have guessed, it was none but he. "I have been long abroad, but I was bred here and know all the streets of the town well."

A few minutes after, Jack entered the church of St. Mary, where a tolerable congregation was assembled. The great Bible, chained safely to its stand, was placed in the open space in front of the chancel, and a young man whom Jack recognized as a former schoolmate was reading from the Gospel of St. John. Around him were grouped people of all classes: gentlemen and ladies, citizens with their wives and children, and sailors from the river, all eagerly listening to the Word of God, while at the edge of the crowd stood two or three priests with scowling brows, evidently highly displeased with the whole affair.

"Oh, Father William, could you but have lived to see this day!" thought Jack. "But you gained your martyr's crown in good time."

Jack had no difficulty in finding out his father, who, with his family, was seated very near the reader. Master Lucas had grown old within ten years, but still looked hale and hearty.

His wife, bright and cheerful as ever, sat by his side, and next her was a very old man in the dress of a priest, who sat leaning his two hands on the head of his staff, and listening evidently with the closest attention. Jack looked at the group, and the tears rose to his eyes as he thought of one who should have been with them. He waited till the reader ceased and the congregation rose to depart, and then drew near his father, who was helping the old man to his feet.

"Let me give you a helping hand," said he, as if speaking to a stranger. "The venerable father seems infirm."

"He can walk very well when he gets to his feet," said Master Lucas. "He is very old, but nothing will keep him from the Bible readings in the church."

"Yes, yes, I am an old man—I am almost ninety years old," said the father, in a feeble but cheery voice. "I am an old man, but I am very well—and everybody is good to me."

"That is the burden of his daily song," said Master Lucas. "Truly, it is a privilege to be allowed to tend him in his age, and I love him like a father."

"It is much to say," returned Jack in an unsteady voice. "I have ever found a father's love the warmest and truest in the world!"

Something in the tone caused Master Lucas to look round suddenly. At the same moment his wife exclaimed—

"Surely, surely—this is our Jack come home. Master Lucas, do you not know your own son?"

We pass over the greetings and questionings, the exclamations and rejoicings on the part of the whole household. Jack soon found himself seated at the family supper table, bountifully spread as in old days, with as many of his favorite dishes as Cicely could provide at such short notice.

"You did not expect to find a step-dame, did you, Jack?" asked his father.

"Why, no, not exactly," replied Jack. "And yet I was no ways surprised, but greatly pleased to find that you had taken our good Madam Barbara to wife. You know I always liked the notion."

"You see the house was very lonely, latterly," said Master Lucas; "and we were both growing older. Then the convents were all broken up, and the nuns had leave to do what they would, so I even broke the matter to the lady, and she was content to take up her living with us. Then our good Father John grew infirm and lonely in his house at Holford, and so we brought him home here, where he is as happy as the day is long. His mind hath grown somewhat dazed the last year, some time ago, and, above all things, he loves the Bible readings. Father John, do you not know our Jack—Jack Lucas, whom you did so much for?"

"Ay, ay," returned the old man readily. "I remember Jack Lucas. A towardly boy he was, and full of good gifts, though he was careless in throwing stones, I remember. They said he was a heretic and that the devil carried him off, but I never believed that."

"If he did, he brought him back," said the baker, laughing, "for here he sits, as you see."

"But Jack was only a lad, and this is a grown man," returned the old priest in a puzzled tone.

"He will get hold of the matter presently," said Dame Lucas, as we must now call her. "I would not trouble him. Never mind, dear father, you will understand all by and by."

"And where have you been all this time, that we have not heard from you?" asked Master Lucas. "We have written again and again, but have heard nothing, and had almost given you up for lost."

"I have been in many lands," replied Jack. "I have been hearing medical lectures in Padua and Milan, and travelling all over Germany—even so far as Hungary and Bohemia. But I have my diploma now, and can settle where like; so I have even come to see whether this town of Bridgewater can afford a living to a poor surgeon."

"You are just in the nick of time, for old Master Burden is dead and there is no one to take his place," said his father. "But do you really mean to settle down here? I thought you would be for going to London or Bristol."

"I wished to be near you, father," said Jack; "and, besides, my chances are better here than in London, where doctors are far more plenty than blackberries."

"Did you see Master Fleming as you came through?" asked Dame Lucas.

"Oh yes, mother—if you care to be called mother by such a well-grown son."

Dame Lucas smiled and nodded, while his father looked greatly pleased.

"I abode a week with the good gentleman, and he hath sent you all various tokens of good will, which are in my mails."

"I warrant he rejoices in the new times," remarked Master Lucas.

"He rejoices, though with trembling, as do all who live near the court," said Jack gravely. "He does think the times are not at all settled, and that the King may yet lay on us a yoke as heavy as that of the Pope. But we will not talk of these things here or anticipate evil. How are the family at Holford?"

"Well and hearty, all that are left. The old knight is gone, but my lady survives and rejoices over the birth of her grandchild."

"What has been done with Uncle Thomas's cottage?"

"Nothing. Old Margery stayed there as long as she lived, and since her death, it has been shut up. Sir Arthur hath ever considered it your property, and he also holds quite a sum of money which Uncle Thomas left you. Sir Arthur is not strong, and I fear will not live many years."

"I will ride out and see him soon," said Jack. "Are the Brents well?"

"Well and flourishing. Davy has a fine vessel and is growing a rich man, and here is Peter to speak for himself," as the tall journeyman entered the room; "and a fine fellow he is, too, as ever kneaded up a batch of dough. He hath been more like a son than a servant to me, and I have used him accordingly. I suppose you heard all about poor Sir William from Master Fleming?"

"Yes, and received the remembrance he left me," replied Jack. "I could but wish as I entered the church this afternoon that he were there to see and hear."

"He is in a better place, if ever man was," said Master Lucas. "His memory is green in this place, I can tell you. When the news came of his death and the manner of it, the people were ready to break their hearts. But it grows late, and the good father is already asleep. I dare say Cicely has your old room ready for you."

A few days after his return, Jack rode over to Holford to visit his friend Sir Arthur, and the place where he had first learned to know and value the Scripture.

"You will find everything as it was in the old man's time," said the steward, as he gave Jack the key of the cottage, "save that the storm last night has somewhat shattered the tree at the house end."

Jack found the place unchanged, as the steward said. A high wind the night before had blown down part of the great old oak, which, no doubt, had been a tree in the time of the Saxons, exposing a hollow in the trunk.

Jack drew near and examined it. Suddenly uttering an exclamation, he put in his hand and drew forth a good-sized square bundle wrapped in leather and carefully secured with thongs of the same. Jack carried his prize into the cottage, and undoing the wrapper with some difficulty brought to view a large volume written on parchment, well bound and clasped with iron.

Reverently, he opened the book. It was the Bible of Wickliffe—the very Bible which had been hidden away a hundred years before, and which had given the crown of martyrdom to both Thomas Sprat and his father.

The Hidden Treasure of the old cottage had become the treasure of all England.

There is little more to add. Father John lived to be a century old, and died, carefully tended by his adopted children, and murmuring with his latest breath that everybody was good to him.

Master Lucas died soon after, leaving his business to Peter Brent, who had long managed it for him.

Madam Barbara lived to teach reading and embroidery to Jack's little girls, cherished as a mother by himself and his wife.

Jack himself survived many perils to see the Protestant religion firmly established in the reign of Elizabeth.

www.ingramcontent.com/pod-product-compliance
Lightning Source LLC
Chambersburg PA
CBHW012151260626
47155CB00020B/3567